FOR GIRLS ONLY

FOR GIRLS ONLY

EVERYTHING GREAT ABOUT BEING A GIRL

LAURA DOWER

ILLUSTRATED BY
HEADCASE DESIGN

FEIWEL and FRIENDS
NEW YORK

for Olivia

A Feiwel and Friends Book
An Imprint of Macmillan

www.feiwelandfriends.com

Design by Headcase Design

Feiwel and Friends logo designed by Filomena Tuosto

ISBN: 978-1-59530-254-0

BOK1149
Printed and bound in China
OCT 09

ACKNOWLEDGMENTS

To Liz Szabla, Allison Remcheck, Jessica Tedder, Dave Barrett, Rich Deas, and all the friends at Feiwel and Friends, but especially, Jean Feiwel, who always believes in me, even when I stumble; to the mega-talented design team at Headcase Design; to everyone who brainstormed with me while writing this book, but especially, the amazing Wohls; to the Bronxville Five writing group: Madisen, Margot, Perry, Madeline, and Lauren (you grrrrls were my inspiration!); to the original "girl" in my life, Mom, who always told me I was smart and pretty, even when I felt the opposite; to any girl with whom I've ever shared a deep secret or stayed up all night, especially Liisa and Melanie; to my non-girl contingent at home: Rich, Myles, and Nate the Great; to Ro Stimo, my über-agent (among other things); and to Ms. Karen Fein, my sounding board and beacon, who proved her true girl power by having baby Noel in the middle of this project.

CONTENTS

A Few Words About Being a Girl 9 • You Go, Girl! Fashion Hall of Fame 10 • Beauty Marks 13 • Got Lipstick? 14 • Brace Yourself 15 • Hair Dos and Don'ts 16 • How to: French Braid Your Own Hair 18 • Crazy Cosmetics 20 • "I Really Do Love My _____." 20 • If the Shoe Fits . . . Random Facts About Footwear 20 • How Much Beauty Sleep Do You Need? 21 • Off to Dreamland 23 • Dream Trivia 23 • What Your Dreams Mean 24 • Games Girls Play 26 • MASH 28 • Love and Marriage 30 • An Apple a Day 30 • By the Numbers 31 • Truth or Dare 32 • Most Popular Classic Board Games 33 • What is Mancala? 33 • Riddle Me This 33 • Five Quick Riddles 33 • Secret Message Rhymes 35 • Calculator Fun 36 • Math Rocks! 38 • Math Phobic No More! 39 • Songs from the Math Vault 39 • I Doku, You Doku, Su Doku! 39 • A Little Friendly Advice 39 • Jump Rope Games 40 • Jump Rope Lingo 41 • Jump Rope Rhymes 42 • Genealogy Made Simple (Sort of) 44 • Whew! Who's Who? 44 • How to: Create Your Family Tree 46 • Autograph-O-Rama 48 • Name Game 49 • To Be or Not to Be . . . A Name from Shakespeare 49 • Around the World in 110 Names 50 • AKA (Also Known As) 52 • Match that Princess! 53 • Birthstones 54 • Deadliest Diamond Ever! 56 • Mood Rings 57 • Fortune-Telling 101: Crystal Ball, Tea Leaves, Runes, Tarot Cards 58 • Wow! Wow! Ouija Board! 62 • How to Tell a Great Ghost Story 64 • The Most Haunted House Ever! 65 • Some Advice from an Expert (Who happens to be a guy, but we won't hold that against him) 66 • Light as a Feather, Stiff as a Board 67 • Sound Effects Everyone Can Make 68 • 6 Ways to Be a Lucky Duck 68 • Lady Luck 69 • Are You Super Superstitious? 70 • A Titanic Coincidence 70 • Achoo! 71 • Lucky Charms: 10 Objects You Might Want to Put in Your Backpack Before that Big Test 72 • Make a Wish 72 • How to: Work a Paper Fortune-Teller 73 • Feeling Fortunate 74 • Invisible Fortunes 74 • How to: Make Your Own Fortune Cookies 75 • 100 + Fantastic (and Fun) People, Places, and Things We Wish Were Real 76 • Revolution Earth 78 • Dot to Dot 80 • Astronomy vs. Astrology 80 • 3 Cool Things Almost Everyone Can Spot in the Night Sky 81 • Maps of the Stars! 82 • Zodiac Attack 84 • Give Yourself a Hand: Palmistry 86 • Doin' the Bump: Phrenology 88 • Sports Superstars 90 • Up Close: Babe, Billie, Mia, and Jackie 93 • What is Title IX? 97 • What Disability? 97 • At the Barre: Basic Ballet Positions 98 • Other Ballet Terms You Should Know 99 • What's Your Point? 99 • The Funky Chicken & Friends 100 • 15 Great Dance Movies to See with Your Friends 101 • Here! Here! Gimme a Cheer! 102 • Famous Folks Who Used to Be Cheerleaders 102 • Bust a Move! Basic Terms and Facts 102 • How to: Ace Your Tryout 103 •

CONTENTS

Bring on the Pom-Poms 104 • How to: Do a Perfect Cartwheel 105 • These Girls Know How to Kick Butt 106 • How to: Tear a Book in Half 108 • Getting Elected Class President 109 • Having Your First (Almost) Real Job 110 • Things You Can Do For $$$ 112 • Babysitting: Just About Everything You Need to Know 113 • Famous Firsts and Founders 116 • The Real Mothers of Invention 120 • Got a Big Idea? 121 • Cool Tech Girls 122 • So Are You a Tech Girl? 123 • Handy-Dandy E-chat Dictionary 124 • Point and Click: Remember This When You Go Online 126 • Netiquette 126 • How to: Write a Letter to the Future 127 • Body Lingo 128 • Cool Lettering 129 • Graphology 130 • A Brief History of Handwriting Analysis 130 • Passing Notes . . . or Not? 132 • How to: Make a Paper Football 132 • Not-So-Practical Note-Passing Ideas 132 • Remembering Your Locker Combination 133 • Other Ways to Improve Your Memory 133 • 4 Really Great Poems You Need to Read Right Now 134 • Write Your Own Poem (or Two) 136 • Alpha-Trivia 138 • 100 Commonly ~~Mispeled~~ Misspelled Words 139 • The Buzz on Spelling Bees 140 • 20 Ways to Jazzify Your Journal 141 • Secret Journal Hiding Places 143 • How to: Make a Cipher Code 143 • How to: Write the Best Thank-You Notes 144 • Yours Till the . . . 145 • Car Games! The Good, the Bad, and the Totally Annoying 146 • Destination Unknown, U.S.A. 148 • Car Tunes 150 • Funny Bumper Stickers 151 • May I Take Your Order, Please? Menu of the ~~World~~ Weird 152 • Move Over, Big Mac 154 • The Real Kings of Chocolate 156 • Just the Chocolate Facts, Ma'am 158 • A Horse Is a Horse, of Course, of Course 160 • Extraordinary Horses 161 • What a Horse Needs to Be Happy 161 • How to: Groom Your Pony 162 • Baby Animals 164 • Popular vs. Wacky Pets 165 • Six More Pets, Virtually 165 • A to Z: Amazing Women Who Changed the World 166 • So YOU Wanna Save the World? 10 Things You Can Do Right Now 174 • What Is Global Warming 176 • Take a Green Seat 176 • Everything You Want to Know About Barbie 177 • Solve a Mystery Like Nancy Drew 178 • 6 Inspiring Women Who Loved Art 180 • 50 Girls You Need to Hear 182 • 5 Can't-Miss, All-Girl Bands 182 • 20 Rocking Grrrl Tunes 183 • The Perfect Pop Star Name 183 • Things to Write a Song About 183 • American Idol for Beginners: Breaking into the Biz 184 • Planning the Ultimate Sleepover 186 • 30 Great Movies to Watch with Girls 189 • How to: Give Someone a Groovy Manicure (or Pedicure) 190 • Tip by Tip: What You Need to Know 190 • Paint a Garden on Your Fingers and Toes 191 • How to Make 3 Awesome Friendship Bracelets 192 • Knot! Knot! 192 • The Incredibly Unscientific, but Surprisingly Accurate, For Girls Only SuperQuiz 195

A FEW WORDS ABOUT
BEING A GIRL

Sugar and spice and everything nice.
That's what little girls are made of.

WAIT A MINUTE. IS THAT REALLY WHAT girls are? Last time I checked in the mirror, I was made of a lot more than sugar or spice.

This nursery rhyme was penned in the early nineteenth century, but it lingers. When I was small, my mom told it to me. Back then, I didn't mind being classified as "everything nice." After all, being made of "nice" was way better than being made of "snips and snails and puppy dog tails," from the boy version of the rhyme.

In elementary school, I decided that I was going to read every book in the library. My friend John did, too. And I won this battle of the fourth-grade sexes, claiming a small victory as the "smart" girl in class. But still, I suffered a little bit from a girl identity crisis. I wasn't just nice or smart or good at softball or piano. Who was I?

When the song "Girls Just Want to Have Fun" came out in seventh grade, I gladly traded my "super-sweet" and "super-smart" and "super-sporty" girl-dentities for something a little more fun and, at the time, cool. My favorite lyric in that song was, "I wanna be the one to walk in the sun." I wanted to be in the spotlight, just like that. Although I like reading serious books, talking about serious feelings, and getting serious about anything, I know I'm also a girl who wants to have fun— and lots of it. I'm guessing you do, too. Go ahead, admit it. I won't tell anyone.

The fact is that girls like us defy expectation and explanation. We can be a kickin', kung-fu mama and a pretty princess all at the same time. A girl can chart her destiny, ace that soccer penalty kick, get an **A** on the science quiz, and plan the best sleepover all in the same day. She can sleep late and daydream about getting a makeover, or she can grow up to be the next conductor of an orchestra or president of the United States. Or she can do it all. Girls really do rule, just not necessarily by following the rules.

A quick note on the book's title: *For Girls Only*. That doesn't mean boys can't read it. They just might not get it. But that's okay. Because, girls, we're just here to have fun. And we don't need boys for that.

Your amigo / friend / buddy / pal / BFF / comrade
in arms (the hugging kind),
—Laura Dower
xox

YOU GO, FASHION HALL

3500–2600 B.C.
Ancient Sumerians, Babylonians, and Assyrians don calf-length sheepskin skirts and shawls over one shoulder. A fashion statement is born.

3000–1000 B.C.
Because the dyeing process is slow to arrive in ancient Egypt, most Egyptians wear white. But they decorate themselves with brightly colored, jeweled collars, otherwise known as ancient bling.

500–1 B.C.
Greeks and Romans wear variations on the tunic including chlamys, chitons, peplos, and togas, all belted fabric of different lengths.

Centuries later, college kids will throw "toga parties" at their Greek fraternities.

1–900
What's that smell? Outer clothing in the Middle Ages is rarely laundered, but some say its super-strong smoke scent (from cooking or tanning) was as good as perfume or deodorant.

950–1100
Although Vikings sewed modest tunics, aprons, and cloaks for practical wear, their wardrobes are anything but ordinary. Vikings bring fine silks, linens, and wools back to Scandinavia from their trades (and raids!) in the Mediterranean and Asia.

1100–1200
The emperor's court in China's Sung Dynasty forces young women to bind their feet with bands of silk or cotton. These bandages are wrapped and tightened every few days for years, until the girls' feet are three or four *inches* long! Some say that the story of Cinderella (and Prince Charming's search for the fair maiden with the smallest foot) actually evolved from this painful, crippling ritual.

1100–1300
During the Crusades, rich Europeans begin to wear more silks, satins, damasks, brocades, and velvets in bright colors. With the invention of the spinning

GIRL! OF FAME

Our closets are crammed with last year's hot looks and this year's cool looks. No matter where we go or what we do, someone will be watching us and our clothes. Personally, I've never really cared what anyone thinks of my fashion choices, whether it be my clogs or too-faded jeans, or the funny-looking, home-made holiday sweater my aunt gave me about ten years ago. But it does make me wonder what counts as "style" through the ages. Here are some hits and misses from ancient tunics to really big hair:

wheel and the loom, clothes become more ornate. Thankfully, it will be many, many years before tacky sequins hit the scene.

1400–1500

Show off your swag! European women wear the fabric-heavy houppelande gown with sleeves that reach the floor. Also all the rage in your medieval town: mantles (cloaks), templets (hair coils), headdresses, and turbans.

1500–1600

From corsets to farthingales (otherwise known as hoop skirts), English women get pinched, poked, and prodded for the ideal Elizabethan look. Best fashion statement of the bunch: ruffs, those honeycomb neckpieces you see in art and movies about Shakespeare.

1600–1700

Real stars of the Baroque period? Curls, curls, curls. Everyone's got long, poofy hair, including the men. Bring on the stylists!

1700–1800

Order in the court? Women wear more elaborate gowns, puffed-up petticoats, and oversized wigs like Marie Antoinette. However, as the century goes on, hoop skirts and high heels morph into narrow skirts and flat shoes. Why the switch? The French Revolution and the American Revolution are partly respon-

sible. Popular fashion is not all about the rich anymore; it's about all the people.

1800–1840

Average women in the early part of the century really go for the layered look. A typical outfit: a chemise (slip), corset, more than one petticoat, underwear (also known as drawers), matching skirt and bodice, stockings, shoes, gloves, bonnet, and shawl. And you think it takes you a long time to get dressed in the morning!

1846

Sew Important Moment: Isaac Singer patents the first-ever sewing machine, which allows mass production of clothing.

1850–1900

In the middle of all the bones and ruffles, a practical, American fashion takes hold. Levi Strauss introduces the first pairs of riveted jeans, and a Wild West style is born. Cartoonist Charles Dana Gibson popularizes the "Gibson Girl," showing a woman who is free to dress in comfortable skirts and tailored jackets. With the invention of the bicycle in 1878, women's sweeping skirts are replaced by bicycle bloomers.

1910s

Fashion kicks into gear mid-decade with World War I, the women's suffrage movement, and the Great Influenza Epidemic of 1918. But get this: Even the strong-willed suffragettes are slaves to fashion. Some wear pencil skirts that are often so tight and restrictive that women can hardly walk in them.

1920s

Prohibition, jazz, and mass media bring a new look and a "Roaring Twenties" voice to fashion. Now women aren't afraid to drink, curse, wear short skirts and flapper dresses, and roll down their stockings to show some knee.

1930s

After the huge Wall Street crash of 1929, fashion falls in line with the Great Depression. More women sew at home and patch old clothes instead of purchasing new ones. One exception: fur. Sable, mink, chinchilla, and silver fox are in demand.

1940s

World War II ushers in the 1940s and Rosie the Riveter's working-class look is considered chic. Although artificial silk had come to the U.S. in 1910 and was named rayon in the 1920s, it isn't until the 1940s when pantyhose production really ramps up. While men are off fighting the war, women back in the U.S. hold down the home and jobs in comfortable, casual clothes. The most outrageous wartime fashion statement? Designer gas masks made to match elaborate eveningwear.

1950s

Television moves fashion into a new zone because now everyone wants to look—and be—like the families they see on TV. Top looks: conservative skirts, sweaters, pumps, and the grey flannel suit. Teens, however, get a little more adventurous. Called "bobbysoxers," they wear Converse sneakers, saddle shoes, ponytails, Levi's, penny loafers, and poodle skirts. And between Elvis Presley's blue suede shoes and beatnik culture, the times are a-changin'. . . .

1960s

Baby-doll minis! Bellbottoms! The Beatles! And don't forget Barbie! Hippies and surfers set the biggest trends this decade. Like, wow, dude.

1970s

"The uglier the better," is the best way to describe this lost decade of fashion. Polyester pants, wide ties, thick platform shoes, sherbet-colored chiffon dresses, Wonder Woman boots with short shorts, and of course, punk. Okay, you can stop laughing. I was there in my too-short plaid pants, blue Winnie the Pooh sweater, and red parka with the fake white fur collar . . . and it wasn't pretty.

1980s

Fashion takes the 1980s by storm . . . a cyclone, in fact! Working women wear men's styles, from suit jackets to trousers to big shirts. If clothing doesn't have shoulder pads or leg warmers, it isn't any good. The biggest trend of all, however, is hair. From moussed-up to mullets, it's all a big tease.

1990–2000

The end of the century is marked by a sort of "anti-fashion" movement. Music dictates a lot of the trends. Grunge means dark colors and flannel shirts and an angsty, "I haven't bathed in a really long time" look. The style shifts to hip-hop with its modern bling. Skater style gets big, too. A look we'd like to forget: sagging, or wearing your pants about five sizes too big, so your underwear shows.

BEAUTY MARKS

AN IMPORTANT THING TO REMEM-ber when talking about style and fashion: One culture's ugly is another's beautiful. You may look at some of the examples here and think, "Ewww, that is soooo freaky!" However, whether women wore incredibly tall wigs or flattened their heads, they thought that particular practice made them love*ier*, not uglier.

For years, women in Chad, Africa, have had their earlobes and lips stretched by metal rings as the ultimate statement of beauty. Today, women in Western countries inject their lips with collagen and Botox. Are these two actions really all that different? Irish novelist Margaret Wolfe Hungerford once said, "Beauty is in the eye of the beholder." For sure.

In ancient Egypt, women wore headdresses that looked purely ornamental, but were not. They were actually "unguent [pronounced 'unjent'] cones," a combination of animal fat and wax mixed together with spices and fragrant oils. After being worn all day, a cone would gradually melt and the odors would cloak the wearer with a strong scent.

In the first century, Roman women boiled walnuts and leeks together and applied the gooey mixture to their hair to make it dark and shiny. In the fourteenth century, women boiled lizards in olive oil to produce their sleek conditioner. Today, people wash their hair with everything from avocados to beer to mayonnaise.

In the Middle Ages, European women carried long, forklike back-scratchers to reach their heads beneath fancy hairdos. What were they scratching? Lice and fleas. Women started shaving their legs and armpits in this era, too, but it wasn't for beauty purposes. It discouraged the bugs from sticking around.

After 1760, the higher the hairdo got, the better it looked. Women piled on horsehair, natural hair, and wooden padded frames to create a tower of hairdo—sometimes their 'dos would be as high as thirty inches! This was, of course, a huge hindrance for women getting through doorways and into carriages. In 1776, the roof of St. Paul's Cathedral in London was raised primarily to make room for women's wigs, which kept catching on fire when they bumped up against the chandeliers!

During the nineteenth century, women used heavy makeup and beauty patches of velvet or silk to cover smallpox scars and large, black skin spots. Sometimes, the spots were "designer," shaped like stars, moons, or hearts. The placement of the patches was significant, too. A patch on your right cheek meant you were married, but a patch near the squint of your eye meant you were having an affair. How scandalous!

In the late eighteenth century, Napoleon's wife, Empress Josephine, thought her hands were so unattractive that she had gloves made to cover her hands and arms up past the elbow. Voila! The opera-length glove was born.

Corsets have been around for thousands of years. Popular legend says that most nineteenth century Victorian women, hoping to have the perfect seventeen-inch waist, squeezed into corsets a few sizes too small and ended up fainting because they cut off their circulation. Although it's true that corsets were hugely popular, none could instantly reduce a waistline to such teeny proportions. It took many years of corseting to train the waist to be smaller and corsets came in a range of sizes all the way up to size forty-two.

In the 1920s, women wore a flapper style of dress. But to make the dress look straight and clean, they also wore a flattener bra. Yeowch! Today, designers promote the opposite kind of undergarment. Women don items like the Wonderbra to lift and enhance their chests. Go figure!

GOT LIPSTICK?

THANKS TO INCREDIBLY WELL-preserved ancient Egyptian tombs, we have untouched evidence of makeup dating as far back as 10,000 B.C. Egyptians wore heavy eye shadow and kohl (black) eyeliner, lip ointments, and henna (reddish-brown) nail stain. They also traced lines of blue paint and liquid gold around their faces and other body parts.

Roman women loved makeup, too. The Roman philosopher Plautus wrote, "A woman without paint is like food without salt." Women applied pastes (made from things like lentils, honey, wheat, eggs, and other ingredients) to make their skin look as pale as possible. Consumption (or, "sickly") was the "in" look. And the paler a woman was, the wealthier she appeared to be. While poorer women worked outdoors under a hot sun, wealthy women had lives of leisure away from the burning rays.

In the nineteenth century, Victorian women carried on the pale tradition at great risk to their own health. Homemade cosmetics included dangerous compounds like arsenic, lead, or mercury. There were many wild ways that women achieved their whiter shade of pale.

• Staying indoors with blackened curtains and no contact with the sun
• Painting their face with paints and white powder
• "Bleeding" themselves with leeches
• Drinking vinegar and avoiding fresh air

• Applying urine to fade freckles
• Painting the veins on their faces to make their skin appear translucent
• Washing the eyes with lemon and orange juice, or rinsing the eyes with belladonna, a dangerous juice from the poisonous nightshade plant—all to make their eyes appear brighter against their pale skin

By the turn of the twentieth century, attitudes about makeup shifted. Women bit their lips or pinched their cheeks to get more color, rather than applying makeup! Between World War I and World War II, there were many developments in the field of cosmetics. Women like Helena Rubenstein, Elizabeth Arden, and Coco Chanel produced an array of lipsticks, blushers, shadows, cleansers, nourishing creams, tonics, lotions, and other makeup and skin-care products.

In the 1950s, color movies influenced the makeup industry. A face appearing on a huge movie screen showed every blemish and wrinkle. How to fix that? Makeup artist Max Factor created "pancake" makeup, a foundation that made all skin look smooth and flawless.

Today, although arsenic drinks, giant wigs, and white-powdered skin are mostly long gone, they've been replaced by a whole new lineup of beauty must-gets: fat-reducing creams, hair extensions, and self-tanner in about fifty different shades. Beauty is big business that keeps on getting bigger.

BRACE YOURSELF

CHANCES ARE YOU MAY HAVE TO get braces—if you haven't gotten them already. A lot of times, our teeth just don't grow in straight. But braces don't have to be scary or painful. I won't go so far as to say, "Braces are the most amazing things EVER!" because then you know I would be lying through my . . . er . . . teeth. But braces have come a long way from the clunky, metal-mouth contraptions of long ago. These days, they're less noticeable, they're available in an assortment of cool colors, and they're doing something fabulous for your smile and your health.

A FEW BRACING FACTS:

• Braces don't hurt—except when they are first fitted and sometimes when they are tightened. Oh, and if you get socked in the face.

• Braces do not usually change the way you talk. You should have the same ability to speak, sing, yell at the cat, and make fun of your little brother.

• Braces are now made with wires from a space-age material that straightens teeth faster and easier than ever before. And (bonus!) they come with rubber bands in colors you love. Pink and green look great together. Or try black and orange for Halloween.

• Braces that come apart in your mouth are not dangerous. This means: If you swallow a piece of your braces by accident, it shouldn't hurt you. You will, however, need to rush to the orthodontist to have it replaced. Braces stay on for an average of two years—if you take care of them.

• Braces last longer if you don't eat gum or gooey candy. And no popcorn! Stuff that sticks in your braces will give you nasty cavities.

• Don't do karate or play contact sports without wearing a mouth guard.

• Today's braces will not pick up radio signals. Years ago, when AM radio was big, people said they could hear radio signals on their fillings. But there have been no recent reports of *American Top 40* coming in loud and clear on braces. Sorry.

• Braces do not have to be clunky or boring. Some designer styles come in gold and sapphire, or bright purple, neon green, pink, or black—with or without sparkles! No one will ever call *you* Metal Mouth or Train Tracks!

• Braces will not embarrass you . . . if you don't let them. So smile, proudly—at school, at your next soccer game, *and* at the school dance. Chances are that your school crush is already wearing braces, too.

• If you have braces and you kiss someone wearing braces, it's unlikely you'll get stuck together. But if, by chance, you do—relax! The meeting of the metal won't last forever.

HAIR

DOS AND DON'TS:

GOING TO THE SALON

We've all lived through the hair horror stories. You go to the hairdresser with hair down your back . . . and leave with a bowl cut. Help! Fear not. There are simple things you can do to make sure you get the look you want. Remember these next time you head into the salon.

1. Your stylist is not psychic. He or she cannot read your mind or tell you what you want. Feeling pressured to make a decision? Maybe you shouldn't get a cut right away. Make an appointment for a consultation first. Talk it out.

2. Show up on time for your appointment. This is one of those Grandma rules. When you show up on time for anything, you're less stressed out and that makes all the difference. Plus, it gives you more time to read those back issues of *Us* and *People* at the salon.

3. Bring a photograph. Having trouble explaining the haircut you want? Try showing your stylist a picture. Maybe it's a photo of the cut you got last time, or maybe it's a photo of your favorite Hollywood star walking down the red carpet. Visual aids are always a good thing.

4. Haircuts aren't always that dramatic. The best kind of cut will make the most of your natural texture and length, but it probably won't change your face or your life. Don't expect too much, unless you're cutting off five feet of long hair in exchange for a pixie cut. As if.

5. You don't have to be all that dramatic, either. Stay cool and calm during your hair salon visit. And be realistic. If you have straight, thin hair, and you want a shimmering, curly 'do, you need to rethink your expectations.

6. Let the stylist do his/her job. Step outside of the box. Just because your hair has been parted in the middle since you were in second grade doesn't mean your hair stylist shouldn't part it on the side.

7. No matter how attached you are to your hair, it's just hair. It will grow back. And it will still be as beautiful as ever. I promise.

8. Visit the salon solo . . . but meet up with your pals afterwards. Let your BFFs see your new 'do when it's all perfect and blow-dried by the professional. That way you can show off and get all the oohs and aaahs you deserve.

Mohawk

Princess Leia

Mullet

Feather-Back

Crimp

Bouffant

Shag

Ringlets

BAD HAIR DAY

HOW TO

FRENCH BRAID

HEADS UP! THERE ARE A FEW important things you need to know about French braiding before you begin.

The key to a perfect French braid is practice, practice, and patience. You can practice while watching TV, listening to music, or in the backseat of the car.

Try French braiding your best buddy's hair first, so you get the hang of all the steps—and practice your hand position.

Don't be afraid to start over.

1. Take a section of hair at the top of your head, on your crown or behind your bangs. Divide the section into three even pieces, separating and holding them between your fingers. This will start off your French braid.

2. Cross the right-hand strand over the middle strand. Now hold all three strands in your left hand.

3. Take a new strand of hair with your right hand and add it to the right strand.

4. Cross the left strand over the middle strand. Now hold all three strands in your right hand.

5. Take a new strand of hair with your left hand and add it to the left strand.

6. Cross the right-hand strand over the middle strand. Now hold all three strands in your left hand.

7. Take a new strand of hair with your right hand and add it to the right strand.

8. Cross the left strand over the middle strand. Now hold all three strands in your right hand.

9. Take a new strand of hair with your left hand and add it to the left strand.

10. Continue to add strands and switch hands, braiding as far down as you can. Remember to keep the braid as tight as possible as you go. Be sure to gather up all the loose hair.

11. When you've braided as far as you can reach, shift the braid to one hand and gently pull it to the side, over your shoulder. Continue braiding at the side of your head. It might feel strange at first, since you are now braiding in the opposite direction. But continue braiding until there is no more hair.

12. Done braiding? Tie it off. Now take a look in the mirror. Congratulations! Sometimes there may be a "lump" of hair at the top of your head where you started the French braid. This is easily smoothed down. Remember: Don't get upset if the braid gets messed up. You can start all over again!

YOUR OWN HAIR

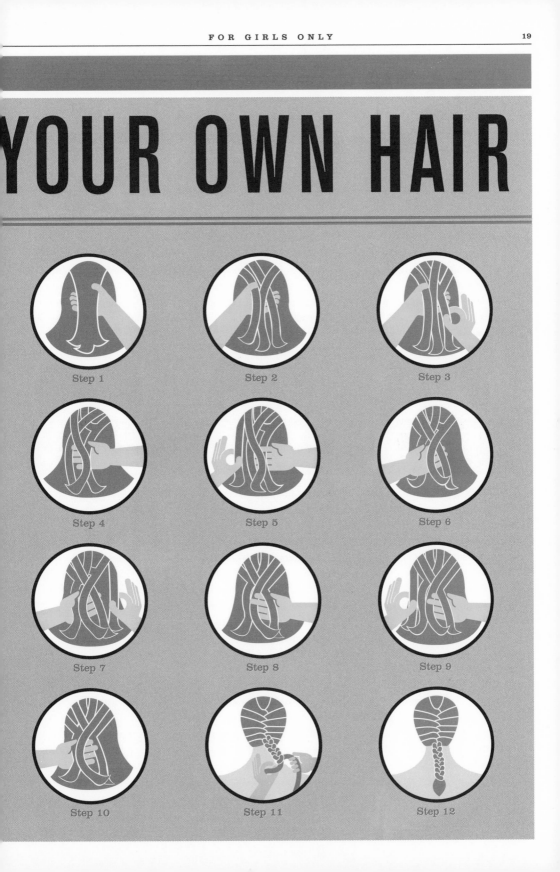

Step 1

Step 2

Step 3

Step 4

Step 5

Step 6

Step 7

Step 8

Step 9

Step 10

Step 11

Step 12

CRAZY COSMETICS!

Absolutely True!

- Chili Pepper Face Wash—hot stuff!
- Cheetos-flavored lip balm—the cheese taste stays with you forevah!
- A chocolate bar that doubles as acne scrub—huh?
- Bubble bath that smells like vanilla pound cake. (Okay, wait . . . maybe that one's not so bad. . . .)

"I REALLY DO LOVE MY _____."

THE NEXT TIME YOU ROLL OUT OF BED and wander into the bathroom, plant your bare feet firmly on the floor in front of the mirror. Now take inventory. Give yourself a morning pep talk. Not to get all touchy-feely on you, but positive affirmations—especially ones said out loud in front of an enormous mirror under fluorescent bathroom lights at the crack of dawn—really DO work.

Sample, starter affirmation (does any of this sound familiar?):

"I know that my tummy isn't perfect, and my toes are too long, and I really need a haircut . . . BUT . . . I really do love my nose. And I love my toes. And I love my hair . . . and my elbows . . . and my eyes . . . and the way I look at the world . . . and . . . well, golly gee, I love being me."

Take a few deep breaths. Say it all over again. Of course, the list can go on and on if you want it to. There's a lot to love about you!

IF THE SHOE FITS . . .
RANDOM FACTS ABOUT FOOTWEAR

OLDEST SHOES? Evidence of Native American shoes found in Missouri dates back to 8000 B.C. When archaeologists uncovered the "Ice Man" frozen in the Alps since 3300 B.C., he was wearing shoes made from bearskin and woven plant fibers. Now those guys had sole!

STRAIGHT SHOE FACTS? As late as 1850, most many shoes were still made on straight lasts. (A last is the oblong block the shoemaker uses to measure, make, and mend shoes.) Why is this so weird? It means no one had left or right shoes until the late 1800s. During the American Civil War (1861–1865), shoes were mass-produced, and a more detailed left and right shoe-sizing system was invented. Each soldier was given a shoe size along with his name tag.

POINTIEST SHOES EVER? First place: The Gothic fifteenth-century garment called a houppelande ended in leather shoes with extremely pointed toes that needed wooden clogs (aka patterns) to support them. Second place: Stilettos. Third place: All shoes belonging to Santa's elves and court jesters.

SMELLIEST SHOE FACT? New Yorker Herbert Lapidus invented the odor-eater insole in the early 1970s, because he claimed his wife had super-smelly feet.

SHOE FACT THAT SOUNDS LIKE AN EPISODE OF *BATTLESTAR GALACTICA*? The manufacturing process of vulcanization, discovered and patented by Charles Goodyear (the tire guy), uses heat to meld rubber to cloth or other rubber components for a sturdier, more permanently bonded shoe.

BEST SHOE NAME EVER? The word "sneaker" was coined by Henry Nelson McKinney, an advertising agent. He said the rubber sole made the shoe quiet when you walked, as if you were "sneaking" around.

HOW MUCH BEAUTY SLEEP DO YOU NEED?

DOCTORS RECOMMEND THAT YOU GET AT LEAST eight hours of sleep per night. The perfect night's sleep is one that leaves you alert and active the following day. But everyone has different sleep requirements. Even animals! What amount is right for you?

ANIMAL	APPROXIMATE TOTAL SLEEP TIME PER DAY
Python	18 hrs
Tiger	16 hrs
Dog	13 hrs
Cat	12 hrs
Chimpanzee	10 hrs
Sheep	4 hrs
African elephant	3 hrs
Giraffe	2 hrs
Shark	0 hrs*

* This is actually a trick answer! The truth is that scientists don't really know how sharks sleep, or if they sleep. Since sharks must maintain a forward motion to keep their gills moving, rest probably isn't the first thing on their minds. Only time—and research—will tell.

Contrary to some beliefs, sleep is NOT a time for the body or brain to shut down and stop. Although the metabolic rate slows down some, the body is still busy. During sleep, your brain's delta waves actually increase dramatically! Your endocrine system (which releases hormones that help us grow) is also very active during sleep. That explains why sometimes kids wake up with literal "growing pains" in their legs during the night.

OFF TO
Dreamland

Having trouble falling asleep? These may be the culprit:

- Watching TV or playing video games too closely to bedtime
- Too much (or too little) light
- Cold or heat
- Too much noise
- Soda with caffeine, or chocolate
- Sirens
- Loud music
- Other noises: your hamster on its wheel, a drippy faucet, the radiator

Next time you get ready for bed, try these simple steps to guarantee happy sleep:

- Try to go to bed at the same time every night.
- Keep your bedroom cool, dark, and quiet.
- Don't eat a big meal before bedtime.
- Run and play for at least three hours every day.
- Take a warm shower or listen to quiet music.

Source: sleepfoundation.org

DREAM TRIVIA

- Ancient Egyptians thought that the gods sent dreams as signs of luck or danger.
- Ancient Greeks decided that it was not the gods, but *people*, who created their own dreams.
- Around a third of dreams take place in houses, and a fourth in trains, buses, boats, cars, or other vehicles.
- Nearly 40% of dreams are about strangers.
- Sometimes people remember their dreams in black and white, even though everyone dreams in color.
- Robert Louis Stevenson wrote his book, *The Strange Case of Dr. Jekyll and Mr. Hyde*, according to nightmares that he had about the future.

WHAT YOUR DREAMS

AIRPLANE—a means of escape for your troubles

APPLE—immortality and love

BABY—something new has begun

BEE—you're too busy jumping from one thing to another

BIRDS—freedom

BOOK—wisdom and information; if the book is hidden, you're seeking something you cannot find

BUTTERFLY—transformation

CHAIR—if you're sitting down, you're repressing something

CLOUDS—you face the unknown and the unknowable

CROSS—you need to make a choice

DANCING—you are moving from one phase of your life to another

DOGS—one dog shows you the right way to do something, a pack of dogs means your situation is out of control

DOOR—there is an opportunity ahead

DROWNING—you are unable to deal with your emotions

FAMOUS PEOPLE—you are connecting with whatever traits and qualities that person has: good looks, fame, wealth, intelligence, etc.

FEATHER—truth

FIRE—you believe in passion and the burning away of bad things

FLYING—you are not stuck; you will find a solution

FOREST—the unknown (offering some shelter and protection)

MEAN

You wake up in a bundle of blankets, your hair is a tangle, and all you can think about is the giant airplane that crash-landed in your bedroom while you were sitting on a chair under a rainbow. Wait a minute. That didn't really happen, did it? But it seemed so real, especially the part about the tidal wave, the volcano, and the birds! That's how dreams work. They throw us vibrant, meaningful symbols and ask us: So, what do you think it all means? Here are some dreamy definitions.

GARDEN—safety and peace is coming your way

HAIR—you are strong; however, loose hair means freedom, while bound hair means loss of power

HATS—you need to share your opinions

HEART—you are holding on to a secret

HORSE—represents the human body; so if a horse is injured in your dream, it could mean that you'll get sick

INSECTS—you are suffering from anxiety

JEWELS OR TREASURE—you are on a spiritual quest

MAP—you are afraid to take risks

MIRROR—your true self

OCEAN—the unknown (offering uncertainty and no limits)

PATH THAT LEADS NOWHERE—you took a wrong turn

RAINBOW—a promise

SNOW—you have feelings that you're keeping to yourself

STAIRS—going up represents growth; going down represents your inner feelings

SWIMMING—you're navigating the unconscious; if you struggle against waves or a sea monster, you're afraid of something

TEETH—losing teeth means that you are growing wiser, although it also could mean that you also may lose power or get injured

TREE—a symbol of growth and branching out

VOLCANO—a great change is about to happen

WINDOW—you can see yourself clearly

GET A GROUP OF GIRLS TOGETHER and you can be assured of a few things.

Gossip. Everyone usually likes to talk about everyone else. Hopefully, all things that are said are nice. Yes, that's a hint.

Makeovers. Everyone enjoys testing out new 'dos and makeup on each other, which is cool as long as no one gets too carried away with the purple glitter eye shadow.

Games. But not just any kind of games. Sure, we like the ordinary playground games like tag and hide-and-seek. And we love board games like Battleship and Monopoly as much as the next kid. But there is an entirely separate category of *girl* games. And we like these best.

MASH

THE GOAL OF THIS GAME IS TO discover who you will marry, where you will live, and some other important details about your future.

Write MASH across the top of a piece of paper. This stands for Mansion, Apartment, Shack, House.

Then write down the names of four boys you like. They do not have to be people in your class at school. You can put down some cute movie star's name if you want. After all, who knows what could happen in ten years?

The short lists of four continue on the page. Write down four places where you would like to go on your honeymoon, four cities where you would like to live, four jobs you would like to have, four pets you would like to own, and four cars you would like to drive.

Now, take a pen and close your eyes. Somewhere on the bottom of the page, begin to draw a spiral. Stop after a few seconds. Now mark each line in the spiral. Count those marks. What number is it? That will be the number to reveal your ultimate MASH results.

Say that the number you got is seven. Now, starting with the M in MASH at the top of the page, count out that number through each item. Each time you get to seven, cross off the item, skipping over the items you've already crossed off. When you get down to one in each group of four, you have the truth about where you'll live, who you'll marry, and so on. But make sure you really like all of your choices before you start to eliminate. One time, I wrote down the North Pole as a place where I wanted to live. And that's what came up!*

Make a MASH notebook. Get your BFFs together and decorate a notebook that you can pass around the group. Inside, keep track of your latest MASH charts. Or make up MASH charts for your friends with people and places they don't expect! Try MASH categories like POP STAR MASH (only famous singers), HOLLYWOOD MASH (only famous actors), or SPORTS MASH (famous sports hunks).

*How to make it interesting: Have your BFF pick one item for each list that's something *horrible*. Have her add in "garbage dump" for a honeymoon destination or put down the boy you like the *least*, and see if his name pops up at the end. It's good for a laugh!

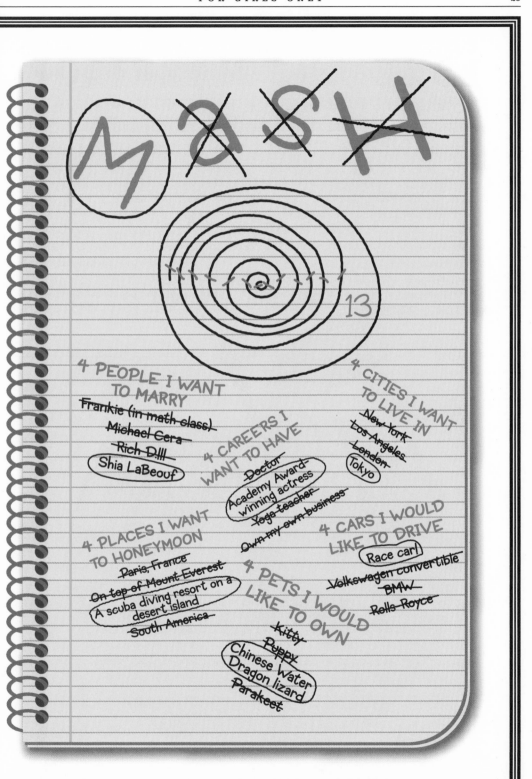

LOVE AND MARRIAGE

♥ ♥ ♥ ♥ ♥ ♥ ♥ ♥ ♥ ♥ ♥ ♥ ♥ ♥ ♥ ♥ ♥

LOOKING FOR LOVE? Look no further than the letters of your own name. Grab a piece of paper and a pen and check the odds of marrying your crush.

Write down your first and last names.

Under your name, write down the first and last names of your friend/crush/person you think you might like.

Do you have any of the same letters in your first name and his last name? Cross those out.

Do you have any of the same letters in his first name and your last name? Cross those out.

Now start to cross off each letter remaining in your name. As you cross off each one, say another word in this sequence: Love, Hate, Friendship, Marriage, Love, Hate . . . and so on. Whatever you say on the last letter of your name says how you really (truly, madly, deeply!) feel about him.

Do the same thing with his name, repeating the same sequence. This tells you how *he* really feels about *you*.

AN APPLE A DAY

DID YOU KNOW THAT YOU CAN FIGURE OUT the name of the person you love with any ordinary apple? Get to the green market and find a firm apple with a strong stem.

Take the stem and twist it in circles while reciting the alphabet. When the stem pops off, the letter you say is the first initial of the FIRST name of the person you will love forever.

Now take the stem and poke it into the apple repeatedly while reciting the alphabet once again. When the stem pokes through into the apple flesh, you have the first initial of the LAST name of the person you will love forever.

Eat the apple.

BY THE NUMBERS

THIS ISN'T REALLY A GAME, but it works a lot like MASH and Love and Marriage. It's adapted from a chain letter that I've gotten in my e-mail at least a bazillion times. Have someone read the instructions to you as you write down what is needed. Then you can read it and ask your friends to do the same.

- On a blank sheet of paper, write the numbers from 1 to 11 down the page.
- Beside the numbers 1 and 2, write down any other numbers you want (your age, your house number, your lucky number). One number per line, please.
- Beside the numbers 3 and 7, write down the names of two members of the opposite sex.
- Beside the numbers 4, 5, and 6, write down the names of family members or friends.
- Beside the remaining numbers, 8, 9, 10, and 11, write down the titles of four songs you like. (Or the first four songs that pop into your head.) When you've finished, here's what your answers tell you:

- The number of friends who are thinking about you right now is what you wrote on line 2.
- The person on line 3 is the person you secretly love.
- The person you like but can't seem to connect with is on line 7.
- The person on line 4 is the one you care about the most.
- The person on line 5 is the one who knows you the best.
- The person on line 6 is your lucky star—and the person who always gives you the best advice.

- The song on line 8 goes with the person on line 3.
- The song on line 9 goes with the person on line 7.
- The song on line 10 is the song that best describes your state of mind.
- The song on line 11 is the song that describes the way you feel about life.
- Finally, the number on line 1 is your lucky number. Keep that in mind if you're ever playing a game of chance—or helping Dad choose numbers for Lotto.

TRUTH OR DARE

YOU NEED A LARGE GROUP OF FRIENDS to play this game. The bigger the group, the more fun the game can get. Sit in a circle. One person volunteers to go first. That person turns to anyone else in the circle and asks, "Truth or dare?" Someone chooses TRUTH to answer a question, or DARE to take a dare. I always opted for dare, fearing mortal embarrassment if I had to face my friends' questions. The goofiest thing I ever had to do on a dare: Yell something dumb out of my friend's apartment window.

Here are some TRUTHS and DARES to get you started.

TRUTH

- What is your biggest secret?
- Have you ever gotten homesick?
- What do you like the least/most about ___ (someone's name here)?
- What is the most embarrassing thing you've ever done?
- What is the silliest thing you've ever said?
- If you could be anyone for a day, who would it be and why?
- What is the worst nickname you ever got?
- Who has the best outfit in the room?
- Who in the room is most likely to succeed and why?
- Who in the room has the best 'do?
- What did you dream about last night?
- If you had two wishes, what would they be?
- What is the strangest thing about you?

DARE

- Recite the alphabet backwards.
- Do a cartwheel. (see page 105)
- Put an ice cube down your T-shirt until it melts.
- Bark like a dog.
- Hop around the room on one foot.
- Lick your knee.
- Kiss your own foot.
- Make a toilet paper turban and wear it.
- Snort like a pig.
- Do a robot dance.
- Sing a silly song.
- Eat a packet of ketchup.
- Blow in someone's ear.
- Kiss your stuffed animal.
- Put on lipstick without looking in the mirror.
- Suck your thumb and cry like a baby.
- Make the weirdest face ever.
- Do the hula dance.

Make sure that all truths and dares are done with the spirit of good fun. Playing this game should never be about exposing, embarrassing, or hurting someone else.

MOST POPULAR CLASSIC BOARD GAMES

Battleship • Chess and Checkers • Chinese Checkers • Clue • Dominoes • The Game of Life • Mancala • Monopoly • Scrabble • Sorry! • Yahtzee

Ranked and rated by boardgameratings.com © 2007

WHAT IS MANCALA?

Mancala is a group of "count and capture" board games from Africa and Asia. In the U.S., the Mancala game played most often is called Kalah. On a Kalah game board, you have twelve small pits in two rows of six, two larger pits (called houses) at either end, and thirty-six beans/seeds (known as counters). Your goal is to get or "sow" the beans/seeds to either end of the board with a series of smart moves. Fun fact: The word *mancala* comes from the Arabic word *naqala* meaning "to move."

RIDDLE ME THIS

CLASSIC AMERICAN FOLKLORE celebrates the days when kids sat around making cornhusk dolls and telling riddles by the fire. And yes, those days really did exist, long before Xbox, the Internet, and digital cable TV. Here's a notion: The next time you're sitting around the cafeteria table picking at your fish sticks that look like cardboard, test out one of these riddles on your friends. Can you stump anyone? (Answers can be found at the bottom of the page.)

Humpty Dumpty sat on a wall
Humpty Dumpty had a great fall.
All the king's horses and all the king's men
Couldn't put Humpty together again.
Riddle 1: Who's Humpty?

As I was going to St. Ives,
I met a man with seven wives.
Each wife had seven sacks.
Each sack had seven cats.
Each cat had seven kits.
Kits, cats, sacks, and wives,
How many were going to St. Ives?
Riddle 2: How many were going to St. Ives?

Big as a barn,
Light as a feather,
And sixty horses can't pull it.
Riddle 3: What is it?

FIVE QUICK RIDDLES

1. What has legs but can't walk?
2. What has teeth but can't eat?
3. Four fingers and a thumb, but flesh and bone, it has none.
4. As long as I eat, I live, but when I drink, I die.
5. What goes up and down and around the house and then sits in a corner?

ANSWERS TO RIDDLE ME THIS: 1. Humpty Dumpty is an egg. 2. Only one person (the narrator) was going to St. Ives. The others were traveling in the opposite direction. 3. The mysterious thing is the shadow of the barn. ANSWERS TO QUICK RIDDLES: 1. Chair, table, or desk. 2. Comb or saw. 3. Glove. 4. A fire. 5. A broom.

SECRET MESSAGE RHYMES

S OMETIMES RHYMES AREN'T AS SIMPLE as they seem. The nursery rhyme "Sing a Song of Sixpence" was supposedly a coded message used to recruit crew members for the notorious Blackbeard's pirate ship expeditions. There is no one true version of the rhyme, but many of the lines have secret meanings that are decoded here.

LINE	SECRET MEANING
Sing a song of sixpence	Sixpence would be the payment per day. That was good money in the 1700s.
A pocket full of rye	A pocket is a leather bag and rye is liquor (which pirates loved).
Four and twenty blackbirds	Blackbeard's crew dressed all in black.
Baked in a pie	Concealing something in a pie was a common way to hide a surprise.
When the pie was opened, the birds began to sing	In this case, the surprise is a pirate crew and their "singing" is the great noise made while attacking!
Was that not a tasty dish	The dish, in this case, is the ship and booty that have just been seized.
To set before the king	And the king is actually Blackbeard, king of the pirates.
The king was in his counting house/Counting out his money	This is Blackbeard counting his loot.
The queen was in the parlor/Eating bread and honey	The queen is actually Blackbeard's ship, the *Queen Anne's Revenge*.
The maid was in the garden	The garden is the area of sea where the crew would scout for other ships to attack.
Hanging out the clothes	Clothes refers to the sails they hoist on their own vessels.
When down came a blackbird and snapped off her nose!	Beware! Blackbeard will strike again!

WITH A CALCULATOR AND A LITTLE IMAGINATION, you can turn numbers into words! The next time you're goofing around with multiplication and division, flip your calculator upside down and see if you can spell a real word. I've included a clever calculator dictionary as your guide and some riddles. Watch out! The fun really adds up.

be 38	go 06	obese 35380
bee 338	gobble 378806	oblige 361780
beg 638	goes 5306	oboe 3080
beige 36138	gosh 4506	oil 710
bell 7738	he 34	ooze 3200
bib 818	heel 7334	see 335
big 618	hello 07734	seize 32135
bill 7718	high 4614	sell 7735
bless 55378	hill 7714	she 345
bliss 55178	his 514	shell 77345
blob 8078	hiss 5514	shoe 3045
bog 608	hobbies 5318804	siege 36315
boggle 376608	hoe 304	sigh 4615
boil 7108	hog 604	sill 7715
boss 5508	hole 3704	silo 0715
bosses 535508	hose 3504	size 3215
eel 733	igloo 00761	sizzle 372215
egg 663	ill 771	sleigh 461375
eggshell 77345663	is 51	slob 8075
else 3573	leg 637	so 05
geese 35336	less 5537	sob 805
giggle 376616	lie 317	soil 7105
gill 7716	log 607	sole 3705
glee 3376	loose 35007	solo 0705
globe 38076	lose 3507	zoo 002
gloss 55076	loss 5507	

Don't forget most words can be made plural simply by starting with a 5, which turns into an S at the end of the word. My stepmother always loved this game, because it could spell her name, Lois (5107)! Can you spell your name?

Try and solve these fun riddles. Then make up new ones on your own.

Riddle: My mother always says I'm a . . .
Answer: Multiply 5 by 12. Add 236. Multiply by 6. Add 8,000. Subtract 1,701.

Riddle: Something gooey this way comes. What am I?
Answer: Multiply 4 by 1,000. Add 39. Multiply the total by 2.

Riddle: Reading all the words in all those book reports will _____ your teacher's mind.
Answer: 217,001 words minus 400 words plus 160,007 words.

ANSWERS: 1. 8075 or SLOB. 2. 8078 or BLOB. 3. 376608 or BOGGLE.

MATH ROCKS!

PICTURE THIS. YOU WALK INTO math class. Your teacher asks everyone to take their seats and then she announces that there will be a pop quiz. Your palms begin to feel sweaty. But then what do you do? Shake off the nerves and wing it? Keel over and pass out? Or do you raise your arms into the air and shout, "Bring it on!"

Whenever it came to math in school, I always felt like I was winging it. Just the thought of geometry gave me little hives. Okay, maybe I'm exaggerating a little, but I didn't have anyone telling me how much math mattered in real life.

The absolute truth is . . . math is power. It's logic, it's number theory, it's chemistry, it's physics, it's the way everything adds up and fits together. And it's fun.

Some simple things you could never do if you didn't know math:

Figure out how much those super-cool $75 platform shoes will cost with the mall's 30% tween discount. ($52.50)

Make the best chocolate chip cookie recipe ever—even though it comes from your European grandmother's cookbook. Convert her liter measurements to cups. Just check out the easy online metric calculator at www.worldwidemetric.com.

Divide one eight-slice pizza into dinner for fourteen. (Just cut each slice into two slices. You'll have two extra slices for the hungriest. You can also have the pizza parlor leave the pie unsliced and then carve up fourteen slices at home using a ruler. Note: Option 1 is easier.)

Know what Mom means exactly when she says she'll take your $10 allowance and give you a 10% increase each year for the next five years. (That'll be $14.64 a week in five years!)

Count the number of cute guys at the school dance. Then add up your chances for getting a dance with the one you really like—ha, ha! Get it?

Did you know that women have been mathematicians since at least the fourth century? Hypatia, an ancient Egyptian, was the first woman mathematician that we know about. She lived from 370–415 A.D.

MATH PHOBIC NO MORE!

Eliminate math nerves (otherwise known as a paralyzing fear of geometry, algebra, and all things mathematic). Get help with your homework and learn a few tricks about doing math from these useful Web sites:

www.mathgoodies.com • www.webmath.com
www.gomath.com • www.algebrahelp.com

I DOKU, YOU DOKU, SU DOKU!

THE LATEST PUZZLE CRAZE is just right for math wannabes. Sudoku (*soo-doh-koo*) is a logic puzzle that originated with Leonhard Euler, a Swiss mathematician who made "Latin Squares" puzzles in the eighteenth century. During the late 1980s, a Japanese puzzlemaker revamped the Latin Squares and started a new trend: Sudoku. In Japanese, *su* means a number, and *doku* roughly translates as "singular" or "unique." The game really skyrocketed in popularity in the 2000s in England. Now, it's something of a puzzle phenomenon. In 2005, some folks in Bristol, England, decided to make the largest-ever Sudoku game. Carved into the side of a hill, the huge puzzle measured more than 240 feet square with 15-foot-high numbers.

SONGS FROM THE MATH VAULT

- *Rikki Don't Lose That Number* (Steely Dan)
- *867-5309/Jenny* (Tommy Tutone)
- *99 Luftballons* (Nena)
- *One* (Three Dog Night)
- *Tea for Two* (Vincent Youmans and Irving Caesar)
- *Knock Three Times* (Tony Orlando and Dawn)
- *Add It Up* (Violent Femmes)
- *30,000 Pounds of Bananas* (Harry Chapin)
- *Love Potion #9* (The Clovers)
- *. . . Baby, One More Time* (Britney Spears)
- *Positively 4th Street* (Bob Dylan)
- *When I'm Sixty-Four* (The Beatles)
- *Edge of Seventeen* (Stevie Nicks)

A LITTLE FRIENDLY ADVICE

ONE OF THE THINGS THAT WILL make you successful with math is not being afraid to admit when you don't know something. It's okay to ask questions. It's okay if you don't understand everything (or anything) at first. It's okay to make mistakes and then go back and see where it all went wrong. The more you ask questions, the more you will learn. Plus, other kids in class, like shy friends or the new kid, will be happier when you ask. The truth is, everyone is wondering the same thing.

You know how sometimes a friend says, "Just deal with it!!!!" when something has gone wrong? Math is one of those things that shows you how to recognize, how to deal with, and how to solve all kinds of problems. It provides us with key reasoning skills that will prove useful now and in the future.

JUMP ROPE
G A M E S

JUMP ROPING STARTED THOUSANDS of years ago as a game for boys to show off jumping skills like crossovers and double jumps. It was girls, however, who raised the stakes. As families migrated from farm towns to cities, girls started doing their own brand of jump roping on smoothly paved sidewalks and playgrounds—adding tricky moves and the nifty rhymes that we love so much.

1-2-3 JUMP ALONE!

These are rope tricks you can do alone. Helpful hint: Before you try it with the rope, try it without, just so you're sure-footed.

SINGLE BOUNCE or DOUBLE BOUNCE: Jump once or twice before the rope rotates all the way around.

SWING TIME: Swing the rope to your left side. As you switch, spread your hands apart and jump. As the rope comes over, swing it to your right side. On the next turn, spread your hands apart and jump.

SKIER: Jump from side to side as you jump, just like you're on a real ski slope.

STRADDLE: Do a little midair split as you jump, but bring your legs back together as you hit the ground again.

HEEL EXCHANGE: As you jump, put one foot forward and touch your heel. Then switch feet.

WOUNDED DUCK: Jump into the air with toes pointed out. Jump again with them pointed inward.

DOUBLE UNDER: Jump up and try to spin the rope around twice before your feet touch the ground again.

PUSH-UP: On the first spin, jump up and then stretch out, facedown. Put your hands and feet into the push-up position. After a few moments, do the push-up and pull the rope around your feet. Repeat.

LEG CROSS: First, jump a single bounce. Then, pull your right leg up and jump over the rope with your left leg, while putting your right arm under your right knee. Now pull your arm out from under your leg and do a side swing.

4-5-6 JUMP TOGETHER!

Two players hold opposite ends of a long rope and turn it, while a third player jumps. The people doing the turning are called "enders." Everyone counts the jumps. A missed jump means the jumper must switch with one of the enders. Some of the tricks you can try:

Double hops or alternating feet (add in claps and twists—anything to move your body around in an interesting way while you jump).

Bounce a ball at the same time as jumping (called "Rock the Boat").

Drop an object and pick it up again—before the rope gets you!

DOUBLE DUTCH

Two enders hold the ends of two ropes. The ropes are turned toward each other so that as one rope is up, the other is touching the ground. It is easier to move into the ropes at an angle, standing with one shoulder next to an ender with the opposite foot slightly forward. Watch the "front door" rope, but be prepared to jump the "back door" rope as you move in.

JUMP ROPE LINGO

Grinding coffee	Porridge	Cut the cheese
Swish-swosh	Wind the clock	Scissors
Baby in the cradle	Split the pie	Lift and lay
Low water	Sweep the floor	Up the ladder
Run through the moon	Baking bread	Hopsies
Blindsies	Feet together and apart	Yokey
Hot peas	Double-French	

JUMP

The best jump rope games are played with nonsense rhymes. Most have funny words, sounds, and body and hand actions. Although some of these scream nineteenth century more than twenty-first, they are all about one thing that doesn't change with time: having fun.

Grandma Moses sick in bed
Called the doctor and the doctor said,
"Grandma Moses, you ain't sick,
All you need is a licorice stick."

Ouch! Touch your side, stomach, and head as you sing these lines.
I gotta pain in my side, Oh! Ah!
I gotta pain in my stomach, Oh! Ah!
I gotta pain in my head 'cause my baby said,
"Roll-a-roll-a-peep!
Roll-a-roll-a-peep!
Bump-te-wa-wa, Bump-te-wa-wa,
Roll-a-roll-a-peep!"

As you sing the rhyme, clap, snap your fingers, and smack your thighs.
Downtown baby on a roller coaster,
Sweet, sweet baby on a roller coaster,
Shimmy shimmy co-co-pop
Shimmy shimmy POP!
Shimmy shimmy co-co-pop
Shimmy shimmy POP!

Acka, backa, soda cracker,
Acka, backa, boo,
Acka, backa, soda cracker,
Out goes you!

Ice cream, soda, Delaware punch,
Tell me the initials of your honeybunch.
A, B, C, D . . .

Take note! Keep jumping until you trip or get tangled in the jump rope. Whatever letter stops you in your tracks . . . that's the first letter of your sweetheart's first name. Jump again until you trip again. That's the first letter of his last name!

ROPE RHYMES

Spell cat. C-A-T.
Spell rat. R-A-T.
Now it's time for exercise:
Hands up, hands down,
Turn around, touch the ground.
Now it's time for Arithmetic:
8 plus 8 is 16, 10 plus 10 is 20.
Now it's time for History:
George Washington never told a lie.
He ran around the corner and stole a cherry pie.
How many did he steal?
He stole 1, 2, 3, 4 . . .

Down in the valley
Where the green grass grows,
There sat [YOUR NAME]
Sweet as a rose.
She sang, she sang,
She sang so sweet.
Along came [YOUR CRUSH]
And kissed her cheek.
How many kisses did he give?
One, two, three, four, five . . .

Test your "High Waters" (that's what the motions in this rhyme are called). Have the enders spin the rope a little bit higher (without touching the ground) each time the word "floor" is said.

Fudge, fudge, tell the judge,
Mama's got a newborn baby.
It isn't a girl and it isn't a boy,
It's just a fair young lady.
Wrap it up in tissue paper
Send it up an elevator.
First floor, miss.
Second floor, miss.
Third floor, miss.
Fourth floor, miss.
Fifth floor, miss.
Sixth floor, baby's floor.
All out!

GENEALOGY MADE SIMPLE (SORT OF)

THERE'S NO CLIMB MORE THRILLING than scaling your own family tree. Is anyone in your family a genealogy buff? Do you know what your great-great-grandfather did? It's time to find out. On the 46-47 is a sample family tree. Can you collect information and create one of your own—complete with roots and branches? Where do you begin? Ask questions! Your parents are a good start, but you can ask your grandmother and grandfather, too, and any other relatives, including aunts, uncles, and cousins. Are you lucky enough to know your great-grandparents? Talk to them about the past and see how far back they can remember. All this information will be the branches of your tree.

What kinds of information do you need to gather? The most important pieces of information are full names, dates of birth, dates of death (if the person has died), and other simple facts. Who did that person marry? How many children did she/he have? What was that person's occupation? Do any photos of that person exist? If photos do exist, you need to make copies. Keep originals in a safe place.

If you aren't having such good luck gathering facts, or you just want to know more, there are lots of other places to look. It's probably the coolest treasure hunt you'll ever do!

- ☑ Check your house for old photographs with writing on the back.
- ☑ Find old notebooks and scrapbooks.
- ☑ Look for old Bibles (long ago, people wrote details of family records in the Bible).
- ☑ Look for letters or diaries with valuable family information.
- ☑ Check the public library for newspaper birth announcements or obituaries (death notices).
- ☑ Visit the county clerk's office (if family members lived in your town) for deeds, notices, and other records, too.
- ☑ Check out www.familysearch.com. The Mormons maintain the best genealogy records for public use. See what you find in their database.

WHEW! WHO'S WHO?

- your mom or dad's mom and dad = **your grandparents**
- your grandparent's mom and dad = **your great-grandparents**
- your great-grandparent's mom and dad = **your second great-grandparents**
- your brother or sister's child = **your niece or nephew**
- your parent's brother or sister = **your uncle or aunt**
- your grandparent's brother or sister = **your great-uncle or great-aunt**
- your uncle or aunt's child = **your first cousin**
- your first cousin's child = **your first cousin once-removed**
- your second cousin's child = **your second cousin once-removed**
- your first cousin's grandchild = **your first cousin twice-removed**

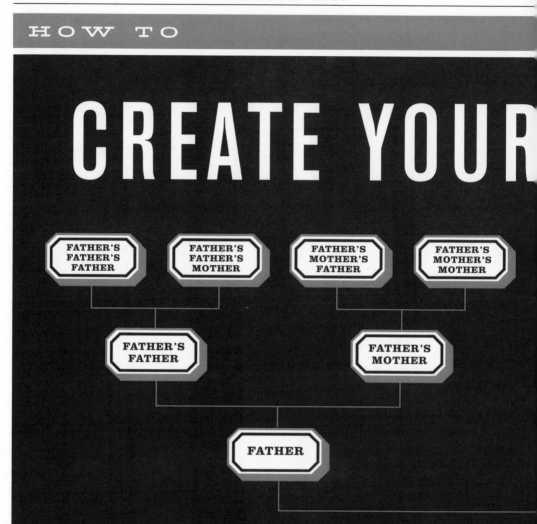

HOW TO

CREATE YOUR

BEFORE YOU START TO fill it in, take a look at the way the tree works. You are the base of the tree and all the branches and leaves going upward show the many members of your family. Directly above you are your parents. And directly above them are their parents. Got it?

As you add people's names, try to include personal notes and details wherever possible. For example, under Aunt Margie Wilmer, if she had a funny nickname, write that down. Did Aunt Margie like to sew? Write it down. Keep track of everything! The fun of genealogy is all about the details. Someday, when you get really good at sewing, you could trace it back to Margie. How cool is that?

The format for the squares, beginning with you and your own parents:

- Your name
- Born when and where
- Also known as (nickname)
- Place where you live
- Job

TAKE NOTE!

All items on your family tree that appear on the same line

FAMILY TREE

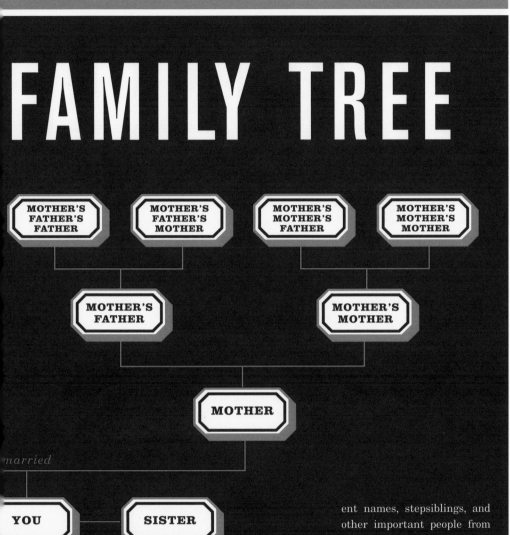

MOTHER'S FATHER'S FATHER

MOTHER'S FATHER'S MOTHER

MOTHER'S MOTHER'S FATHER

MOTHER'S MOTHER'S MOTHER

MOTHER'S FATHER

MOTHER'S MOTHER

MOTHER

married

YOU

SISTER

level, are considered members of the same generation.

If someone is still alive, just leave the date of death blank.

Use abbreviations to make things easier to read. B = Born; D = Died; M = Married; and P = Place.

If you're adopted, fill in the names of your adoptive mother and father, and so on. And if you happen to know or have a relationship with your birth mother and father, find a place on the tree for their names, too.

If you have a stepparent, make sure to add in stepparent names, stepsiblings, and other important people from your family.

Family trees don't just have to feature facts. Turn your tree into a family memory forest. If genealogy is all about your roots, that includes culture, upbringing, traditions, and more. So dig down deep! Take notes about your experiences, memories, and life lessons learned from various family members.

AUTOGRAPH-O-RAMA

IN A WORLD OF BLOGS AND MySpace pages, some old-fashioned traditions like writing letters (on paper! oh my!) are getting lost. But autographs—in little books, in yearbooks, and even on casts—still survive. Usually, the greetings go something like this: 2 Good 2 Be 4 Gotten! C U Next Yr! xox Susi! And of course there's the beloved, "Roses are red, violets are blue. . . ."

Many years ago, when the fine art of autographing was in full bloom, rhymes were a way to be clever and witty—and make up a ditty. Some classic examples:

It tickles me and makes me laugh
To think you want my autograph.

Remember Grant. Remember Lee.
To heck with them. Remember me.

Your future lies before you like the freshly fallen snow
Be careful where you walk, for every step will show.

Every time it rains I think of you:
Drip, drip, drip.

God made the rivers, God made the lakes.
God made you. We all make mistakes!

Your album is a golden spot
In which to write Forget Me Not.

If U B U and I B I
It's EZ to C the reason Y
I like U and U like I.

Maybe next time you sign a yearbook or write a message on the belly of a stuffed Build-A-Bear, you can surprise everyone with an alternate greeting from another era. If you're looking for even more autograph ideas, check out the list of "yours till the . . ." sign-offs on page 147.

NAME GAME

W HEN I WAS IN FIFTH GRADE, I had autograph books, for sure. But I also kept a separate, tiny notebook of names. I considered myself a genuine collector. If I heard a weird name, I wrote it down (over and over again!). For example, if I liked someone named John Smith*, my notebook page would look a little something like this:

> Laura Smith   MRS. JOHN Smith!   Laura + John
> Laura & John Smith   Mrs. Dower-Smith ♡   ♡♡♡
> Mrs. Laura Smith   Ms. Laura Dower-Smith   LD+JS

And so on. Sometimes I'd doodle about 100 possible child names, too, also with the last name Smith. This could go on for hours. You know what I'm talking about. I read somewhere that author J. K. Rowling kept a name notebook, too—and look where it got her!

The truth is, names are incredibly revealing, and playing any kind of name game says a lot about who we are. I always loved names like Hamlet and Ophelia and so many others from William Shakespeare's plays (see below). I also love names from different places around the world. Do you see *your name* anywhere on the next pages?

You may think about using some of these names for
   a) your very, very far-off-in-the-future offspring
   b) your top-secret alias
   c) the next character in your creative writing assignment

* Actual names of my die-hard childhood crushes have been changed to protect the embarrassed; namely, me!

TO BE OR NOT TO BE . . . A NAME FROM SHAKESPEARE

Aemilia	Cordelia	Hamlet	Nathaniel	Rosalind
Angus	Cymbeline	Hermione	Nerissa	Stephano
Antipholus	Desdemona	Hortensius	Ophelia	Timon
Balthazar	Dogberry	Juliet	Orsino	Toby
Bardolph	Elbow	Laertes	Othello	Tybalt
Benedick	Fabian	Leontes	Perdita	Ursula
Bianca	Ferdinand	Lysander	Pistol	Valentine
Caliban	Florizel	Malvolio	Portia	Viola
Cassio	Goneril	Miranda	Roderigo	

AROUND THE WORLD IN 110 NAMES

Here are some of the twenty-first century's top names from across the globe. Is your name here? Do you know what your name means?

ARABIC NAMES, 2006

RANK	GIRL NAME	MEANING	BOY NAME	MEANING
1	A'idah	Reward	A'waan	Helper
2	Afra	White	Xavier	Bright
3	Bilqis	Queen of Sheba	Aadam	Earth
4	Ra'eesa	Leader	Amjad	Rewarding
5	A'ishah	Lively	Ayman	Lucky

ENGLAND & WALES, 2006

RANK	GIRL NAME	MEANING	BOY NAME	MEANING
1	Olivia	Olive tree	Jack	God is gracious
2	Grace	Good will, agreeable	Mohammed	Praiseworthy
3	Jessica	God sees	Thomas	Twin
4	Ruby	Red	Joshua	God is salvation
5	Emily	Rival	Oliver	Olive tree

FRANCE, 2006

RANK	GIRL NAME	MEANING	BOY NAME	MEANING
1	Emma	Entire, whole	Enzo	Crowned with laurels
2	Lea	Weary	Mathis	Gift of God
3	Manon	Beloved	Lucas	Light
4	Clara	Bright	Hugo	Heart and mind
5	Chloe	Blooming	Matheo	Gift of God

GERMANY, 2006

RANK	GIRL NAME	MEANING	BOY NAME	MEANING
1	Anna	Favor, grace	Lucas	Light
2	Leoni	Lion	Leon	Lion
3	Lea	Weary	Luca	Light
4	Lena	Short for Helena, Magdalena, etc.	Tim	God's honor
5	Hannah	Gracious, merciful	Paul	Small

ICELAND, 2004

RANK	GIRL NAME	MEANING	BOY NAME	MEANING
1	Guðrún	God	Jón	God is gracious
2	Anna	Favor, grace	Sigurður	Protector in a battle
3	Sigríður	Beautiful victory	Guðmundur	Hand of God
4	Kristin	Follower of Christ	Gunnar	Warrior
5	Margret	Pearl	Olafur	Ancestor

ISRAEL, 2005

RANK	GIRL NAME	MEANING	BOY NAME	MEANING
1	Noa	Movement	Uri	My light, flame
2	Shira	Poetry	Noam	Pleasantness
3	Agam	To be sad	Itai	Friendly
4	Maya	Water	Ido	To be mighty
5	Tamar	Palm tree	David	Beloved

JAPAN, 2005

RANK	GIRL NAME	MEANING*	BOY NAME	MEANING*
1	Hina	Sunlight & greens	Yuuki	Gentleness & hope
2	Yui	Superiority & clothing	Haruto	Sunlight & to soar
3	Miyu	Beautiful superiority	Souta	Smoothly & big
4	Haruka	Distant, spring flower	Yuuto	Gentleness & to soar
5	Sakura	Cherry blossom	Haruki	Clear up life

* Japanese names are typically a combination of two symbols with distinct meanings

SPAIN, 2005

RANK	GIRL NAME	MEANING	BOY NAME	MEANING
1	Lucia	Light	Alejandro	Protector
2	Maria	Beloved	Daniel	God is my judge
3	Paula	Little	Pablo	Humble
4	Laura	Crowned with laurels	David	Beloved
5	Marta	Lady	Adrian	From Hadria

SWEDEN, 2006

RANK	GIRL NAME	MEANING	BOY NAME	MEANING
1	Emma	Entire, whole	Lucas	Light
2	Maja	Mother	Oscar	Spear of the gods
3	Agnes	Chaste, holy	William	Strong-willed warrior
4	Julia	Youth	Elias	Lord is my God
5	Alva	Elf	Filip	Horse lover

UNITED STATES (TOP NAMES OVERALL), 2006

RANK	GIRL NAME	MEANING	BOY NAME	MEANING
1	Emily	Rival	Jacob	Supplanter or literally, "holder of the heel"
2	Emma	Entire, whole	Michael	Who is the God
3	Madison	Son of Matthew/Maud	Joshua	God is salvation
4	Isabella	God is my oath	Ethan	Solid, enduring
5	Ava	Like a bird	Matthew	Gift of God

UNITED STATES (TOP HISPANIC NAMES), 2005

RANK	GIRL NAME	MEANING	BOY NAME	MEANING
1	Maria	Star of the sea	José	Of God
2	Sofia	Wisdom	Angel	Messenger
3	Isabel	God's promise	Juan	God is gracious
4	Adriana	From Hadria	Diego	He who succeeds
5	Daniela	God is my judge	Carlos	Free man

For more information on these and other names, including your own, you can surf some great sites on the Internet: www.20000-names.com, www.babynames.com, www.behindthenames.com

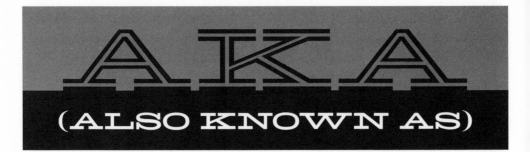

(ALSO KNOWN AS)

SOMETIMES PEOPLE ALTER THEIR NAMES for movie, modeling, or musical stardom. When they do this, they adopt a false name or a pseudonym. Stars have even been known to make up additional pseudonyms, when checking into hotel rooms to protect their identities! Here's a short list of famous gals and the names they were really born with:

Jennifer Aniston	Jennifer Anastassakis
Carmen Electra	Tara Patrick
Gloria Estefan	Gloria Maria Milagrosa Fajardo Garcia
Jodie Foster	Alicia Christian Foster
Whoopi Goldberg	Caryn Johnson
Audrey Hepburn	Edda van Heemstra Hepburn-Ruston
Billie Holiday	Eleanora Fagan
Diane Keaton	Diane Hall
Tea Leoni	Elizabeth Tea Pantleoni
Courtney Love	Courtney Michelle Harrison
Andie MacDowell	Rosalie Anderson MacDowell
Elle MacPherson	Eleanor Gow
Madonna	Madonna Louise Ciccone
Joni Mitchell	Roberta Joan Anderson
Marilyn Monroe	Norma Jeane Mortenson
Demi Moore	Demetria Guynes
Julianne Moore	Julie Anne Smith
Natalie Portman	Natalie Hershlag
Meg Ryan	Margaret Mary Emily Anne Hyra
Winona Ryder	Winona Horowitz
Meryl Streep	Mary Louise Streep
Donna Summer	LaDonna Gaines
Tina Turner	Anna Mae Bullock
Shania Twain	Eilleen Regina Edwards
Reese Witherspoon	Laura Jeanne Reese Witherspoon

MATCH THAT PRINCESS!

YOU CAN'T HAVE A BOOK ABOUT GIRLS without mentioning princesses, can you? Some are made up from books or movies. Others are found in real life. But all seem to have one thing in common: a range of power, strength, wit, smarts, and beauty. Can you match each princess with her description?

Princess Caraboo 1	a Chinese princess who fought the Huns
Pocahontas 2	b Her beautiful voice is stolen by Ursula, the sea witch
Diana, Princess of Wales 3	c Indian chief Powhatan's daughter, whose name means "playful girl"
Princess Diana of the Amazon 4	d Hates Prince Humperdinck in *The Princess Bride*
Ariel 5	e She tames the Beast
Aurora 6	f Princess of video game fame
Belle 7	g She wore the glass slipper
Cinderella 8	h Nineteenth-century maid pretending to be from the exotic land of Javasu
Jasmine 9	i Also known as Sleeping Beauty
Mulan 10	j Falls for Aladdin
Snow White 11	k She's from outer space
Princess Leia Organa 12	l Main character in Meg Cabot's *The Princess Diaries*
Princess Zelda 13	m Also known as Wonder Woman
Princess of Genovia 14	n She lived with seven dwarfs
Princess Buttercup 15	o Married Prince Charles of England
Princess Fiona 16	p Moves to the swamp with Shrek

Answers: 1h, 2c, 3o, 4m, 5b, 6i, 7e, 8g, 9j, 10a, 11n, 12k, 13f, 14l, 15d, 16p

BIRTHSTONES

What would a princess be without the jewel in her crown? Each of us has at least one birthstone that relates to the month of our birth. What does yours say about you?

JANUARY
GARNET

The word *garnet* comes from the Latin word *granatum*, which means seed. This stone looks a lot like a deep, red pomegranate seed. Way back in 3100 B.C., Egyptians used garnets in their jewelry. It stood for eternal friendship, trust, and strength.

FEBRUARY
AMETHYST

Amethyst is a light purple quartz stone that is supposed to protect you from poison. Ancient Greeks and Romans thought the stone would keep the wearer clearheaded. Put an amethyst under your pillow to bring about pleasant dreams.

MARCH
AQUAMARINE

The name for this gemstone comes from the Latin words *aqua*, meaning water, and *marina*, meaning the sea. Its beautiful pale, blue-green color is supposed to keep the wearer cool and calm. Ancient people thought it protected sailors from harm.

APRIL
DIAMOND

Diamonds stand for inspiration. They may appear colorless, but they actually come in a rainbow of hues including yellow, red, pink, blue, and green. Here's the rule: The deeper the color of the diamond, the higher its value. Diamonds are a typical stone found in engagement rings and in tiaras, and they are the hardest gemstone in existence. A diamond can cut right through a piece of glass!

MAY
EMERALD

Derived from the Latin word *smaragdus*, an emerald is a green stone that comes from the mineral beryl. The stone, mined in Egypt as early as 330 B.C., was the sacred stone of the goddess Venus. It has been known for centuries as a symbol of rebirth, and the person who wears it will have good fortune.

JUNE
PEARL OR MOONSTONE

Pearls, the only stones made inside a living creature (the oyster), have been treasured for centuries. The 1500s were known as the Pearl Age. Moonstones have a floating play of color and light inside the stone (called *adularescence*), but they stand for confidence. The Roman natural historian Pliny named the stone for the changing cycles of the moon.

JULY
RUBY

Rubies are supposed to bring health, wisdom, wealth, and success in love to whoever wears them. The deep, red color of the gem is most important to its value. It is the second-hardest stone after the diamond. What are some the most famous rubies ever worn? That has to be Dorothy's ruby slippers in *The Wizard of Oz*!

AUGUST
PERIDOT OR SARDONYX

Got nightmares? Peridot is supposed to protect you! This gemstone (ranging in colors from olive to lime green) comes from volcanoes. Legend says the stone is actually the tears of Pele, the goddess of fire and volcanoes. Sardonyx, with its alternating layers of reddish brown and white banding, was carried into battle by ancient Greeks and Romans. They engraved the stone with images of Mars, the god of war, and Hercules, known for his supernatural strength.

SEPTEMBER
SAPPHIRE

According to folklore, sapphire will protect you and your loved ones from jealousy. To medieval people, the stone represented the skies and heaven. Fun fact: Although it is the most common color, not all sapphires are blue. There are red, pink, and green sapphires, too.

OCTOBER
TOURMALINE OR OPAL

Tourmaline comes in different color combinations like watermelon tourmaline that has green, pink, and white color bands sliced to look just like the fruit! The word *opal* comes from the Greek *opallos*, meaning "to see a change (of color)." Centuries ago, a kind of crystal gel flowed into gaps in sedimentary layers of earth. With time, heat, and shifts in the ground, the gel hardened into the iridescent opal stones we see today.

NOVEMBER
TOPAZ OR CITRINE

For thousands of years, all yellow gems in antiquity were called topaz, but this isn't entirely right. For one thing, not all topaz is yellow. Imperial topaz, named after the Russian czars of the 1800s, comes in brilliant orange and pink. Also, some yellow stones are actually quartz. Citrine (aka "healing quartz") will give you health and positive energy.

DECEMBER
TURQUOISE OR ZIRCON

Although turquoise comes from the French for "Turkish stone" and is one of the oldest gemstones—dating back to the thirteenth century—we probably know it best from the jewelry of the American Southwest. Zircon comes from the Arabic words *zar* and *gun*, meaning gold and color, although the red variety of the stone is the most prized color. A colorless zircon stone called *cubic zirconia* is used to imitate diamonds.

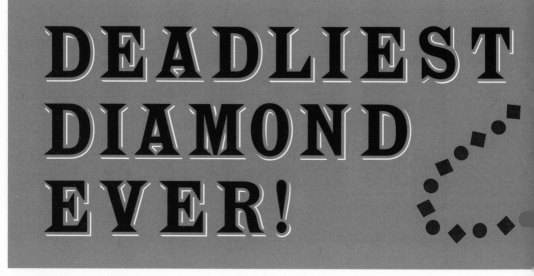

DEADLIEST DIAMOND EVER!

THERE ARE MANY legends (some fact, most rumor) about one of the most famous gemstones in the history of the world, known to us now as the Hope Diamond. The big question on everyone's mind is: can one stone curse more then 10 generations of people who came into contact with it? Or is all this one gem of a tall tale?

OWNER #1:
A statue of the Hindu goddess Sita. Her curse? Having a beautiful, enormous blue diamond stolen from her forehead.

OWNER #2:
Jean Baptiste Tavernier, a French jeweler traveling in India, lifted the 112 ³⁄₁₆ carat blue diamond and pocketed it. His curse? Some stories say he was eaten by wolves and died shortly after selling the stone.

OWNER #3:
Louis XIV, the Sun King, who bought the large, blue diamond and had it re-cut in 1673 to enhance its brilliance. At a new 67 ⅛ carats, he named it the "Blue Diamond of the Crown" and wore it on a long ribbon around his neck. He was the first of many generations of French Kings (Louis XIV, Louis XV, and Louis XVI) to own the stone. His curse? He lost all of his teeth and then died a slow, painful death from gangrene.

OWNERS #4:
Louis XV was only five years of age when he came into power. The stone wasn't a major player in his reign. His curse? Out of his ten children only two were boys and only one of those survived. The remaining son would be Louis XVI.

OWNER #5:
In the 18th century, Louis XVI became king of France with Marie Antoinette as his queen, the diamond came back! The curse? While the diamond was in their possession, king and queen met cruel fate . . . at the guillotine. They were both beheaded during the French Revolution. Then the blue diamond disappeared.

OWNER #6:
King George IV of England, whose jeweler recut it again to mask its identity. It now weighed approximately 44 carats. His curse? Massive debt. After his death, the diamond was sold to pay off his creditors.

OWNER #7:
Henry Philip Hope, banking heir and collector of fine art and gems got the famed blue diamond. It was then nick-

named The Hope Diamond. His curse? Irresponsible descendants (see Owner #8).

OWNER #8:

After the eldest Hope's son, Henry Thomas Hope, inherited the stone, it passed through the hands of a few other Hope family members, before landing in the jewel box of grandson Francis Hope. His curse? A serious gambling and high spending problem. The jewel was sold again.

OWNER #9:

Evalyn Walsh McLean came into the stone via Pierre Cartier, a jeweler in the U.S. A very rich woman, McLean fiercely believed that objects usually considered bad luck turned into good luck for her. So she wore the famed Hope Diamond all the time. She didn't even take off the necklace for an operation on her throat! Unfortunately, she was to have the worst luck of all. Her first born son, Vinson, died in a car crash when he was only nine. Her daughter committed suicide at age twenty-five. And her husband was declared insane and confined to a mental institution! After so many years, the curse was alive and well—and the name Hope Diamond probably should have been changed to Hopeless.

OWNER #10:

Harry Winston, a jeweler, got the stone and immediately donated the Hope Diamond to the Smithsonian Institution in Washington, D.C. It became the focal point of a newly established National Gem and Mineral Collection in the National Museum of Natural History. You can still see it today . . . if you dare to see the cursed jewel up close and personal!

MOOD RINGS

A MOOD RING ON YOUR finger can say a lot about how you're feeling and what's humming inside your head. Here's how it works: The stone set in a mood ring is actually a hollow glass shell with liquid crystals inside that change and twist as temperatures change. For example, if your finger is hot, a mood ring may change to red, purple, or green. Without heat, the ring may stay a cold, black color. The fun part: Every color is associated with a particular "mood" or trait. And the ring won't lie (at least it usually works for me!).

RED = Excited, Feeling Adventurous

ORANGE = Big Ideas, Daring

GREEN = Hopeful, Not Stressed

YELLOW = Imaginative, Wondering

LIGHT BLUE = Calm, Relaxed, Lovable

DARK BLUE = In Love, Very Happy

PINK = Afraid, Lots of Questions

PURPLE = Not Sure How You're Feeling

BLACK = Tense, Nervous

WHITE = Frustrated, Bored

LIGHT BROWN = Restless, Waiting for Something

FORTUNE-T

THERE ARE SO MANY WAYS TO READ and tell fortunes. Some people use Magic 8-Balls, although I always seem to get the same, lame answer whenever I use mine: *Reply hazy, try again*. The twenty standard Magic 8-Ball responses are:

> As I see it, yes
> Ask again later
> Better not tell you now
> Cannot predict now
> Concentrate and ask again
> Don't count on it
> It is certain
> It is decidedly so
> Most likely
> My reply is no
> My sources say no
> Outlook good
> Outlook not so good
> Reply hazy, try again
> Signs point to yes
> Very doubtful
> Without a doubt
> Yes
> Yes–definitely
> You may rely on it

But isn't there something more that fate has to tell me? There are fancier—and more tried and true—ways to explore your fate. Take your pick.

CRYSTAL BALL

What it is: A glass orb with special power, usually made from rock crystal.

What it does: Lets you "see" the future, literally. This is called "scrying."

How to use: Rub your hands over it, say a few incantations (spells), and focus your gaze on the ball.

The inside scoop: Celtic priests called Druids began using crystals to divine the future in the fifteenth century. (Fun fact: Druids were also the guys who supposedly built that mysterious landmark in England called Stonehenge, way before they used crys-

ELLING 101

tal balls). Other common crystal users from medieval times: gypsies, psychics, and wizards.

Extra credit: Best movies with crystal ball scenes: *Big, Fantasia, Harry Potter and the Sorcerer's Stone, Sleeping Beauty,* and *Snow White and the Seven Dwarfs.*

TEA LEAVES

What they are: You can "read" tea leaves as they settle on the bottom of your teacup.

What they do: Predict your future.

How to use: Make a piping hot cup of loose tea in a white cup. Wait until the leaves sink, then drink the liquid. "Read" the leaves that have settled on the bottom. You need to be familiar with all the possible symbols and their interpretations. Even more than that, you need to be able to distinguish and identify one clump from another. That's the real trick. An easy "clump" detecting chart is shown below.

The inside scoop: In *Harry Potter and the Prisoner of Azkaban,* Hermione is upset by Professor Trelawney's predictions from a cup of tea leaves. What appears? A wicked dog called the Grim. Its appearance is an omen that Harry will die.

WHAT YOUR CLUMPS MEAN

Arrow . . . you're getting some big news
Bell . . . someone is giving you good news
Boat . . . a friend is coming to visit

Bridge . . . you're going on a journey
Butterfly . . . happiness is on the way
Circles . . . you will be getting money
Crescent moon . . . good fortune
Forked line . . . you need to make a decision
Heart . . . Love is coming your way
Squares . . . you will get comfort and peace
Star . . . excellent luck
Triangles . . . one point up = good luck, but one point down = bad luck
Volcano . . . you're going to be so mad
Wavy lines . . . you will suffer a loss
Zebra . . . you'll be traveling far and wide*

*I'm sorry, but if you can see a zebra in a clump of tea, you are a total genius.

RUNES

What they are: Viking alphabet used for writing and magic. But they aren't your usual ABCs. Instead, the Runic alphabet is called FUTHARK after its first six letters/sounds (see the chart below).

What they do: Rune masters are specially trained to bring runes into play for divination and sorcery. A Viking poet once said, "Let no man carve runes to cast a spell, save first he learns to

Rune Symbol	Rune Name	Meaning	Sound
ᚠ	Fehu	Money, new start	F
ᚢ	Uruz	Strength, health	U
ᚦ	Thorn	Force	TH
ᚨ	Ansuz	Intellect	A
ᚱ	Raidho	Power, control	R
ᚲ	Kenaz	Artistic ability	K
ᚷ	Gebo	Generosity, honor	G
ᚹ	Wunjo	Joy, luck, prosperity	W
ᚺ	Hagalaz	Harmony	H
ᚾ	Nauthiz	Necessity	N
ᛁ	Isa	Unity, self-control	I
ᛃ	Jera	Peace	J
ᛈ	Pertho	Good omen	P
ᛇ	Eiwhaz	Protection	E
ᛉ	Algiz	Awareness	Z
ᛋ	Sowelu	Hope, success	S
ᛏ	Tiwaz	Truth, victory	T
ᛒ	Berkano	Birth, freedom	B
ᛖ	Ehwaz	Trust	E
ᛗ	Mannaz	Humanity	M
ᛚ	Lagiz	Flow, growth	L
ᛜ	Inguz	Resting	ING
ᛟ	Odala	Home	O
ᛞ	Dagaz	Happiness	D

read them well." Each of the twenty-four runes has a special meaning based on a) what is inscribed on the rune, and b) the rune material (ceramic, stone, wood/bark, or even metal). Viking warriors would sometimes carve runic inscriptions on their swords to protect them.

How to use: Cast runes on the ground and then read them from left to right to tell someone's fortune. But you might want to get one of those rune masters to help you!

The inside scoop: Check out a book of Norse mythology and read the story of Odin, who was speared to a tree for nine windy nights while he learned the mysteries of the runes—and then passed those mysteries onto his people.

TAROT CARDS

What they are: A tarot deck consists of seventy-eight cards. There are the twenty-two Major Arcana cards (Arcana means "life secrets"). The Major Arcana cards include the Fool, the Wheel of Fortune, and the Magician. There are also fifty-six Minor Arcana cards. The Minor Arcana are like a modern card deck with four suits. But the suits here are not clubs, hearts, spades, and diamonds. The tarot suits are cups, wands, swords, and pentacles.

What they do: Tarot tells you what's going on in your life right now.

How to use: The cards tell stories based on their placement in the spread. A person who wants his or her cards read (called a "seeker") must focus on an important question. Sometimes, the reader will let a seeker shuffle or cut the deck so the cards can "get" the question firsthand.

The inside scoop: Tarot symbols are thought to have originated in ancient China, India, or Egypt, but there is little evidence of the formal use of tarot cards before the eighteenth century. Two cool (and random) superstitions about tarot: 1) You should let someone else buy your first deck of cards; and 2) If you keep a deck, you should wrap it in silk and store it safely in a little box.

Extra credit: Don't get tarot mixed up with taro root, a potatolike starchy food found in West Africa, Hawaii, and the Polynesian Islands.

Lay it out there: One of the most common tarot card layouts is called the Celtic Cross. See the diagram below.

To read the cards, you must interpret them in order based on the face value of the card. Each card has its own story.

Card 1: This card represents the seeker's overall personality. It is sometimes called the Significator card.

Card 2: This card shows the most important things that influence the seeker. That's why it's placed over the first card in the layout.

Card 3: This card shows the things the seeker is striving for. That's why it is placed above the other cards in the layout.

Card 4: This card represents the foundation of the seeker's question and/or background. That's why it is placed beneath the other cards in the layout.

Card 5: This card shows the things that have already happened.

Card 6: This card shows what lies ahead.

Card 7: This card represents the seeker's disposition or attitude about things.

Card 8: This card represents the seeker's influence on others.

Card 9: This card represents hopes and fears.

Card 10: This card is the overall outcome of the reading.

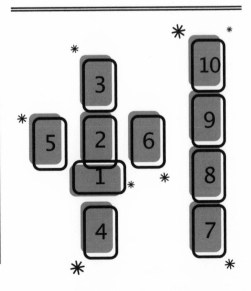

WOW! WOW! OUIJA BOARD!

THE OUIJA BOARD GOT ITS NAME FROM the combination of the French and German words for "yes," *oui* and *ja*.

Popular use of Ouija (pronounced "weejee") boards started with the American Spiritualism movement in the mid-nineteenth century. Peo-

Fig. 1 **The Ouija has a flat surface printed with letters, numbers, and other symbols that are meant to reveal secret messages from the spirit world.**

Fig. 2 **The sun means "yes," or conditions favorable.**

Fig. 3 **The moon with the single star means "no," or conditions unfavorable.**

Fig. 4 **GOODBYE on the board means stop your session. No one is listening.**

Fig. 5 **The people in the lower corners don't mean much of anything and are just part of the design.**

Fig. 6 **A planchette is a little triangular piece that moves around the board. The word planchette is French for "little plank." You and everyone else who is playing press gently with your fingertips on this piece to see where it goes.**

Fig. 7 **Wherever the planchette moves (and stops), that reveals a particular letter or number. The same process is repeated again and again until the letters and numbers spell out a message.**

Fig. 2

Fig. 1

YES

ABCDEF

NOPQRS

1 2 3 4

GOO

Fig. 5

ple liked to divine (or tell) the future using different techniques. Some would swing a pendulum over a plate with letters around the edge, and wherever the pendulum swung spelled out a message.

One of the coolest rumored Ouija board encounters comes from the White House! During sleepovers with her friends, President Jimmy Carter's daughter, Amy, reportedly used a Ouija board to contact the spirit of Abraham Lincoln, who is believed to haunt the Lincoln Bedroom.

HOW TO TELL
A GREAT GHOST STORY

1. Turn out the lights. Darkness is the most important tool you have to get everyone's imagination churning.

2. Hold a flashlight up to your face while you tell the story. For a real air of mystery, like a creepy spotlight, hold it above your head. For an air of terror, so your face looks weird and distorted, hold it under your chin.

3. As you speak, use your best voice distortions like the cackle, the whisper, and the rasp. Speak in a soft voice whenever possible. That way, everyone has to pay extra close attention to your words— and it increases the chance that they'll be caught off guard with a scare tactic.

4. Build tension from the start. Open your story with a happy, ordinary setting like your own town or school. Remember that you want to start slow and build suspense, keeping everyone on the edge of their seats. Tell the story of how you and your friends are just hanging out when . . . [insert cliff-hanger here!]

5. Plan your chilling cliff-hangers in advance. Samples:
   - . . . they hear a strange noise (you make a noise).
   - . . . someone screams (you scream).
   - . . . the lights go out (you turn off your flashlight).

6. Become a master of cool sound effects. A good "WHAM!" in the middle of a calm storytelling moment really makes people jump. Some sounds you can make with your body; others may need to be prerecorded. See the list on the next page.

You're setting the scene for a pretty fearful experience, but one thing you don't have to worry about with your best pals is PARTHENOPHOBIA. That's the fear of *girls*!

7. Introduce your scariest character and describe that person in detail. Include every oozing wart, the bad breath, deep rattling voice, and whatever else makes him or her scary.

8. Build one cliff-hanger upon another, building to key moments in your story.

9. Alternate plan: Start your story, but instead of doing all the work yourself, get *everyone* involved. Everyone adds a detail as you go around the circle. Many imaginations are better than just one. Or you could get an accomplice to help tell your story. That person could flicker a light or slam a door while you're speaking.

10. Whether you tell the story alone or as a group, remember your key goal is to scare. Think about the plots and characters in TV, movies, and books that have given you goose bumps before now. Some spine-tingling stuff:

- Heavy rain
- Screeching bats
- Rattling chains
- Howling wolves
- Squirmy worms
- Sharp, gnashing teeth
- Angry aliens
- Mad scientists
- Thunder and lightning
- Squeaking doors

THE MOST HAUNTED HOUSE EVER!

BELIEVE IT OR NOT, ONE of the most haunted places in the U.S. is the White House! There have been more than eight ghosts seen there over the years, including Abigail Adams doing her laundry in the East Room, Dolley Madison watching over the Rose Garden, President Andrew Johnson pacing and laughing in the Rose Room, and President William Henry Harrison hunting through boxes in the attic. Of course, Harrison *was* the first president to die in office, so his ghostly presence makes sense.

But the biggest apparition seen at Pennsylvania Avenue has to be Abe Lincoln. He's been spotted by numerous heads of state and visitors to the White House over the years, looking concerned as he stared through the Oval Office windows, knocking on guest bedroom doors, or taking off his boots before going to bed. President John F. Kennedy's butler said that Lincoln appeared often and was always polite. He'd tap you on the shoulder or cough slightly so you would notice his presence.

SOME ADVICE FROM

(WHO HAPPENS TO BE A GUY, BUT WE WON'

Mark Twain (also known as Samuel Langhorne Clemens) was clever, funny, and above all else, he knew how to tell a terrific story. His nineteenth-century book *The Adventures of Huckleberry Finn* has been called The Great American Novel. Here is some advice from this expert about how to put the s-s-scare in your story. Twain often wrote stories using a dialect like the people in his small town in Missouri.

"I do not claim that I can tell a story as it ought to be told. I only claim to know how a story ought to be told, for I have been almost daily in the company of the most expert storytellers for years. . . .

"The pause is an exceedingly important feature in any kind of story, and a frequently recurring feature, too. It is a dainty thing, and delicate, and also uncertain and treacherous; for it must be exactly the right length—no more and no less—or it fails of its purpose and makes trouble. If the pause is too short the impressive point is

passed, and the audience have had time to divine that a surprise is intended—and then you can't surprise them, of course. . . .

"I used to tell a . . . ghost story that had a pause in front of the snapper* on the end, and that pause was the most important thing in the whole story. If I got it the right length precisely, I could spring the finishing ejaculation with effect enough to make some impressionable girl deliver a startled little yelp and jump out of her seat—and that was what I was after. This story was called *The Golden Arm*, and was told in this fashion. You can practice with it yourself—and mind you look out for the pause and get it right."

THE GOLDEN ARM

ONCE 'PON A TIME dey wuz a monsus mean man, en he live 'way out in de prairie all 'lone by hisself, 'cep'n he had a wife. En bimeby she died, en he tuck en toted her way out dah in de prairie en buried her. Well, she had a golden arm—

all solid gold, fum de shoulder down. He wuz pow'ful mean—pow'ful; en dat night he couldn't sleep, caze he want dat golden arm so bad.

When it come midnight he couldn't stan' it no mo'; so he git up, he did, en tuck his lantern en shoved out thoo de storm en dug her up en got de golden arm; en he bent his head down 'gin de win', en plowed en plowed en plowed thoo de snow. Den all on a sudden he stop (make a considerable pause here, and look startled, and take a listening attitude) en say: "My lan', what's dat!"

En he listen—en listen—en de win' say (set your teeth together and imitate the wailing and wheezing singsong of the wind), "Bzzz-z-zzz"—en den, way back yonder what de grave is, he hear a voice!—he hear a voice all mix' up in de win'—can't hardly tell 'em 'part—"Bzzz-zzz—W-h-o—g-o-t—m-y—g-o-l-d-e-n—arm?—zzz—zzz—W-h-o g-o-t m-y g-o-l-d-e-n arm?" (You must begin to shiver violently now.)

En he begin to shiver en shake, en say, "Oh, my! Oh,

---

*Pssst! A "snapper" is like a punch line or an "a-ha!" moment in the story.

AN EXPERT

HOLD THAT AGAINST HIM)

my lan'!" en de win' blow de lantern out, en de snow en sleet blow in his face en mos' choke him, en he start a-plowin' knee-deep toward home mos' dead, he so sk'y-erd—en pooty soon he hear de voice agin, en (pause) it 'us comin' after him! "Bzzz—zzz—zzz—W-h-o—g-o-t—m-y g-o-l-d-e-n—arm?"

When he git to de pasture he hear it agin—closter now, en a-comin'!—a-comin' back dah in de dark en de storm—(repeat the wind and the voice). When he git to de house he rush up-stairs en jump in de bed en kiver up, head and years, en lay dah shiverin' en shakin'—en den way out dah he hear it agin!—en a-comin'! En bime-by he hear (pause—awed, listening attitude)—pat—pat—pat—hit's a-comin' up-stairs! Den he hear de latch, en he know it's in de room! Den pooty soon he know it's a-stannin' by de bed! (Pause.) Den—he know it's a-bendin' down over him—en he cain't skasely git his breath! Den—den—he seem to feel someth'n c-o-l-d, right down 'most agin his head!

(Pause.)

Den de voice say, right at his year—"W-h-o—g-o-t—m-y—g-o-l-d-e-n arm?" (You must wail it out very plaintively and accusingly; then you stare steadily and impressively into the face of the farthest-gone auditor—a girl, preferably—and let that awe-inspiring pause begin to build itself in the deep hush. When it has reached exactly the right length, jump suddenly at that girl and yell, "You've got it!" If you've got the pause right, she'll fetch a dear little yelp and spring right out of her shoes. But you must get the pause right; and you will find it the most troublesome and aggravating and uncertain thing you ever undertook.)

By the way, Mark Twain says in a few places here that the goal is to frighten the girl in the group. As if we're all chickens? Puh-lease! That is sooooo nineteenth century.

Main text excerpted from *How to Tell a Story* (1897) by Mark Twain

LIGHT AS A FEATHER, STIFF AS A BOARD

SLEEPOVER PARTY alert! You must try this at your next get-together. A little mood lighting and music will help set the stage. Your goal: levitation. Yes, you can lift your friend into the air with little more than your fingertips.

The most common version of this "trick" requires at least five people. One person (let's call him or her THE BODY) lies relaxed on the floor with eyes closed. The other four participants surround THE BODY, one on each side, one at the head, and one at the feet. Each of the participants places two fingers of each hand beneath THE BODY. With eyes closed, they begin to chant, "Light as a feather . . . stiff as a board . . ." over and over. With just the slightest effort, the participants should be able to raise THE BODY off the floor. Whoa! Talk about gravity-defying! Is something supernatural helping you?

SOUND EFFECTS EVERYONE CAN MAKE

- **RAIN** Shake rice in a pan or spray water into a bucket.
- **RAINSTORM** You need a larger group for this one to work best. Have a few people rub their palms together softly so it sounds like rain; then someone starts to snap, and then another person stomps her feet. With all the noises working together, it simulates the sounds of a real storm.
- **TRAIN** Put a handful of paper clips into a metal box or coffee tin and shake. It sounds like the chug-a-chug on the train track.
- **FIRE** Crumple cellophane or plastic to imitate the sound of crackling flames.
- **PLANE** Whistle high, and then get softer as if the plane sound gets lower.
- **MOTOR** Stick cardboard pieces between your bike spokes and spin the wheel. Or, turn on a blender.
- **WIND** Blow air into a microphone. This works well if you blow into a mic on a stereo or even on one of those cheap, plastic microphones you can get at the dollar store.
- **GALLOPING HORSE** Slap your hands on your thighs, one at a time.
- **PUNCH** Actually punch one fist into your palm.
- **THUD** Pound your fist into a cushy pillow.
- **FOOTSTEPS** Make actual footsteps with a shoe that has a hard heel (or any hard object) on a hard floor.
- **SWAMP MUSIC** In a high and then a low voice, say over and over again, "knee-deep, knee-deep, ribbit, ribbit, knee-deep . . ."
- **EXPLOSION** Blow up a plastic bag and then pop it.
- **SHIP'S HORN OR ELEPHANT** You need: a cardboard paper towel roll, a manila folder, masking tape, and a big breath. Wrap the folder around one end of the tube so it looks like a funnel and tape it in place. Blow through the opposite end.

6 WAYS TO BE A LUCKY DUCK

FRENCH DICTATOR NAPOLEON BONAPARTE did not look for courageous generals or brilliant generals. Instead he said "give me *lucky* generals." But how does a person get to be lucky?

1. Take risks. Trust your gut feelings and go for it. On a test, if you think you know the answer, write it down. Try not to second-guess yourself.
2. Expect the best. My old philosophy was to expect the worst. This way, I figured I could never be disappointed. Ha! Fat chance! What kind of backwards thinking was that? Now I expect better than the best.
3. Share. You can't let in luck if you're keeping all your toys and good ideas to yourself. There is an old saying that when one door closes, another one opens. The more doors and windows that you open, the more great stuff will come flying through.
4. Know what to say. When something lucky comes your way, be gracious. Sample: "Aw, shucks, I can't believe the sweepstakes committee came to my house with balloons and cameras and a check for ten million dollars! Fancy that!"
5. Know when to zip your lip. Listening is one of the most important life skills you can possess. If you listen real close, you'll hear luck coming.
6. Never take off your lucky purple socks. Ever.

LADY ✤ LUCK

WHENEVER SOMETHING GOOD would happen, my grandmother would say, "Lady luck must be smiling on me today." Do you think such a lady exists? The following cases seem to prove she's out there somewhere.

THE CASE OF THE SEVEN LIGHTNING STRIKES

Roy Sullivan was hit seven times by lightning and lived to tell the tale. He was even nicknamed the "Human Lightning Rod," with the scars to prove it.

- 1942: A lightning bolt struck him in a leg, and he lost a nail on his big toe.
- 1969: The second bolt hit him in his truck when he was driving on a mountain road, knocking him unconscious and burning his eyebrows.
- 1970: The third strike, in his front yard, burned his left shoulder.
- 1972: The fourth strike set his hair on fire. After that, Roy got a little worried. He carried a pitcher of water with him at all times.
- 1973: Propelled from his car by lightning.
- 1974: The sixth bolt struck Roy in a campground. He attempted to outrun a cloud he thought was following him and injured his ankle.
- 1977: After a direct hit while fishing, Roy was hospitalized for burns in his chest and stomach. As far as we know, it was his last encounter with lightning. He died in 1983.

THE CASE OF THE DOUBLE LOTTO WINNERS

Who says you can't beat the odds? Eugene Angelo Sr., 81, and his wife Adeline, 74, won the lottery in 1996 ($2.5 million) and then again in 2007 ($5 million), just a month shy of their fiftieth wedding anniversary. A New York State lottery spokesman said that the chances of winning the lottery once are 22 million to 1, so the odds of doing it twice are "galactically astronomical." The Angelos are "living proof that lightning, or in this case, random luck, can strike twice."

THE CASE OF THE MISSING RING AND THE JUNK MAIL CLUE

In Northport, NY, a man found a wedding ring in a floorboard in his home. He used the inscription in the band (Kitty to Johnny—3/31/51) to track down the ring's owner. First, he asked neighbors and used the Internet to try to find the family who had once lived in his home. But no luck. Then he phoned previous owners. No luck. Then, out of the blue, he got a piece of junk mail addressed to a Kitty Zenkus. Fireworks went off. Had he found his missing owner—fifty years later? With some detective work he located 74-year-old Catherine Zenkus, aka Kitty. Tearfully, Kitty explained that finding the ring was like getting a piece of her husband back, since he'd been dead for some eighteen years.

THE CASE OF THE BARGAIN HUNTER AND THE OLD PICTURE

Imagine buying an ugly, framed piece of art at a yard sale for a mere $4.00—and then later discovering it was worth millions. That's exactly what happened to a financial analyst in 1996. He bought an old piece of art because he liked the frame. But as he removed the muddy, worthless painting, he realized that the frame was a hunk of junk, too! And then he found something stuck inside the frame—a document hidden between the canvas and its backing. The man opened the paper and read, "In Congress, July 4, 1776 . . ." He gasped. Could it be true? An expert later confirmed the page's identity: This was one of only 500 copies of the original Declaration of Independence. Eventually, the financial analyst sold that $4.00 paper at auction for $2.42 million!

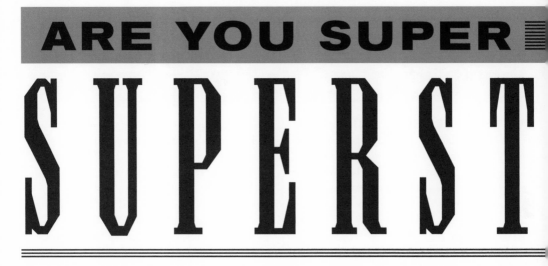

ARE YOU SUPER

SUPERST

SUPERSTITIOUS FOLKS ARE EVERYWHERE, not stepping on sidewalk cracks and totally avoiding ladders. Alas, I'm a member of that superstitious crowd. I still have one pair of ripped jeans that I keep in the bottom drawer because I aced a test once while wearing them and now I'm too afraid to toss 'em. Oh, and I cross my fingers a lot. That's a habit I picked up back in first grade.

So what's *your* superstition?

One of the coolest books on the topic of superstition is called *Cross Your Fingers, Spit in Your Hat: Superstitions and Other Beliefs* by Alvin Schwartz. I read it for the first time when I was nine. Check it out.

A TITANIC COINCIDENCE

MOST PEOPLE KNOW THAT THE *TITANIC* CRASHED into an iceberg and sank on her maiden voyage. Over 1,500 people died on that tragic April 15, 1912. But did you know that fourteen years *before that happened*, Morgan Robertson published a novella named *Futility* featuring a large ship that crashed into an iceberg on its maiden voyage? The name of Robertson's fictional ship? The *Titan*!

Another titanic coincidence involves the screening of a movie aboard the real *Titanic*. The night of the disaster, there was a screening of a little-known movie by a director named D.W. Griffith, who would later go on to make numerous acclaimed films. His movie was *The Poseidon Adventure*, about a group of six passengers and crew members who struggle to stay alive after the ocean liner in which they're traveling is capsized by a tidal wave. Some say that because *Titanic* passengers were enjoying the film so much, they didn't notice the shudder of the iceberg impact and didn't realize their own ship was sinking fast.

ITIOUS?

SUPERSTITIONS FOR BAD LUCK

- Friday the 13th
- Walking under a ladder
- Black cats
- Spilling salt on the dinner table
- A bat flying into the house
- An owl hooting three times
- A five-leaf clover
- Breaking a glass while proposing a toast
- Putting a shirt on inside out
- Putting a hat on a bed
- Breaking a mirror
- Opening an umbrella indoors
- Stepping on cracks in the sidewalk
- An itch inside your nose
- Crossed knives on the dinner table
- Mending a garment while wearing it
- Fastening a button into the wrong buttonhole
- Leaving new shoes on a table

SUPERSTITIONS FOR GOOD LUCK

- Crossed fingers (and toes)
- Knocking on wood
- Saying "God bless you" when someone sneezes
- A robin flying into the house
- Sneezing three times before breakfast
- Meeting three sheep
- Looking at the new moon over your right shoulder
- Finding a four-leaf clover
- Putting a dress on inside out
- Hearing crickets singing
- Cutting your hair during a storm
- Picking up a pencil in the street
- Walking in the rain
- A ladybug on you
- See a penny, pick it up, and all day long you'll have good luck.

SOME GOOD LUCK superstitions have been around for centuries—and longer. At the time of the Great Plague in medieval Europe, if someone sneezed, you knew that he or she was sick and probably had the plague. The Pope passed a law that required everyone to "bless" a sneezer. That's how "Bless you!" got popular.

LUCKY CHARMS

10 OBJECTS YOU MIGHT WANT TO PUT IN YOUR BACKPACK BEFORE THAT BIG TEST

- Rabbit's foot
- Keys on a silver ring
- Peanut (or, if you're allergic, acorns)
- Horseshoe
- Dice
- Spinning top
- Feather
- Ankh (Egyptian symbol for life)
- Copper penny (try to get one of the "wheat" pennies minted before 1958)
- Wishbone (dried out)

MAKE A WISH

MOST OF US MAKE WISHES ON OUR birthday cakes or when we see the first star in the night sky. But there are oodles of other ways to get your wishes to come true.

When you and your friend say the same thing at the same time, hook pinkies and silently make a wish. When you let go, it will come true.

If a ladybug lands on you, wait for it to spread its wings and just as it flies away . . . make a wish.

If you see more than three birds on a telephone wire, make a wish before they fly away.

If you see a duck, make a "quack" noise.

Does the duck talk back? If it does, your wish will come true.

Blow a dandelion so the seeds scatter. Your wish will come true if they all blow off at the same time.

Stick a watermelon seed to your forehead. If it sticks when you make a wish, your wish will come true. If it falls off, just try again!

Don't be afraid of black cats, especially ones with green eyes. Pet one ten times and make a wish.

Can you peel an apple all in one peel? If you can, your wish will come true.

Find a penny heads up and make a wish on it.

When you get a new pair of shoes, make a wish. When the shoes get too small, the wish will come true.

HOW TO

WORK A PAPER FORTUNE-TELLER

MAKE IT:

Start with a standard sheet of paper. Make it square by folding one corner over to the edge and cutting off the extra flap. (Fig. 1)

Unfold it and you have a square. Fold it the other way and crease again. (Fig. 2)

Unfold so you are back to the square. (Fig. 3)

Next, fold each corner point into the center of the creases. (Fig. 4)

Fig. 1   Fig. 2   Fig. 3   Fig. 4

With all four corners folded it should look like this. (Fig. 5)

Next, flip it over and fold all four corner points into the center again. (Fig 6)

With all of the corners folded in it will look like this. (Fig. 7)

Fig. 5   Fig. 6   Fig. 7   Fig. 8

Write the numbers 1 through 8 on each of the triangles. (Fig 8)

Lift up the flaps and write fortunes under here. Check the list on page 74 for ideas.

Flip it over and color or write the name of a different color on each flap.

Flip it back over and stick your two thumbs and two forefingers into each of the four flap pockets. Fingertips should press center creases so that all four flaps meet at a point in the center.

PLAY IT:

Have a player choose one of the top four squares. For example, he or she might choose RED.

Spell the color the person chose while you open and close the Fortune-Teller once for each letter in the color they selected. Open and close up and down and side to side. R-E-D.

Let the person select one of the four visible numbers on the inside. Seven.

Open and close as before as you count to the number. When you've stopped counting, look inside and let the player choose a number again.

Open and close the right number of times, then choose once more. Open the panel under the number and read the fortune under the panel. Play again and again.

CHANGE IT:

Instead of colors on the top squares, write down the name of something else, like animals, weather, planets, or TV characters!

FEELING FORTUNE-ATE

WRITE THESE MESSAGES ON the paper fortune-teller, or on slips of paper, for fortune cookies (see recipe that follows). Add more fortunes to the list. Copy down some of the ones you get at a Chinese restaurant.

- Answer the door. Opportunity is knocking.
- You will travel somewhere cool.
- You will travel somewhere hot.
- You will help someone.
- You will be a great leader.
- There is a great hair day in your future.
- You will meet a new friend.
- You will get a raise in your allowance.
- You will learn a new skill.
- You will receive a surprise.
- Trouble is headed your way.
- Let a smile be your umbrella.
- Good luck awaits you.
- Your wish will be fulfilled.
- Someone you don't know will bring happiness.
- You will receive an important letter.
- You have a secret admirer.
- You believe in yourself.
- You will do a good deed.
- Someone will tell you a secret.
- You will forget something important.
- You will celebrate something special.
- Someone with the initial "S" (insert your own letter here) is thinking about you.

INVISIBLE FORTUNES

WHEN YOU REALLY NEED TO BE hush-hush, make your messages with invisible ink! Well, it's not really ink. It's lemon juice. But it knows how to disappear. First, get a bowl and pour the juice in. Next, write out your secret fortune using a toothpick dipped in the lemon juice. After about thirty minutes, the juice should be dry. Hold the fortune near something warm (a radiator cover or a soft lightbulb, for example.) Once the paper is slightly warmed the "ink" should turn darker—revealing your magical message.

For more idea about writing and notes, turn to page 132.

HOW TO

MAKE YOUR OWN FORTUNE COOKIES

FORTUNE COOKIES ARE TRICKY TO get just right! A few things you need to remember before you bake:

Make sure that each spoonful of batter is spread out evenly on the baking sheet.

Instead of using the back of a wooden spoon to spread the batter, tilt the baking sheet back and forth as needed.

Use cold baking sheets so everything stays unstuck.

Although it's time consuming to make only two or three cookies at a time, it's the best way to go. Otherwise, cookies become stiff very quickly and when cooled are too brittle to bend into their familiar shape.

To handle the hot cookies, wear white, cotton gloves.

Don't forget! Very important! Get permission to cook and make sure an adult supervises you in the kitchen. I can think of nothing worse than having an accident while making fortune cookies! What kind of omen would *that* be?

Now, get your ingredients:

1 ¼ cup flour
2 tablespoons cornstarch
½ cup sugar
½ teaspoon salt
½ cup vegetable oil
2 egg whites
1 teaspoon water
2 teaspoons vanilla extract

And make the cookies!

1. Preheat oven to 350 degrees.
2. In a large bowl, sift together the flour, cornstarch, sugar, and salt.
3. Stir in the oil, egg whites, water, and vanilla.
4. On a well-greased, cold baking sheet, drop spoonfuls of batter into circles. (You might want to do 2 for the first batch and then more as you get better at folding them.)
5. Bake circles for 15 minutes, or until golden.
6. Have an adult help you remove the pan from the oven and immediately flip cookies onto your cotton-gloved hands.
7. Hold fortune in center of bendable cookie while folding cookie in half. Watch out if it's hot!
8. Grasp ends of cookie and draw gently down to crease at center of cookie. It should hold this shape while it cools.

- Unicorns
- Mermaids
- Sprites
- Brownies
- The Shire
  (from *The Hobbit*)
- Watership Down
- Bigfoot
- Leprechauns
- Faeries
- C-3PO
- R2-D2
- Shrek
- Dumbo
- Puff the Magic Dragon
- Peter Pan
- Tinker Bell
- Jiminy Cricket
- Loch Ness Monster
- Peter Cottontail
- Mickey and Minnie Mouse
- Abominable Snowman
- E.T.
- Gryphons
- The Lost City of Atlantis
- Avalon

- The Bat Cave (in *Batman*)
- Bikini Bottom (home to
  SpongeBob, Patrick,
  Squidward, and friends)
- Candy Land
- Dinotopia
- The Emerald City
- Sim City
- Hundred-Acre Wood
  (Winnie the Pooh, Piglet,
  Eeyore, and everybody else)
- Mount Olympus
- Sesame Street (starring
  Elmo, Kermit, Oscar,
  Snuffleupagus and every-
  body else)
- *Where the Wild Things Are*
- Spiderman
- Wonder Woman
- Superman
- Barbie and the Twelve
  Dancing Princesses
- The Incredibles
- Woody
- Buzz Lightyear
- Hogwarts

- Ewoks
- Willy Wonka's factory
  (with all the Fizzy Lifting
  Drink, Everlasting Gob-
  stoppers, and more)
- X-ray Glasses
- Lightsabers
- Bedrock (home of the
  Flintstones)
- Jellystone National Park
  (home of Yogi Bear)
- Invisibility Cloak
- Platform 9 ¾
- Teleportation
- Quidditch
- Centaurs
- Pegasus
- Hercules
- Popeye (and Olive Oyl)
- The Indian in the Cupboard
- Gizmo (the good gremlin)
- Nemo
  (and Dory, of course)
- Lilliput
- The Care Bears
- The Smurfs

FANTASTIC (AND FUN)

PEOPLE, PLACES AND THINGS

WE WISH WERE REAL

- Strawberry Shortcake
- Curious George
- The Time Machine
- The Mystery Machine
- Scooby Doo
  (and Shaggy, too)
- Magic carpets
- Magic wands
- Magic mirrors
- Genies in bottles
- Fairy godmothers
- Xanadu
- Gilligan's Island
- Shangri-La
- Angelina Ballerina
- Mary Poppins
- Babar
- ESP
- UFOs
- Imaginary Friends
- The Mad Hatter
- Alice in Wonderland
- Tweedledum
- Tweedledee
- Charlotte (the spider)
- Wilbur (the pig)

- The Force
- Gandalf
- The Cat in the Hat
- The Lorax
- Sneetches
- Heffalumps
- The Grinch
- Harold and his Purple
  Crayon
- Xena the Warrior Prince
- The Magic School Bus
  (with Ms. Frizzle aboard)
- Sailor Moon
- Sabrina, the Teenage Witch
- Buffy, the Vampire Slayer
- Camelot
- The Bionic Woman
- Narnia
- The Golden Compass
- Little Miss Muffet
- Snow White
  (and the dwarves)
- Sleeping Beauty
- Ariel
- Cinderella
- Little Red Riding Hood

- Goldilocks
  (and the bears, too!)
- The Old Woman in the
  Shoe
- Rapunzel
- Jumanji
- Supergirl (Oh, wait!
  That's YOU, isn't it?)

There are so many other people, places, and inventions from books and movies that could be included here. Make your own list. Try to think of places you'd like to explore, or other fantastic characters you wish you could invite to your next sleepover. I used to dream about Luke Skywalker (from *Star Wars*) asking me to marry him—in space. Wait. Did I really just admit that out loud? Sheesh. I'm baring my soul here. Your turn.

R E V O L

FULL NAME:

PLANET EARTH

NICKNAMES:
Big Blue (because 97% of me is covered with water)

HOW OLD AM I?
I look great for my 4.5 billion years, don't you think?

HOW BIG AM I?
196,950,711 square miles (510,100,000 square kilometers)

HOT OR NOT?
Are you kidding!? HOT! Near my center, I'm about 7,000 degrees.

BASIC COMPOSITION:
Volcanic rock. But don't forget all the other stuff that's living on me! As of 2007, my human population is 6,627,854,547 people—and there are at least five to ten million kinds of insects and other animals here, too. (That's not total bugs or creatures by the way. You need to multiply those millions by millions to get a total critter count. Yeeps!)

Check out pages 174–176 for some things you can do to help keep me in the best shape I can be.

SOMETHING TO THINK ABOUT
Our planet has been here for 4.5 billion years. Dinosaurs were here for 250 million years. But Homo sapiens have only walked on Earth for 100,000 to 200,000 years! How on Earth (pun intended) are we supposed to think we're the center of anything when, compared to all that's come before, we've only been here for a blink of an eye?

HAS YOUR MOM OR DAD ever said these words to you? *The world doesn't revolve around you, dear. So stop acting like it does.*

Ha! Mine sure did. And you can laugh all you want, but for years, I thought—quite innocently—that the world did indeed revolve around me. Why not? I didn't know anything about orbits or gravitational pull or asteroids or whatever else is spinning out there in space.

Earth and I share a similar story—because for centuries of recorded history, Earth was named the precise center of the universe . . . even though it wasn't. How did scientists figure it all out in the end? Well, Earth's tale is far from over, but here are a few key moments along the way:

• Aristotle wrote in the fourth century B.C. that Earth must be a sphere because different stars could be seen as you move north and south, and the shadow of Earth on the moon during an eclipse was curved.

• In the second century A.D., Ptolemy made star catalogs. He said the solar system was like a carousel with Earth as the center. Planets, stars, the sun, and the moon were like the painted horses going around and around. Unfortunately, it didn't work that way. Although his wrong theory lasted for some 1,400 years, it was quickly booted by Nicolaus Copernicus. But (here comes the silver lining): If Ptolemy hadn't been so wrong, the next guy wouldn't have been so right. . . .

• "Right guy" Nicolaus Copernicus used math to explain how the sun, planets, and stars moved. He said the sun was the center of our solar system (thus naming it solar—*sun*—system). But he wasn't 100% right. This guy also believed Earth was flat. So there were still a lot of questions waiting to be answered.

• Johannes Kepler used elliptical orbits to predict plane-tary motion. When he wasn't predicting orbit paths, Kepler was predicting his next sneeze. He had a notoriously runny nose.

• Galileo Galilei proved that the sun was in the center of the solar system, and other planets (including Earth) orbited it. He was the first guy to spot craters on the moon by introducing the telescope into astronomy. He also discovered moons near other planets, too, like Jupiter.

• Isaac Newton proposed a theory of gravity to explain how the planets were held in place. Legend says he got hit on the head with an apple and cried, "Eureka! Gravity!" But the truth is, he probably just observed a falling apple (like so many other natural objects) and came up with his theory.

• Edmund Halley figured out that comets orbit the sun like planets do. Plus, he figured out the paths of *returning* comets, including Halley's Comet (named after him, of course).

DOT TO DOT

A GROUP OF STARS LOOKS LIKE the biggest connect-the-dots puzzle ever. Draw imaginary lines between them, and see a picture of an object, animal, or person otherwise known as one cool constellation.

But here's the weird part: Even though we see constellations as a pattern in our sky, their stars may not be near one another! Stars appear to have the same brightness, but each of the "dots" is actually a different distance from Earth. Although we see stars shining brightly, they are many light-years (one light-year = almost 6 trillion miles) away. That kind of distance is impossible to imagine. But all that distance is a good thing! Because stars are so far away, the sky moves and changes very, very slowly. And for centuries, sailors, astronauts, and all humans have been able to use the slow-moving stars as guides.

ASTRONOMY
vs.
ASTROLOGY

I MPORTANT! IN CASE YOU DIDN'T know this: Astronomy is the scientific study of stars. Astronomy and astrology are not the same thing! Scientists try to understand how stars are born and how they survive. They do not believe that things in space, especially ones positioned light-years from Earth, can affect our daily activities.

VS.

Astrologers think that stars, no matter how far away, determine our fates. An astrologist tries to predict the future or describe what people are like based only on their birth date and the position of stars.

3 COOL THINGS ALMOST EVERYONE CAN SPOT IN THE NIGHT SKY

hen you look up at the sky at night, if it's clear outside, you can almost always count on a moon
ew. Sometimes it's full; other times it's crescent-shaped. You also probably know how to find the
orth Star, one of the brightest spots in a dark sky. But what else can you train your eyes to spot?

NDROMEDA
WHEN? November or December
WHERE? High in the northern part of the night sky
WHAT? The largest galaxy (bigger and more visible than the Milky Way galaxy), Andromeda can be seen without a telescope. It may look like a small-ish, fuzzy star to the naked eye, but it's actually a vast spiral of light that is about seven times as big as our moon.
LEGEND? In Greek mythology, Andromeda was the beautiful daughter of Cepheus and Cassiopeia. Likewise, this is known as one of the most beautiful sights in the night sky.

HE BIG DIPPER
WHEN? Mid-summer
WHERE? The northern part of the night sky
WHAT? Shaped like a ladle, two of the stars in its "cup" point the way to the North Star. This is close to north on a compass, so it can help you find your direction in the darkness.
LEGEND? The Big Dipper was known as the Drinking Gourd for slaves trying to make their way to freedom. They used it as a guidepost to find their way north to escape the bonds of slavery.

RION
WHEN? Very early morning, August through December; Evening, December through May
WHERE? Rising in the east and setting in the west
WHAT? Shaped like the giant figure of a hunter, the easiest way to spot this constellation is by its "belt." The belt is made up of three bright stars—Alnitak, Alnilam, and Minatka—that form one of the most recognizable patterns in the sky.
LEGEND? The mythological hunter Orion is accompanied in the sky by his faithful dogs Canis Minor and Canis Major, waiting at the right "foot" of the great hunter.

MAPS OF THE STARS!

No, we're not talking about Hollywood stars. Check it out!

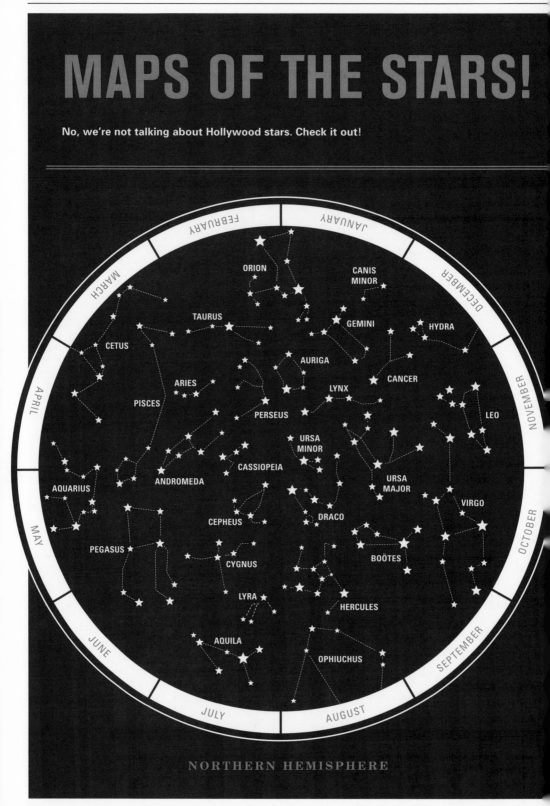

NORTHERN HEMISPHERE

NASA's (National Aeronautics and Space Administration) Web site has nifty printable star maps. Check it out. Soon, you'll be able to identify all the stars in your night sky.

Go to: http://spaceplace.nasa.gov/en/kids/

Click on PROJECTS

Click on STAR FINDER

Have a blast (or should I say have a blast-*off*)!

SOUTHERN HEMISPHERE

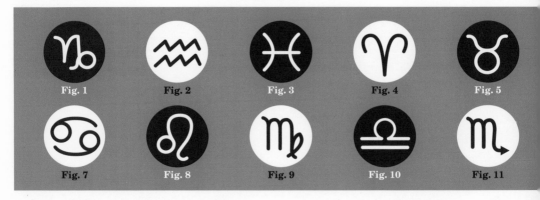

Fig. 1   Fig. 2   Fig. 3   Fig. 4   Fig. 5

Fig. 7   Fig. 8   Fig. 9   Fig. 10   Fig. 11

MORE THAN 3,000 years ago, the Babylonians used a twelve-month calendar based on the different phases of the moon. At some point, they divided the sky into twelve pieces*, naming each piece of sky after one of their months. Each month was assigned a unique animal or symbol called a zodiac sign. The word *zodiac* comes from the Greek *zidoakos*, which means "circle of animals."

CAPRICORN (Fig. 1)
The Goat 12/23–1/20
- Traits: Practical, responsible, wise
- Likes: Good manners, punctuality, expensive stuff
- Dislikes: Being embarrassed in public, surprises
- Most likely to: Be an accountant, jeweler, art dealer, or anything out of the spotlight
- Famous Capricorn Girls: Mary J. Blige, Kate Bosworth, Diane Keaton

AQUARIUS (Fig. 2)
The Aquarian 1/21–2/18
- Traits: Strong-willed, eccentric, dependable
- Likes: Fame, magic, surprises
- Dislikes: Show-offs, violence, aggressiveness
- Most likely to: Do something that requires innovation, like dance or invent
- Famous Aquarius Girls: Judy Blume, Alicia Keys, Oprah Winfrey

PISCES (Fig. 3)
The Fish 2/19–3/20
- Traits: Shy, caring, creative
- Likes: Make-believe, poetry, romantic places
- Dislikes: Dirty, crowded places and voices of authority
- Most likely to: Be in film, theater, TV, and advertising work
- Famous Pisces Girls: Drew Barrymore, Jessica Biel, Queen Latifah

ARIES (Fig. 4)
The Ram 3/21–4/20
- Traits: Active, takes risks, likes to explore
- Likes: Being liked, books, new clothes
- Dislikes: Being ignored, waiting, secondhand stuff
- Most likely to: Lead a group
- Famous Aries Girls: Mandy Moore, Mariah Carey, Posh Beckham

TAURUS (Fig. 5)
The Bull 4/21–5/21
- Traits: Materialistic, organized, cautious
- Likes: Nature, romance, doing the same thing over and over
- Dislikes: Chaos, change, being late
- Most likely to: Be an investment banker
- Famous Taurus Girls: Kirsten Dunst, Janet Jackson, Kelly Clarkson

GEMINI (Fig. 6)
The Twins 5/22–6/21
- Traits: Curious, charm-

---

* Some ancient stories say the Babylonians actually started with thirteen constellations in the zodiac, but they later dropped one called Ophiuchus.

Fig. 6

Fig. 12

ZODIAC ATTACK

ing, optimistic, coopera-
tive
* Likes: Gossip, talking on
the phone, hanging with
friends
* Dislikes: Being stuck in
the same place for too
long, getting bored
* Most likely to: Be a
teacher or politician
* Famous Gemini Girls:
Anne Frank, Angelina
Jolie, Paula Abdul

CANCER (Fig. 7)
The Crab 6/22–7/23
* Traits: Sensitive, nostal-
gic, dreamy
* Likes: Hugs, hard work,
romance
* Dislikes: Insults, rejec-
tion, betrayal
* Most likely to: Be a social
worker or chef
* Famous Cancer Girls:
Meryl Streep, Liv Tyler,
Lindsay Lohan

LEO (Fig. 8)
The Lion 7/24–8/23
* Traits: Show-off, popular,
proud
* Likes: Elegance, admira-
tion, loyalty
* Dislikes: Boredom, apolo-

gies, not being center of
attention
* Most likely to: Act, direct,
or sell something
* Famous Leo Girls: J. K.
Rowling, Jennifer Lopez,
Madonna

VIRGO (Fig. 9)
The Virgin 8/24–9/23
* Traits: Gentle, modest,
dedicated
* Likes: Working hard,
making lists, grooming
* Dislikes: Talking about
feelings, crowds, whiners
* Most likely to: Do something that seems hard to
most people
* Famous Virgo Girls: Shania Twain, Cameron
Diaz, LeAnn Rimes

LIBRA (Fig. 10)
The Scales 9/24–10/23
* Traits: Artistic, fair, opin-
ionated
* Likes: Looking good,
cleaning up, playing by
the rules
* Dislikes: Change, sloppi-
ness, loud arguments
* Most likely to: Be a
lawyer or diplomat
* Famous Libra Girls: Sere-

na Williams, Gwyneth
Paltrow, Kate Winslet

SCORPIO (Fig. 11)
The Scorpion 10/24–11/22
* Traits: Protective,
attached, determined
* Likes: A good fight, win-
ning, mysteries
* Dislikes: Nosy people,
competitors, flattery
* Most likely to: Be a detec-
tive or scientist
* Famous Scorpio Girls:
Jodie Foster, Hillary Rod-
ham Clinton, Julia
Roberts

SAGITTARIUS (Fig. 12)
The Archer 11/23–12/22
* Traits: Open, honest,
overly enthusiastic
* Likes: Flirting, moving
around, freedom
* Dislikes: Confinement,
doubt, tight clothing
* Most likely to: Be a per-
former, travel, and be
multilingual
* Famous Sagittarius Girls:
Miley Cyrus, Raven-
Symoné, Britney Spears

GIVE YOURSELF A HAND

PALMISTRY

DID YOU KNOW YOUR PALM IS LIKE a fingerprint and a snowflake? No two are exactly alike. But your palm tells the story of your life. Lines on the left hand show the past. Lines on the right hand show your future. Open your hands and take a look. What do you see?

"A wise person rules by his destiny . . . but is not ruled by it." —CONFUCIUS

LIFELINE (Fig. 1)
- **Long and curved:** Good health and life
- **Short and strong:** Energetic and strong-willed
- **Thin and wavy:** Health problems
- **Wide semicircle:** Enthusiasm for life
- **Straighter line:** Cautious

HEARTLINE (Fig. 2)
- **Long line:** Idealistic
- **Straight:** Hard to love
- **Curved and long:** Affectionate
- **Curved and going up:** Do anything for love
- **Short:** Overly emotional

HEADLINE (Fig. 3)
- **Head and lifelines linked:** Deep thinker
- **Head and lifelines separate:** Adventurous
- **Long and straight:** Good memory
- **Long and curved:** Imaginative
- **Light and wavy:** Can't concentrate
- **Short:** Indecisive

HEALTHLINE (Fig. 4)
No line actually means good health. A strong line means good sense. Heads up for a wavy health line. It could mean some health problems.

FAMELINE (Fig. 5)
Your fame line goes up the palm and ends at the ring finger. Do you have one? A broken line means ups and downs in your career, but a straight one means you will have a public life. Cover of *People* magazine anyone? Bring on the paparazzi.

DOIN' THE BUMP
PHRENOLOGY

WHAT PHRENOLOGISTS SAW INSIDE THE NINETEENTH-CENTURY HEAD

1   Hope
2   Self-esteem
3   Love of truth
4   Cautiousness
5   Friendship
6   True wit
7   Prudence
8   Courage
9   Parental love
10   Idealism
11   Imitation
12   Philoprogenitiveness (love of kids)
13   Secretiveness
14   Eventuality (knowledge that something is about to happen)
15   Language
16   Amativeness (love and attraction)
17   Sublimity (morals)
18   Veneration (awe)

WHAT PHRENOLOGISTS MIGHT SEE INSIDE YOUR TWENTY-FIRST-CENTURY HEAD

A   Wishing I were taller
B   Crushing on some boy in class who doesn't know my name
C   Gotta see the new episode of my fave show
D   Gotta memorize a monologue for drama club
E   Wishing I were more popular
F   Obsessing about the pimple on my chin
G   Wondering how I will tell Mom about the C+ on my report card
H   Studying for tomorrow's math test
I   Shuffling tunes on my iPod
J   Dreaming about the candy bar in my locker
K   Mentally planning my laps for the swim meet on Saturday
L   Cleaning my closet before Mom does it for me—and tosses everything out
M   Crushing on a different boy at lunch who does know my name
N   Wondering why no one has IMed me
O   Imagining what it would be like to be chased by paparazzi
P   Realizing I left my notebook in class
Q   Thinking about how much I love my BFFs

Here's a new word for you: *phrenology*. No, it's not green stuff that comes out of your nose when you have the flu. And it's not the name of a new flick over at the multiplex. Phrenology is the old-time practice of studying the bumps and lines on your head to determine character and personality traits. Not to be confused with craniometry, the study of skull stuff, or physiognomy, the study of your facial features.

While all this may sound like a bunch of gobbledygook, it's one example of a way in which people have tried to unravel some of the mysteries of the human mind. And no, current brain science doesn't really consider phrenology to be useful today. But it sure can be fun! The next time you and your friends are hanging out, check for bumps. It's just one more way to get inside each other's heads.

SPORTS SU

FOR CENTURIES, social conventions tried to tell women they were not as strong or agile as men. Thankfully, some women didn't listen! They stepped up, flexed their muscles, and set an example for the rest of us. It's been a slow but steady climb to the top of the record books, onto the Olympic podium, and into the hearts and minds of girls everywhere.

The timeline here shows a few ways in which women's sports have proven that girls can do whatever they want to do—even when faced with controversy and conflict. But remember this as you read some of these stats: Much of the progress in women's sports has taken place in the last twenty-five years. That isn't very long, is it? You may *think* women have had equality for a long time now, but the truth is . . . we're still fighting for it in a lot of places, including courts and stadiums all over the world.

What do you think women will do *next*?

776 B.C. Although women were not allowed at the first Olympics, they had their own Games of Hera, with footraces just for women.

1567 Mary Queen of Scots is the first woman to play golf in Scotland. Her achievement is somewhat overshadowed by the fact that she plays her game only days after her husband Lord Damley's murder.

1784 Elizabeth Thible of France is the first woman to soar in a hot-air balloon.

1851 Amelia Jenks Bloomer invents the shorts that will bear her name (bloomers!)— and make it easier for women to run, jump, ride, and be more active in sports of all kinds.

1856 Catharine Beecher publishes the first exercise manual for women.

1873 A mile-long swimming contest is held in New York's Harlem River. Ten women compete, and the winner is Delilah Goboess. Her prize? A $175 silk dress.

1882 The first athletic games for women are held at the YWCA in Boston, Massachusetts.

1885 At age twenty-five, Phoebe Ann Moses (also known as Annie Oakley) becomes the sharp-shooting star of Buffalo Bill's Wild West Show. She could shoot a moving target while riding a galloping horse, shoot a cigarette out of her husband's mouth, and hit a dime in midair!

1895 Annie Smith Peck is the first woman to climb to the top of the Matterhorn. But what do the newspapers focus on? Her clothes! She wore knickerbockers, not a dress or a skirt.

1900 Women compete in a few Olympic events in Paris: croquet, golf, and tennis.

1902 Madge Syers of Britain enters the all-male world figure skating championships and places an incredible *second*! However, after her finish, officials announce that

PERSTARS

women are banned from the tournament. No way! It will be a few years until a separate women's event is planned in 1905. But Madge strikes back in 1908, winning the gold Olympic medal.

1917 Lucy Diggs Slowe becomes the first African-American woman to win a title in any sport. Her triumph? The American Tennis Association (ATA) tournament.

1918 Proving that women really *can* do it all, Eleanora Sears (who just happens to be a great-granddaughter of Thomas Jefferson) participates in all kinds of sports. She wins more than 240 career trophies in squash, baseball, golf, field hockey, auto racing, swimming, tennis, yachting, and speedboat-racing. What is considered her most scandalous achievement? Sears rides astride her horse (rather than side saddle, the "ladylike" convention for women at the time) while playing polo.

1926 Gertrude Ederle is the first woman to swim across the English Channel.

1928 Sonja Henie brings a womanly touch to ice-skating, introducing ballerina-like moves and dance choreography. Girls everywhere are inspired to take up skating! Throughout her career, Henie wins more than 1,500 medals and trophies, including three consecutive Olympic Gold Medals.

1928 Women are finally allowed to participate in track and field events at the Olympics.

1931 Seventeen-year-old pitcher Virne Beatrice "Jackie" Mitchell becomes the first woman to play professional baseball—and what a start she has! While playing in an exhibition game for the Chattanooga Lookouts, she strikes out Babe Ruth and Lou Gehrig! Aghast, the baseball commissioner bans women from professional baseball for the next sixty years (the ban was lifted in

1992). His reason: Baseball is just too strenuous for women. His real reason: The sport can't risk having a woman like Mitchell strike out a man again!

1943 The All-American Girls Baseball League is formed to fill baseball stadiums emptied out by male players leaving for World War II.

1948 Alice Coachman is the first black woman to win an Olympic gold medal—in the high jump.

1948 Patty Berg and others found the Ladies Professional Golf Association (LPGA).

1953 Maureen Connolly is the first woman to win a Grand Slam (all four major tennis championships: the Australian Open, French Open, Wimbledon, and U.S. Open).

1960 Wilma Rudolph is the first woman to win three Olympic gold medals in track and field at the Olympic Games. It's an impressive feat made more incredible by the fact that she once had polio as a child—and needed leg braces to walk!

1964 Soviet gymnast Larissa Latynina finishes her Olympic career with eighteen medals— more than any other athlete in Olympic history.

1970 Diane Crump is the first woman to ride in the Kentucky Derby.

1972 The Constitution's Title IX of the Educational Amendments is passed. Girls in schools everywhere breathe a sigh of relief. (See page 97 for the whole story).

1973 Billie Jean King defeats Bobby Riggs in a tennis match that is dubbed the "Battle of the Sexes."

1974 Girls are (finally!) permitted to play Little League Baseball.

1974 Formation of the National Women's Football League, the first professional tackle league for women.

1976 Krystyna Choynowski-Liskiewicz of Poland is the first woman to sail around the world solo.

1978 Ann Meyers becomes the first woman to try out and sign an NBA contract for the Indiana Pacers (although she later won't make the cut

to the final team). In 1993, she is inducted into the Basketball Hall of Fame.

1982 Shirley Muldowney becomes the first person (woman or man) to win three National Hot Rod Association titles (in 1978, 1980, and 1982).

1983 Tamara McKinney becomes the first American female skier to win the Alpine World Cup overall championship.

1984 Joan Benoit-Samuelson wins the first women's Olympic marathon.

1985 Libby Riddles is the first woman to mush her way to an Iditarod (dogsled race) win.

1987 Jackie Joyner-Kersee is the first woman athlete to appear on the cover of *Sports Illustrated* magazine.

1991 The United States soccer team wins the first Women's World Cup.

1994 Speed skater Bonnie Blair wins five gold medals in three Olympics (1988, 1992, and 1994) and becomes the most decorated female American athlete in the history of the Olympic Games.

1994 Tennis great Martina Navratilova retires with an all-time record (male or

female) of 1,438 match wins.

1999 Two sisters dominate tennis: Serena Williams wins the U.S. Open; the next day, she and her sister Venus take the women's doubles title.

2002 Americans Jill Bakken and Vonetta Flowers win the first women's Olympic gold medal in bobsledding.

2003 Annika Sorenstam becomes the first woman to play in a PGA tournament in fifty-eight years.

2003 The University of Connecticut Lady Huskies rack up seventy straight wins— the second longest streak in college basketball history.

2005 Tennessee basketball coach Pat Summitt gets her 880th win and becomes the winningest (for both men and women) coach in NCAA history.

2005 Danica Patrick has a fourth-place finish in the Indianapolis 500—the best showing ever by a woman.

2006 Effa Manley, who played in the Negro Leagues Newark Eagles, is the first woman elected to the National Baseball Hall of Fame. She used her team to forward causes of the civil rights movement in addition to women's rights.

UP CLOSE:

BABE, BILLIE, MIA, AND JACKIE

SETTING THEMSELVES APART from the ranks of other women superstars are women whose actions on and off the court and field made a HUGE difference in the future of girls sports. This is not a stand-alone list by any means. You probably have your own personal female sports heroines. Go dig up their star stats and post them on your bulletin board for inspiration. We girls have to stick together!

WHO?	Mildred Ella Didrikson (nicknamed "Babe" after Babe Ruth)
FACTS?	Born 1911, Port Arthur, Texas; Died 1956, Galveston, Texas
HER STORY?	Babe is the first girl who proved that she could be as impressive an athlete as any man. She played and competed in every sport: basketball, track, golf, baseball, tennis, swimming, diving, boxing, volleyball, handball, bowling, billiards, skating, and cycling. From childhood, she had her goal set: to be the greatest athlete who ever lived. When asked if there was any sport she *didn't* do, Babe thought for a moment and said, "Yeah, dolls."
HER STYLE?	Tough and self-centered. Many said she was cocky about her abilities. But that didn't alienate George Zaharias, a wrestler who fell in love with Babe in 1938.
BIG WINS?	Olympic medals, basketball and golf tournaments, and 6-time Female Athlete of the Year
BEST ACHIEVE-MENT?	After winning a golf tournament in 1953, Babe learned she had a tumor—and the cancer spread to her lymph nodes. But fourteen weeks later, she was back on the golf course—and a year later she won the U.S. Women's Open by twelve strokes!
LEGACY FOR GIRLS TODAY?	Never give up. Don't be afraid to be strong and bold. Play more than one sport well—and be proud of it.

WHO?	Billie Jean King
FACTS?	Born 1943, Long Beach, California
HER STORY?	Ranked number one in tennis and listed in the top ten for seventeen years, King started a professional women's tour, sports magazine, and sports foundation. She won the famed "Battle of the Sexes" match against Bobby Riggs, making it clear that women could be jocks. She said, "In the '70s, we had to make it acceptable for people to accept girls and women as athletes. We had to make it okay for them to be active."
HER STYLE?	Determined, visionary, and willing to lead, King is a member of numerous Halls of Fame and was named one of the 100 Most Important Americans of the Twentieth Century by *Life* magazine.
BIG WINS?	King is the only woman to win the U.S. Open on all four surfaces (clay, grass, carpet, and hard court). She won twenty Wimbledon titles, including six singles. As a coach, she led the U.S. Olympic and Fed Cup teams to numerous wins.
BEST ACHIEVE-MENT?	Although her personal achievements on the tennis court rank among the best-ever players, it is her accomplishments *off* the court that count as her greatest contribution to women's sports. In 2006, the USTA National Tennis Center, home to the U.S. Open, was renamed the USTA Billie Jean King National Tennis Center.
LEGACY FOR GIRLS TODAY?	Demand gender equality in all sports.

WHO?	Mariel Margaret Hamm (Mia)
FACTS?	Born 1972, Selma, Alabama (the same year that Title IX is enacted, see page 97)
HER STORY?	One of the best all-around female soccer players in the world.
HER STYLE?	Team player, pioneer, and believer in the abilities of young girls everywhere to be future sports leaders and stars.
BIG WINS?	The youngest player ever to be on a national team (she was fifteen); she retired in 2004 after winning two world championships, two gold Olympic medals, and many MVP awards. She was the first female player to reach the 100-goal mark. She scored a total of 158 goals throughout her career in international competition.
BEST ACHIEVE-MENT?	Demonstrating great leadership, she led her U.S. soccer team to a gold medal in the centennial 1996 Summer Olympics in Athens, Georgia. The coolest fact? 80,000 fans turned up to see it happen—the most spectators ever for a women's sporting event. In 2007, she was rightly inducted into the National Soccer Hall of Fame.
LEGACY FOR GIRLS TODAY?	She is a founding member of the Women's United Soccer Association—and an advocate for young athletes every-where.

WHO?	Jackie Joyner-Kersee
FACTS?	Born 1962, East St. Louis, Illinois
HER STORY?	One of the greatest Olympic athletes in history, Joyner-Kersee was one of the first generation Title IX girls (she was ten years old when it was enacted). Sports stars like Mia Hamm and other women athletes claim her as their primary role model.
HER STYLE?	She never flagged during competition: She fought back sickness, asthma attacks, debilitating heat, and more to triumph in sport—and in spirit.
BIG WINS?	Countless world track and field records (her 7,291 points in the 1992 Seoul Summer Olympics heptathlon still stands as the best ever), and nail-biting victories, including a long jump in the 1996 Atlanta Olympics that sent her from seventh place to the Olympic medal podium for a bronze medal.
BEST ACHIEVE-MENT?	Six Olympic medals—including three gold. Plus, wide-ranging philanthropic work, especially in her hometown of East St. Louis.
LEGACY FOR GIRLS TODAY?	There is no shame in being proud of your ability. Give it your all, even when you have to dig deep.

WHAT IS TITLE IX?

THE CONSTITUTION'S TITLE IX OF THE Educational Amendments of 1972 is landmark legislation that bans sex discrimination in schools, whether in academics or athletics.

𝕹o person in the 𝖀.𝕾. shall, on the basis of sex, be excluded from participation in, or denied the benefits of, or be subjected to discrimination under any educational program or activity receiving federal aid.

Why was this so important? Before 1972, schools would regularly discriminate against girls or refuse to admit them altogether, making it difficult or impossible for them to succeed in their studies and sports. In 1972, a mere 9% of medical school graduates were women. In 1994, that number jumped to 38%. Since Title IX was enacted, female high school athletic participation has increased by a whopping 847%. In 1972, only 1 in 27 high school girls played varsity sports. By 2001, 1 in 2.5 high school girls played varsity sports.

WHAT DISABILITY?

Nothing is more inspiring than women (and men) who beat incredible odds and turn themselves into uber-athletes. In 1948, Sir Ludwig Guttman of Great Britain made a separate Olympics especially for the disabled, called the Paralympics. The number of athletes participating in Summer Paralympic Games has increased from 400 athletes from 23 countries in Rome in 1960 to 3,806 athletes from 136 countries in Athens in 2004.

Some of the sports categories seem familiar, but some have a twist to accommodate a person's disability, like sitting volleyball or wheelchair fencing, rugby, basketball, curling, and tennis. One of the most important things you can know about a Paralympics: these athletes are the real deal. They overcome disability, sure, but they have the same—if not more—guts and natural ability as non-disabled athletes. Although American sprinter Tony Volpentest has an artificial limb, he raced to a time 1.52 seconds shy of Donovan Bailey's 100-meter Olympic and world record. American swimmer Trischa Zorn has collected more than 41 Paralympic gold medals. Repeat after me: WOWZA.

Source: www.abilitymagazine.com

AT THE BARRE
BASIC BALLET POSITIONS

PROFESSIONAL BALLERINAS BELONG to an elite group, but many girls take ballet class at one time or another in their lives. Why do so many of us want to be ballerinas when we grow up—at least for a little while? Is it because we want to be lighter than a feather, flying through air? Is it because we all want to know what it feels like to spin around and never get dizzy? Or is it all that pink, tulle, and ribbons? Model Elle Macpherson said, "I wanted so badly to study ballet, but it was really all about the tutu."

The art of ballet dance officially began sometime around the late sixteenth century in Italy, but classical ballet became popular in the French courts in the seventeenth century. Into the eighteenth and nineteenth centuries, classical ballet evolved. By the twentieth century, Russian ballet showcased a wider range of technical strength and drama. Ballet was not just a pretty dance, it was about power, grace, and control.

Despite all the shifts, however, certain things about ballet do not change. Every move in ballet—classical or contemporary—is based on one of the five key positions for feet and hands.

FEET AND LEGS

First In this position, the feet are placed heels together and the legs are turned out so that the feet are as close to 180 degrees as the dancer is able.

Second Again the feet are in line like first position, but this time they are spaced apart; sometimes it is described as shoulder-width spacing and sometimes a foot's length apart.

Third In this position, the legs are turned out and the heel of one foot fits in front of the instep of the other foot.

Fourth This position is similar to fifth position (see below) but instead of the feet being tight together, they are spaced apart to the front and back. Again the description of the distance varies.

Fifth The feet are turned out, with one fitted snugly in front of the other. How much they overlap is dictated by the method being taught; in the Russian method they are heel to toe.

All feet and leg positions should be practiced in one of three ways:

1. Flat feet
2. Demi-pointe (half-toe, standing on the

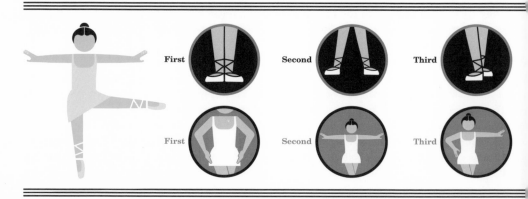

First   Second   Third

First   Second   Third

balls of the feet with the heel raised as high as possible)

3. En pointe (straight up on your toes)

ARMS AND HANDS

During all of your leg and foot positions, you must carefully watch the placement of your hands.

First   The arms are held in front of the body slightly curved so that the tips of the fingers almost meet, resting on the thighs.

Second   Both arms are held out to the side slightly below shoulder level. How curved they are depends on the style being taught; in the Russian method, they only have a slight curve.

Demi-second   *Demi* is French for "half." This is a position, as the name says, halfway between first and second. The arms are lifted to about 45 degrees and held away from the body.

Third   The hands and arms are kept in the same shape as first position, but raised up in front of the body to just below shoulder height.

Fourth   In this position, one arm is in fifth position and the other in second. Which arm is in fifth position relates to which foot is in front. The choreography will dictate whether this will be the same arm as the front foot or the opposite arm.

Fifth   The hands and arms are in the same shape as first position, but raised above the head. In this position the hands should be held with the palms turned away from the audience.

OTHER BALLET TERMS YOU SHOULD KNOW

As most ballet schools originated in France, terminology referring to jumps and bends are French words.

- Arabesque (*ara•besk*) Stand on the right leg while the left leg is raised straight out behind.
- Emboite (*em•bwaht*) Move forward while jumping on alternate toes.
- Jeté (*zhe•tay*) Leap from one leg to another.
- Pirouette (*peer•ooh•ett*) Turn or spin.
- Pas de chat (*pah de shah*) Jump to the side.
- Plié (*plee•ay*) Bend the knees.
- Relevé (*ray•leh•vay*) Rise up on the tiptoes.
- Port de bras (*por de bra*) Move the arms through various positions.
- Sauté (*sew•tay*) Jump.

WHAT'S YOUR POINTE?

The first pointe shoes were soft slippers, heavily darned at the toes, but today's pointe shoes are made of multiple layers of burlap, paper, and hardened glue.

How does a dancer dance on her toes? By contracting the muscles of her feet, ankles, legs, and torso, she is able to pull herself up on pointe. Inside the shoe, her foot is supported underneath the arch by a stiff sole or shank that encases the toes and lets her weight rest on a platform inside the shoe.

A prima ballerina can complete thirty-two Fouette turns while staying in the exact same spot on the floor. After the turns, her pointe shoe tip is actually HOT to the touch. It is also so worn out that it is used then only for rehearsals. Most ballerinas get ten pairs of pointe shoes from their dance company *per month*. In 2003, the English National Ballet went through 3,546 pairs of pointe shoes.

Fourth

Fifth

Fourth

Fifth

THE
FUNKY CHICKEN
& FRIENDS

SOMETIMES A DJ WILL TROT OUT the funny music to get a crowd dancing silly moves. Check out this collection of fad dances. You'll probably know a few. (I mean, is there anyone alive who doesn't know the Electric Slide?) For the ones you don't recognize, ask your mother or grandmother to remember. Maybe they can give you a little shake-your-hips demonstration of the ones they knew?

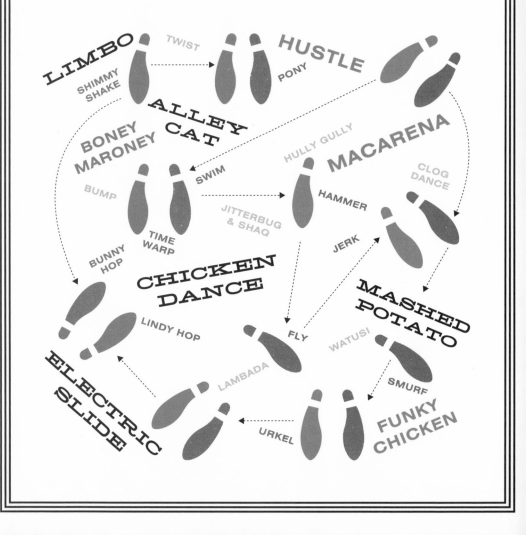

Singin' in the Rain All-time dancing great Gene Kelly sways with his umbrella under a street lamp and sings, "What a glorious feeling . . . I'm happy again!" as he leaps into a puddle. Nothing better! When planning a dance flick-a-thon, don't forget classics like this.

Dirty Dancing "Nobody puts Baby in the corner." See it and you'll know what I'm talking about.

Flashdance After hearing the title track, I admit that I ran through the streets of New York in a ripped sweatshirt, thinking I could dance like Jennifer Beals (the movie's star). Haven't you ever left a movie wishing you were the star at the center of all the drama? Sigh.

Center Stage Ballerinas duke it out for the best roles at a fictional ballet school.

Footloose Dancing is outlawed in this small town, but Kevin Bacon is about to change all that.

Top Hat, Shall We Dance, and *Swing Time* Rent black-and-white classics from the 1930s with Fred Astaire and Ginger Rogers, the greatest pair of dancers ever.

Grease Sandy in leather pants, the guys jumping around to "Greased Lightning," and the "Born to Hand Jive" dance scenes at the prom make this movie a must-see.

15 GREAT DANCE MOVIES TO SEE WITH YOUR FRIENDS

Newsies The true story of a courageous group of newsboys who become unlikely heroes when they team up to fight a mean old newspaper tycoon. Oh yeah, and they dance a lot.

Hairspray See the version from 2007, with John Travolta and Nikki Blonsky dancing their way around in Technicolor outfits and to-die-for wigs.

Strictly Ballroom A hilarious Australian flick about two dancers who come together to find their own dance style, with the best hair and makeup you'll never, *ever* want to have for yourself.

Billy Elliot Billy's a boy who can do ballet and tap dance so well you'll be cheering for him throughout the film.

Swing Kids Friends in war-torn Nazi Germany rebel against the times with swing and jitterbug dancing. Sounds like an odd mix of subjects, but it's a fascinating flip side (and footnote) to history—and the dancing is great.

High School Musical Though I'm sure everyone has seen this crew do their thing in HSM #1 and #2, it's worth repeated viewings. Just because we can't get enough Sharpay.

Save the Last Dance Emotional tale of a ballerina who uses hip-hop to become a better dancer.

Fame Join the kids from the New York High School for the Performing Arts as they dance in front of their school, and everywhere else for that matter. The movie's opening song wails, "I want to live forever!" Hmmm. Maybe dancing is the key.

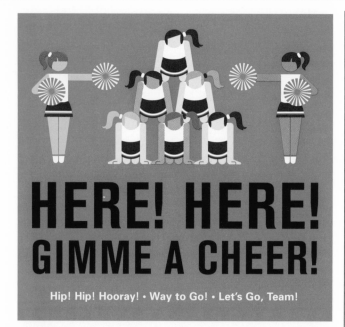

HERE! HERE! GIMME A CHEER!

Hip! Hip! Hooray! • Way to Go! • Let's Go, Team!

FAMOUS FOLKS WHO USED TO BE
CHEERLEADERS

WHO?	WHERE ARE THEY NOW?
Paula Abdul	*American Idol* Judge
Halle Berry	Academy Award–Winning Actress
Sandra Bullock	Actress and Producer
George W. Bush	President of the United States
Katie Couric	News Anchor
Jamie Lee Curtis	Actress and Author
Michael Douglas	Academy Award–Winning Actor and Producer
Dwight D. Eisenhower	Former President of the United States
Ruth Bader Ginsburg	Supreme Court Justice
Madonna	Pop Star and Author
Steve Martin	Actor, Author, and Comedian
Reba McEntire	Country Singer and TV Star
Mandy Moore	Singer and Actress
Franklin D. Roosevelt	Former President of the United States
Aaron Spelling	Legendary TV Producer
Meryl Streep	Academy Award–Winning Actress
Vanna White	*Wheel of Fortune* Hostess

BUST A MOVE!

BASIC TERMS AND FACTS

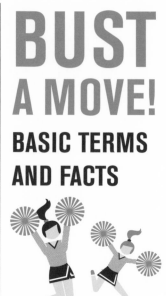

- *Attack the Crowd:* Technique to get the audience involved in a cheer or song.
- *Base:* The person (or people) down on the floor who lift a flyer into a stunt.
- *Candlesticks:* Cheer motion where you extend your arms out in front of you with your fists facing each other as if you were holding a lit candle in each hand.
- *Cradle Catch:* An end movement where a base catches a flyer after tossing her in the air. The base holds the flyer under her thighs and around her back.
- *Cupie:* The base's arm is fully raised up and both of the flyer's feet are in the base's one hand. Also known as Kewpie or Awesome.
- *Double Hook:* A jump where one leg is bent in front of you and the other leg is

bent behind you, while your arms are in a high V. Also known as a Pretzel, Abstract, or Table Top.

• *Facials:* Facial expressions that show how eager and involved you are, like winks, wide smiles, or head bobs.

• *Flyer (sometimes called floater):* The person who is elevated into the air by the bases; the person on top of a pyramid or stunt.

• *Herkie:* Cheerleading jump where one leg is bent towards the ground and the other is out to the side as high as it will go in the toe touch position.

• *High V:* Both arms are up, locked, in a V shape.

• *K Motion:* One arm forms a High V and the other arm rotates across your body on the right or left side (like a windmill).

• *Peel Off/Reload:* A squad splits into two or more groups to do the same motion, skill or step at different times.

• *Spankies:* Another word for briefs or underwear. Also called lollipops, bloomers, and tights.

• *Squad:* A group of cheerleaders.

• *Suck It Up:* When a flyer is up in a stunt, the base must suck it up, or hold it and not fall.

• *Tick-Tock:* When a flyer switches feet in a stunt.

• *Touchdown:* Motion with both arms held up high against your head.

• *Tuck:* Jump where you bring both knees up to your chest; sometimes precedes a flip.

HOW TO

ACE YOUR TRYOUT

CHEERLEADERS ARE, ABOVE EVERYTHING ELSE, *leaders*. They are meant to show the highest level of skill, sportsmanship, athletics, and spirit. If you're serious about becoming a cheerleader, you need to get serious about your health (cheerleaders are fit!) and your attitude (cheerleaders have positive energy!).

When going out for the cheering squad, there are a few things you want to do *ahead of time*:

• Get set to do more than yell and jump around. Familiarize yourself with basic cheers and cheerleading moves.

• You need to be physically strong. Regularly eat a balanced diet, exercise, and get a good night's rest.

• Learn specific jumps. You need to be able to do basic gymnastics and dance, and be a strong tumbler, too. Check local gyms, recreation departments, and colleges for classes you might take to better your skills.

• Learn about the sport you'll be cheering for. Ask questions, read books, watch videos, use the Internet. Never be afraid to say "I don't know" or "I don't understand," and "Can you show me?"

• Practice motions, cheers, jumps, and facial expressions, too. You want to leave a good impression. You might want to videotape yourself and then watch it to catch mistakes. Practice in front of a mirror.

On the day of the tryout, there are a few more things you need to do:

• Keep your hair away from your face and tuck in your shirt (in upside-down stunts, everything shows). Consider wearing a bow in the school colors. Wear clothes in your school colors, too.

• Don't wear jewelry, chew gum, or wear a lot of makeup.

• Try not to play around with your friends or talk too much.

• Keep that smile pasted on your face, no matter what. Think peppy.

• Make eye contact with the judges. Look ahead. Never look down or at the floor.

• Think sharp. Make sure all your motions are clean.

• Take your time when you say the cheers (and don't sing; say the words loud and clear).

• Ignore mistakes. Keep going. Use the opportunity to show you can recover from a mistake.

• Be confident. Believe in yourself. You can do it! Yeah!

BRING ON THE POM-POMS

Bow and Arrow　　　Daggers　　　Right L　　　Left L

Go or Punch　　　Hands on Hips　　　Touchdown　　　Low Touchdown

High V　　　Low V　　　T　　　Half T

Left Diagonal　　　Right Diagonal　　　Right K　　　Left K

HOW TO

DO A PERFECT CARTWHEEL

1. Make sure you have plenty of room. Start on soft grass, mats, or carpet while you perfect your moves.

2. Extend your arms straight above your head. Keep your hands turned in towards your head, with your arms against your ears. Reach for the sky, but keep your arms straight at all times.

3. Point one foot in the direction you will be going. Turn the other foot slightly outward, for better balance.

4. Pick a spot in front of you where you will land. Reach your hands out in the direction of the pointed foot. If you pointed your left foot, your left hand will touch the ground first (and vice versa). Your other hand will follow.

5. While the first hand is going down, the opposite foot should come up. Pretend you are landing on a straight line. Keep both hands on the same imaginary line that your feet started from. Just make sure to keep that leg straight.

6. Push yourself and kick powerfully so your legs come off the ground. Balance your weight on both of your arms, like a handstand, with your legs straight in the air, but out in a straddle/split position. Try to keep your back straight. This will help you to stay up; not to fall. What you want to look like is a bicycle wheel with its spokes turning one over the other.

7. Now that you've flipped around, land on the opposite foot. Do this facing the direction you came from, front leg slightly bent. You should be in the same position you started in, but with the opposite leg pushed forward.

P.S. Don't forget to tuck in your shirt.

THESE GIRLS KNOW

The best part about being an animated action girl: Cartoons are invincible. They can do a zillion flips, and never get dizzy, and look ultra-cool while doing it. Here are a few popular (and not-so-popular) girls who've been animated to fame. Do you count anyone as your alter ego? Who would you want to be your best friend at school? Who would make your enemies run in the opposite direction?

	POWERPUFF GIRLS	KIM POSSIBLE
REAL NAME(S)	Blossom, Bubbles, and Buttercup	Kim Possible
HOMETOWN	Townsville	Middleton
OUTFIT	Multicolored dresses with black stripes	Stylin' black T-shirt and cargo pants
SUPER SKILL	X-ray vision and assorted super-strengths (plus, Bubbles speaks squirrel!)	She can do anything
X FACTOR	Chemical X	Kimmunicator
SIDEKICK	Professor Utonium	Wade the genius
EVIL VILLAIN	Mojo Jojo	Dr. Drakken
WEAKNESS	Their curfew	Ron Stoppable
QUOTABLE QUOTE	"And so, once again, the Powerpuff Girls save the day."	"What's the sitch?"
VOTED MOST LIKELY TO...	Save the day. Duh.	Save the world.

HOW TO KICK BUTT

PEPPERMINT PATTY	LARA CROFT, TOMB RAIDER	SAILOR MOON	PEBBLES FLINTSTONE
Patricia Reichardt	Lara Croft, daughter of Lord Henshingly Croft	Serena "Bunny" Tsukino	Later, Pebbles Flintstone-Rubble
Wherever the Peanuts lived, U.S.	London, England, and all over the world	Azabu Juban, Japan	Bedrock (and later, Hollyrock)
Tomboy look: striped shirt and sneakers	Ripped T-shirt and strap-on weapons	Odango hairdo & clothes with moons and ribbons	Designer cave dress circa 1 million B.C.
Superstar athlete	Fearless solver of traps and puzzles	Magic and moon-light attacks	Wearing a bone in her hair
Bat & ball	Archaeology smarts	The silver crystal	Dino the dinosaur
Marcie	Werner Von Croy	Tuxedo Mask	Bamm-Bamm
Lucy	Gangsters, super-natural beings, and prehistoric creatures	Dark Kingdom, Black Moon Clan, and others	Her Dad, Fred, when he gets mad
Doesn't get it	Reckless	Eating cake	Getting her pals Wiggy, Moonrock, and Penny into trouble
"You kind of like me, don't you, Chuck?"	"This is where I start to have fun."	"Moon prism power, makeup!"	"Abba Gabba Goo." (And later, "Abba Dabba Doosie.")
Crush on Charlie Brown.	Globe-trot.	Become sovereign of Earth by the thirtieth century.	Pursue a career in advertising. (She really did!)

HOW TO

TEAR A BOOK IN HALF
AMAZE FRIENDS WITH YOUR SUPER-GIRL STRENGTH!

START SMALL! YOU WILL BE ABLE to tear a huge telephone book in half eventually, but first try a smaller, thin telephone book that's out of date.

Sit in a chair. With both hands, hold the book firmly across the long, open edge. See fig A.

Keep your palms on one side and put your fingers on the opposite side, with the spine of the phone book on your lap/knee. See fig B.

Pull your fingers up and push your palms down, spreading out the long, open edge of the telephone book. The pages should be in a slanted position so that each one just slightly overlaps the one next to it.

Start to tear the pages, one at a time gradually, so you're not actually tearing the thickness of the whole book at once. See fig C. Once the pages begin tearing, the entire book should tear apart more quickly.

Twist your hands in opposite directions, slanting the pages as much as possible as you tear. See Fig D.

Watch your position! The audience can't see the slanted side of the book that's facing you. They think you're ripping apart a huge book. See fig E, the audience's view of you and fig F, the view from your side.

Once you've torn the book into two pieces, say to your audience, "But wait! There's more!" Then, tear the book into two more pieces. Your audience will be amazed! Note: This trick may take a little practice to get it just right. But don't rip apart all the paperback books on the bookshelf. Ask friends if you can use their old phone books.

If for some reason your superpowers fail you while executing this feat, simply shrug it off. Even supergirls have off days, right?

Fig. A　Fig. B　Fig. C

Fig. D　Fig. E　Fig. F

GETTING ELECTED

CLASS PRESIDENT

IF MY RESEARCH IS CORRECT, I may possess the lamest slogan ever offered by a class presidential candidate. The year was sixth grade and I ran with the clever phrase, "Laura, We're For Her." Catchy? Um . . . nope. Rhyming? Sorta. The thing was, despite my sappy slogan, I put stickers with the slogan onto pencils that I handed out in class. And I frosted the slogan onto a batch of cookies. Now everyone knows that free cookies = victory, right?

What are some of the best pointers you'd offer a pal trying to get elected class president at your school? What winning strategies worked for you? Here are a few more of the tried and true:

- You need good ideas about how to bring the class together and get students involved. Organize your ideas. Create a list of "talking points" for yourself, so you are able to think clearly and answer questions.

- Be an awesome listener. You can't do all the talking.

- Don't stop smiling. Ever. Half-grins don't count. Teeth showing at all times! Oh, and with that in mind, you must remember to brush and floss a lot. You never know what's sticking out of your gums after lunch.

- Come up with a GREAT slogan. (Oh, and try to make your rhyme a little more exciting than mine.)

- Really care. No, really. CARE.

- Press the flesh. This means lots of hand shaking. It also means you should carry around a little container of that antibacterial gel because, well, you just never know.

- Make dozens of posters to plaster the halls. Just make sure you use bold, big letters, and add a photo of yourself looking class presidential (whatever that means!)

- During the election, don't try for any crazy fashion statements. You want to appeal to the widest base possible.

- Think about your campaign speech more than five minutes before you deliver it. In other words, you need to plan, write, rewrite, and practice in front of your friends. Being a presidential candidate is tough stuff. Just think how it'll be when you're actually elected president? You'll be making speeches all the time.

HAVING YOUR FIRST
(ALMOST) REAL JOB

CHANCES ARE THAT YOU GET SOME kind of allowance. Maybe Mom and Dad give you $5.00 a week just for being you. Or maybe you have to clean the basement, do the dishes, take out the trash, polish the car, and weed the garden before you even see fifty cents. Or maybe you get bupkus, nada, not a cent. Everyone's situation is different when it comes to making, saving, and spending money.

So when you wake up one day and decide, "I want a *real* job," you're probably thinking about the money part of it. If you work hard, you can add to that pile o' cash that's growing in your savings account. And that's true. But here's another truth: Getting a job is about a lot more than money. It's about independence, responsibility, experience, and self-confidence.

Deciding what kind of job you might want to take on is tricky. You have a lot of things to think about.

1 **What kind of services can you offer?** Make a list of all the things you can do and like to do. If you like plants, you could offer to water your neighbor's plants or mow their lawn. If you like dogs, you could walk your neighbor's pet. Are you crafty? Maybe you need to make something and sell it.

2 **Ask your family and neighbors what kind of things they need help with.** Maybe your neighbor needs someone to help them wash the car or clean out the basement. You're just the person for the job! These days, a lot of people have busy households and can always use an extra hand. Don't rule anything out. Someone may need help doing a load of wash—or taking the dog for a long walk.

3 **How much time do you have?** Considering whether to take on a job depends on your other commitments. Will you have time to finish your homework, clean your own room, and get to soccer practice *first*? Those are your top priorities. It's a good idea to ask your parents for advice in figuring out how to make your schedule work. Sometimes weekends are a good time to take on small jobs, but weekends are also family time for a lot of people. And yes, you want to work, but you also need to play. Don't overschedule or overbook yourself. A lot of kids try to do too much. Give yourself a chance to just chill out, too.

4 **Make a real plan.** If you're serious about offering your services, then get serious about making a business plan and put it into action.

   a. *Write down all the details of your business.* Describe what you want to do and how you expect to do it. For example, say you want to shovel driveways when it snows. How much money do you want to make? Are you trying to save for something specific? Write it all down.

   b. *Make a list of all the materials you need.* If you're shoveling snow, you will obviously need a few important things: a good shovel and sturdy, warm gloves. What else?

c. *Identify your competition.* **Are** there other kids who shovel snow? Do some neighbors usually shovel themselves? Does someone hire a service to plow his driveway? Consider all the competition—and see what you can do to make your service better than their service.

d. *Where will your business be located?* It's easy to imagine your snow-shoveling business based in your house because you're not dealing with a lot of materials or products. But if you decide to embark on a business with a lot of stuff to store, Mom and Dad may not be so happy about its taking over the garage or your bedroom. You need to find the right place to make and store your stuff.

e. *Figure out your sales plan.* Figure out how much you would like to charge each house to shovel their driveway based on the size and time you will have to put into the job. Multiply that by the number of people in your neighborhood. Consider working on the next block, too. If your job is shoveling, you need to consider the fact that it may not snow—or it may snow *a lot*. Are you willing to work harder sometimes—or deal with no work sometimes? What will you do when it doesn't snow? Perhaps you need to be a raking *and* shoveling business. Maybe, in the spring and summer, you can offer to water and weed, too. Should you go into business with a friend or two in case the workload gets too big? Try not to get overwhelmed by all the possibilities. Start simple and build your plan as you go.

f. *Advertise your business.* Come up with a memorable name. Make a flyer to deposit in everyone's mailbox. (Just make sure you clear all the information posted on the flyer with an adult first.) Post or put a flyer on the local post office bulletin board. Hopefully, once your business gets going, customers will recommend you to their neighbors and friends. "Word of mouth" is the best kind of advertising.

g. *Prepare for the worst.* There will be times when you have no business at all. Someone may not need your services or maybe it's not snowing—even though your shiny shovel is just raring to pick up some newly fallen snow. Don't lose faith in your ability as a good businessperson or a smart worker. Don't give up. Re-evaluate your business plans and consider other jobs. Team up with a friend to brainstorm and get out of a slump.

5 **Don't ever forget your number one priority: YOU.** It may be tempting to work all the time. There's a chance your business plan may really take off and you're flush with cash. But you need to learn how and when to say "No, thanks" as well as "Yes." You can't do it all. Your homework, your sleep, your health — all of these things must come first. No matter what kind of job you do, keep tabs on your other responsibilities. Check in with your parents often. Take care of yourself.

6 **Be responsible about the money you do make.** Don't let money burn a hole in your pocket. Save some—or *all*—of it. Spend it on things that really matter. Take your time to value what you've earned and how you've earned it.

HOW MUCH?

Negotiating how much you will be paid for your time and services can be tricky. Here's a good rule of thumb: Find out the "going" rate for your type of service. What do local babysitters get paid? How much does the kid down the block get for each lawn he mows? Your salary will be based on age, experience, location, and obviously, your skills. The more you know, the more you get!

THINGS YOU CAN DO FOR

$ $ $

IF YOU'RE ARTISTIC . . .

- Make and sell stuff like greeting cards, pot holders, decorated T-shirts, flip-flops, or even friendship bracelets (see pages 197–198).
- Paint a mural on a child's bedroom wall using those fabulous art class skills!
- Paint wooden picture frames—and then personalize them for customers.

IF YOU LIKE GREEN STUFF (AND WE'RE NOT TALKING ABOUT MONEY, WE'RE TALKING ABOUT THINGS THAT GROW) . . .

- Plant or tend a garden for your neighbors. (One idea: In late summer/fall you could offer a yard cleanup and bulb planting service.)
- Plant watering (indoor or out).

IF YOU LIKE FOOD . . .

- Bake and sell cookies with cups of lemonade at a sidewalk stand.
- Offer to help neighbors serve food and clean up at a birthday or graduation party.

IF YOU'RE SUPER-ORGANIZED . . .

- Basement or garage picker-upper.
- Organize recyclable materials the day before curbside pickup.
- Help with laundry: washing, drying, and folding.

- Run errands for senior citizens or any neighbors who can't do it themselves. This works best if you have stores within walking distance, or if you can get a ride to the store from an adult. With permission, you could also take a local bus or train. Just figure its cost into the cost of your services.

IF YOU LIKE ANIMALS . . .

- Think about dog, fish, or other pet sitting (and feeding!) while someone is at work or on vacation.
- Dog walking.

IF YOU LIKE FLEXING YOUR MUSCLES* . . .

- Snow shoveling.
- Car washing/waxing.
- Sidewalk or patio sweeping.
- Leaf raking.
- Fence painting.

*Note: A lot of times it's the *boys* who get these gigs. But girls have just as much muscle! *And* they have a reputation for being thorough and neat. Emphasize what you can offer that girls and boys do differently.

IF YOU LIKE LITTLE KIDS . . .

- Mother's helper.
- Babysitting (read on for useful tips about this popular choice).

BABYSITTING

JUST ABOUT EVERYTHING YOU NEED TO KNOW

Congratulations! You're ready to babysit. Now what? Let's break it down.

THE KIND OF PERSON YOU NEED TO BE

Respectable: Listen to what the parents instruct you to do and respect their wishes.

Responsible: You need to show up on time, ready to get to work. Although most of the experience may turn out to be more like playtime, think about it as a job.

Loving: You must like kids. That's the number one job requirement. As if you didn't know. You also need to know *how* to act with kids.

Self-confident: The kids you are watching will be able to tell how you are feeling by your words and actions. Let them know you're feeling good about you.

Mature: If there is any kind of emergency, you need to be able to stay clearheaded and manage the scene, which includes tending to the sick or injured kid *as well as* continuing to watch the other kids, if necessary.

Well-Mannered: Set a good example by saying please, thank you, and excuse me.

Adaptable: Just when you think everything is under control, something crazy is bound to happen. One of the most likely scenarios: The kids will miss Mom and Dad. How will you deal with tears—sometimes hysterical, red-in-the-face ones? Plan to be comforting, entertaining, and safety-conscious all at the same time. And remember: Distraction is your best friend. When he or she starts bawling, try to get your charge interested in something else like a game or snack.

ADVERTISE YOUR SERVICES

- Lead off with a friendly message. (Fig. 1)
- Put your name in a bold, bright color to make it the focus. (Fig. 2)
- Add some quick points about your credentials (Fig. 3) with a message to call for more information. (Fig. 4)
- Put your phone number here, maybe in the same bold color as your name. (Fig. 5)
- End the flyer with a friendly closing note. (Fig. 6)
- Always check with a parent before advertising anything, especially your services.

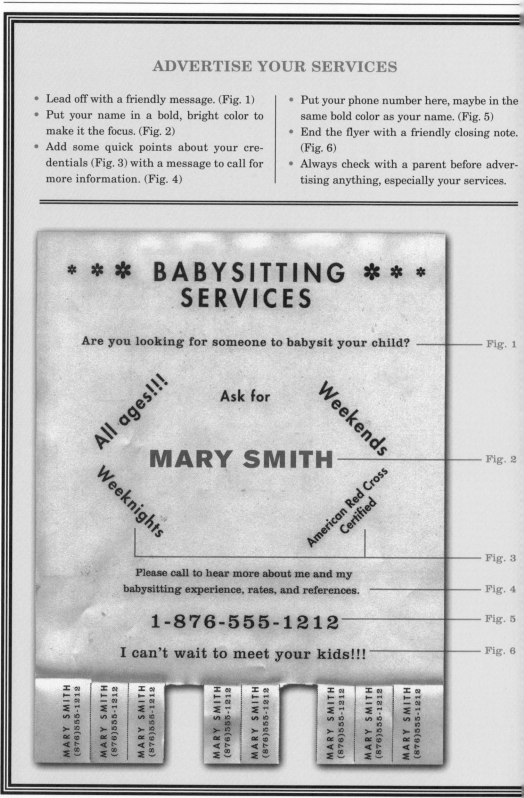

YOU GOT THE JOB, NOW GET THE FACTS

Before you start any babysitting job, meet with the parents and the child or children you'll be watching. You're the babysitter; the child is called your "charge." (That's because you're the one *in* charge! Got it?) There are essential questions to consider. Write information down on a babysitting "cheat sheet" so you can refer to it now and later. Trust me . . . the parents will be impressed by your attention to details.

☑ TIME
- How long will I be babysitting? When should I arrive? When should I plan to be picked up?

☑ CONTACT INFO
- Where will you be? How can I reach you? Ask for telephone numbers, including cell phones. Make sure they leave a list of emergency numbers, including the doctor, 911, and another adult who can help if there is any problem.

☑ FOOD & MEDICATION
- Do I have to serve a meal? When do I serve it? What do I make? Does the child have any eating problems/likes/dislikes/allergies? What about snacks and drinks? Am I allowed to cook with stove or microwave? Am I allowed to eat something from the fridge, too?
- Are there any things you usually do at mealtime like saying grace or playing a game at the table?
- Is the child in good health? If there is any chance that the child needs medication, you need to know the dose and the time it needs to be given.

☑ PLAYTIME
- Where can the children play inside the house? Outside? Will any friends be available for play dates while I am babysitting? Can the child use the computer or watch TV? What about video games—even handheld ones? What can the child watch? Are there any toys or games that are off-limits?
- Ask about favorite games, books, and play spots for each kid you are watching. Are there any other favorites or play routines you need to know about?

☑ BED & BATHTIME
- Do I need to give the child a bath? Can the child do any of the washing herself? Can the child brush his teeth or does he need help? What clothes does the child get into after the bath?
- Do I need to put the child to bed? What does the child wear? What time is lights out? What is the usual routine? Does the child have a "lovey" like a pacifier or blanket that she needs to fall asleep?

☑ DIAPERING AND DRESSING
- Where are the children's clothes? Do I need to change diapers? Where are extra diapers, baby wipes, or powder?

☑ ALL AROUND THE HOUSE
- Does the child have any other special needs? Are there any other house rules that I should know about?
- Where are flashlights and batteries in case the power goes out?
- Where are the Band-Aids and antiseptic ointment in case someone gets a boo-boo?
- What else am I not allowed to touch or use in the house/apartment? Can I turn on the air conditioner or fan if it gets hot?
- Do I get a set of house keys? Are we allowed to go into the yard or to the playground?
- What else should I know about?

FAMOUS FIRSTS

1773
PHYLLIS WHEATLEY
- First African-American published poet
- Although she came to the United States, Wheatley's book of poems was first published in England.

1792
MARY WOLLSTONECRAFT
- First feminist author
- Her work, *A Vindication of the Rights of Woman*, talked about inequality between the sexes like no one had done before.

1849
ELIZABETH BLACKWELL
- First woman physician in the modern era
- When she applied to medical school in Geneva, NY, the school endorsed admission only because they believed she was playing a joke on them. Ha! Who got the last laugh?

1849
AMELIA JENKS BLOOMER
- First woman U.S. newspaper editor
- Founded *The Lily*, a semimonthly women's periodical in 1849.

1865
MARY EDWARDS WALKER
- First woman to receive the Congressional Medal of Honor
- This army surgeon was awarded the medal for her service during the Civil War, but in 1910, it was stripped from her because she had not served active military duty. Half a century later, in 1977, the medal was reinstated by the Army board.

1866
LUCY HOBBS
- First woman dentist
- After marrying Civil War veteran James Taylor, Hobbs taught him how to be a dentist, too—and opened their dental practice together.

1869
ARABELLA MANSFIELD BABB
- First woman admitted to the bar (lawyer)
- In college, Belle (her nickname to family and friends) and her brother, Washington Irving, were the best students. She was valedictorian (top student) and he was salutatorian (second-best student).

1881
CLARA BARTON
- Founder of the American Red Cross
- During the Civil War, President Abraham Lincoln placed Barton in charge of the search for missing Union army men. Her group was able to locate 30,000 men!

1881
VICTORIA CHAFIN WOODHULL
- First woman U.S. presidential candidate
- Many people cite reasons why she should not officially be considered a candidate: She was under the age of 35, her name was

AND FOUNDERS

not put on the ballot, and, *of course*, she was a woman!

1887
SUZANNA MADORA SALTER
- First woman mayor
- After marrying Civil War veteran James Taylor, Hobbs taught him how to be a dentist, too—and they opened a dental practice together.

1888
LOUISE BLANCHARD BETHUNE
- First woman member of the American Institute of Architects
- During her career, she designed schools, factories, hotels, housing developments, and one of the first U.S. structures with a steel frame and poured concrete slabs, now commonplace.

1904
MARY MCLEOD BETHUNE
- First woman to establish a four-year college
- One of seventeen children of slave parents, Bethune went on to become vice president of the NAACP.

1910
BLANCHE STUART SCOTT
- First woman to fly an airplane (unofficially)
- In 1910, Scott was also the second woman to drive a car coast to coast.

1912
JULIETTE GORDON LOW
- Founder of Girls Scouts of America
- She is the eighth woman ever to be honored with a stamp.

1917
JEANETTE RANKIN
- First woman in Congress (Montana)
- Rankin was the only member of Congress to vote against the United States' entry into World War II—an unpopular decision that cost her a lot of support.

1917
KATE GLEASON
- First woman bank president
- The first woman to enter Cornell University's engineering program, she was good friends with suffragette Susan B. Anthony.

1922
FLORENCE E. ALLEN
- First woman judge
- Friends called her a "two-fisted" woman, meaning that she fought for her principles. When she was just eleven, her mother took her to hear Susan B. Anthony speak at a meeting celebrating the victory for women's suffrage in Utah.

1925
NELLIE TAYLOE ROSS
- First woman governor (Wyoming)
- Happy as a wife and mother, Ross inherited the governorship after the death of her husband; but found that politics suited her. Years later, she was named director of the U.S. Mint.

1931
JANE ADDAMS
- First woman to win the Nobel Peace Prize
- In 1889, she founded Hull House, one of the first settlement houses offering neighborhood services like day care, classes, and more.

1932
AMELIA EARHART
- First woman to fly solo across the Atlantic Ocean
- How weird is this: Earhart met Orville Wright (one of the brothers who flew the first plane) the year she disappeared! She also had a great relationship with Eleanor Roosevelt and planned on teaching her how to fly.

1933
RUTH BRYAN OWEN
- First woman foreign diplomat
- Daughter of William Jennings Bryan (famous Democratic politician), she was inducted into the Florida Hall of Fame in 1992.

1938
PEARL S. BUCK
- First woman to win the Nobel Prize for Literature
- Buck's won this (and the Pulitzer Prize, 1932) for her book *The Good Earth*, the story of a peasant farmer whose love for his land sustains him through hard and good times.

1930s
MAE WEST
- First woman to make $1 million per movie
- Starred with W.C. Fields in *My Little Chickadee* . . . and she wrote the screenplay, too!

1949
GEORGIA NEESE CLARK
- First woman treasurer of the United States
- She started her career as an actress in New York and spent ten years touring the country for $500 week.

1953
JACQUELINE COCHRAN
- First woman to break the sound barrier
- Also the first woman to: take off and land on an aircraft carrier; pilot a bomber; and the only woman in the Aviation Hall of Fame, among other achievements.

1963
VALENTINA TERESHKOVA
- First woman in space

- A crater on the far side of the moon is named after Tereshkova.

1967
MURIEL SIEBERT
- First woman to sit on the New York Stock Exchange
- What are the odds? Siebert's seat was one among 1,365 men's seats on the Exchange.

1975
JUNKO TABEI
- First woman to climb Mr. Everest
- She is also the first woman to have reached the summits of all the highest peaks on the seven continents.

1981
SANDRA DAY O'CONNOR
- First woman Supreme Court Justice
- An accomplished lawyer and jurist, O'Connor served on the court for more than twenty-four years.
- Fun Fact: In 2002, O'Connor was inducted into the National Cowgirl Hall of Fame!

1983
SALLY KRISTEN RIDE
- First American woman to fly into space
- She started up www.sallyridescience.com, a science company dedicated to supporting interest in science, math, and technology for girls.

1984
JOAN BENOIT SAMUELSON
- First woman to win an Olympic marathon
- Benoit originally took up long-distance running to help recover from a skiing injury.

1986
ANN BANCROFT
- First woman to cross the ice to the North Pole

- An avid naturalist, Bancroft led her family on mini-excursions into the Minnesota wilderness as early as the age of eight.

1992
MAE JEMISON
- First black woman to fly into space
- Jemison speaks fluent Russian, Japanese, and Swahili, as well as English.

1997
MADELINE ALBRIGHT
- First woman Secretary of State
- When Albright became a U.S. citizen in 1957, she was twenty and spoke four languages: Czech, her mother tongue, Serbo-Croat, French (from schooling in Switzerland), and English (learned in London, where the family evacuated to during World War II).

2003
JULIA ROBERTS
- First woman to earn $25 million for a movie
- Roberts has been named one of *People* magazine's most beautiful people in the world eleven times.

2007
NANCY PELOSI
- First woman Speaker of the House
- She grew up in a political family (her dad was mayor during her entire childhood); however, she waited until the youngest of her five children was a high school senior before she ran for Congress in 1987.

????
YOU
- First woman President of the Universe
- What's *your* greatest achievement so far? What do you have to say?

THE REAL MOTHERS OF INVENTION

ALEXANDER GRAHAM BELL invented the telephone. Thomas Edison discovered electricity. George Washington Carver could make everything from butter to plastic—all with a pile of peanuts.

So, what's wrong with this picture?

There are no women in it! And U.S. patent office records show that women have been just as active as men in developing useful objects and ways to do things. Some of the inventions are wild and crazy. In 1873, a woman invented sunshades to keep the sun out of her horses' eyes. At the Chicago Exposition in 1893, women presented inventions for a combined sofa and bathtub (yes, together), and a combination dress stand and fire escape. A woman named Bertha D. Lilly invented a collar and diaper for her parakeet in 1959. (Hey, it cut down on the mess in the birdcage.)

Of course, there are numerous inventions by women that have left a more lasting mark on our world. Some of these women have been inducted into the National Inventors Hall of Fame. A few of the standouts:

MARY DIXON KIES, 1809
- Weaving straw with silk
- Kies was the first woman to apply for and receive a U.S. patent in her own name. The New England hat-making industry adopted her patent for a process that wove straw with silk. At a time when the U.S. had stopped importing European goods (during and after the Napoleonic wars), her patent and ideas were invaluable. First Lady Dolley Madison credited Kies with giving a boost to the hat industry at a critical moment in history.

AMANDA THEODOSIA JONES (with Professor Leroy Cooley), 1872
- Vacuum process for preserving food
- Jones's important invention, the vacuum process for canning, paved the way for her Women's Canning and Preserving Company in 1890, the first business ever staffed and run by women only. Although the company failed, Jones went on to patent another important invention: the oil safety valve. This device ensured that a reasonable supply of oil went into lamps and other tools, reducing the danger of things catching fire.

JOSEPHINE GARIS COCHRAN, 1886
- Automatic dishwasher
- Socialite Cochran (sometimes spelled Cochrane) was tired of her servants chipping all her dishes, but she hated washing them herself. A solution? Invent a machine that safely washed dishes for her! At the Chicago Exposition in 1893, Cochran's incredible invention (the Garis Cochrane Dish-Washing Machine) was not only put on display, but was also put to use by almost every restaurant in the Chicago area. The company she founded to manufacture these machines later became KitchenAid.

GRACE HOPPER, 1943
- COBOL computer language
- Hopper created a program that translates instructions for a computer from English to machine language. Computer pioneer Howard Bromberg called her "a mathematician, computer scientist, social scientist, corporate politician, marketing whiz, systems designer, programmer," and,

always, a "visionary." But when did Grace really know she'd made it big? In 1996, the U.S. Navy named a ship after her—the USS *Hopper*, nicknamed Amazing Grace.

MARION O'BRIAN DONOVAN, 1949

* Disposable diapers
* Thanks to Donovan, you don't have to worry about washing and drying cloth diapers when you babysit. This stay-at-home mother revolutionized baby care with the creation of a moisture and leakproof diaper that used snaps instead of pins. How did she come up with the idea? She made the first one using a shower-curtain liner. It took her three years to get it just right!

BETTY NESMITH GRAHAM, 1956

* Liquid Paper
* Graham's mother was an artist and she wanted to be one, too, but after a bad divorce, she got a secretarial position instead. Frustrated with erasing her typing errors on the job, Graham revived some of her art techniques and began covering errors in ink with tempera paints. The formula caught on! Eventually, she began making her invention in her kitchen, with her son and other family members helping to mix it and put it into bottles.

STEPHANIE LOUISE KWOLEK, 1965

* Kevlar
* Kwolek's teachers encouraged her to pursue science and chemistry when she was a child. After years of school, she ended up in the lab at Dupont, asked to make long molecules called polymers that could be made into fabric or plastics. Always up for a challenge, Kwolek created Kevlar, a synthetic thread that is five times stronger than steel at the same weight. Kevlar is used in bulletproof vests, canoes, skis, boat hulls, firefighter suits, and radial tires. In 1995, she was inducted into the National Inventors Hall of Fame.

ANN MOORE, 1969

* SNUGLI, the baby carrier
* Moore, a nurse who lived in French West Africa for a time, got her idea for a baby "backpack" from watching African women carry their babies securely on their backs. SNUGLI reached enormous popularity with parents in the late 1980s. Today, Baby Bjorn and other carriers are popular with moms and dads everywhere.

GOT A BIG IDEA?

WHAT DOES A PATENT DO? IT legally clears the way for you—and only you—to own (and profit from) your invention for twenty years.

In addition to patenting your own clever inventions, you can enter contests and even go to invention camp. There are cool scholarships and awards available to kids of all ages, too, like the Partnership in America's Future (K-12), or the Duracell/NSTA Scholarship. NSTA stands for National Science Teachers Association, so ask your own science teacher to help you get the details you need. Check statewide for smaller contests that encourage young inventors, too.

Other great resources:

* www.uspto.gov (information on patents and trademarks)
* www.girltech.com (cool facts about girl inventors)
* www.invent.org/camp (how to go to inventor camp)

COOL TECH GIRLS

TECH GIRLS DO WAY MORE THAN GO online or work with computers. Jobs in engineering and technology include everything and anything: designing a rollercoaster, making weather predictions, developing new medicines, controlling and preventing pollution, and exploring new worlds under a high-powered microscope or in outer space. How do you get to be a tech girl?

When her husband, Washington Roebling, became ill in 1872, **EMILY ROEBLING** took over as day-to-day supervisor of Brooklyn Bridge construction. What a job! She had to supervise hundreds of men working dangerous conditions and long hours on the bridge, in addition to making sure all the construction was just right. Of course, she'd studied many engineering topics related to bridge construction, including mathematics, strength of materials, and cable construction. You can find her name on the plaque dedicating the bridge.

ADA BYRON LOVELACE, daughter of the English poet Lord Byron, designed the first "computer program" in 1843, more than a hundred years before the computer was even invented! Her program calculated certain numbers, called Bernoulli numbers. She also wrote a paper that predicted the development of computer software, artificial intelligence, and electronic music. Next time you think your imagination has gone wild . . . go with it. Ada did!

In the 1940s, movie star **HEDY LAMARR** had another major accomplishment: She held a technology patent. Her big idea: frequency hopping, or switching from frequency to frequency in split-second intervals over lines of communication (so messages could not be detected!). In World War II, her technology was used to transmit messages safely. Today, it is the foundation for wireless networks. Next time you talk on a cell, think of Hedy.

When she was only eight, a young girl named **VALERIE THOMAS** bought a book called *The Boy's First Book on Electronics*. Unfortunately, her dad didn't want to do the projects with *her*. In her all-girls school, no teachers encouraged Valerie to take advanced courses in science or math, but Valerie persevered! She attended Morgan State University and was one of two physics majors. Out of college, she landed a job with NASA and invented an illusion transmitter, a device that uses mirrors to produce optical illusion messages.

TECH-CRAZY FACT

The U.S. Department of Labor reports that the top five fastest-growing occupations are computer-related. According to the Pew Research Center-Internet and American Life Project, if current trends continue, Internet use is likely to equal that of the telephone (94%) or television (98%) within the next fifteen to twenty years.

So Are You a Tech Girl?

DO YOU LIKE USING COMPUTERS? Would you consider attending a summer robotics camp? Do you play video games? How would you design a video game just for girls? How many tech items do you use in one day?

Girl Scouts of America have patches that you can earn in just about every area, including technology. In order to earn the I.T. patch, you need to complete a short quiz. Some of the selected questions are below. To find out the answers, see the bottom of this page, or surf around for them on the Girls are I.T. Web site at www.girlsareit.org.

What does I.T. stand for?
The first PDA was created in what year B.C.?
Who was the first computer programmer?
What important technological invention arrived in 1969?
When was the first computer bug found?
What kind of bug was it?
In what year did "You've Got Mail" begin?
To see a nanochip, you must use what?

HANDY-DANDY E-CHAT DICTIONARY

DO YOU AND YOUR PALS TALK ONLINE or TEXT using shorthand? Many of these acronyms are in popular use all over the Internet. You can also make up your own online e-chat or invent your own emoticons (faces made from lines, dashes, and dots).

2C4W	Too cool for words		GR*	Great
AFK	Away from keyboard		GTG	Got to go
BCNU	Be seeing you		HHOK	Ha ha, only kidding
BFN	Bye for now		HIG	How's it going?
BIFF	Best Internet friend forever		HTH	Hope this helps
BRB	Be right back		IDGI	I don't get it
BTDT	Been there, done that		IYSS	If you say so
BTW	By the way		J/K	Just kidding
CSL	Can't stop laughing		J/J	Just joking
CUL8R	See you later		J/W	Just wondering
DBEYH	Don't believe everything you hear		KIT	Keep in touch
			LMK	Let me know
DGT	Don't go there		LOL	Laugh out loud
DLTM	Don't lie to me		LTNE	Long time no e-mail
DTRT	Do the right thing		LYLAS	Love ya like a sister
FC	Fingers crossed		NBD	No big deal
FTBOMH	From the bottom of my heart		N2M	Not too much
GL	Good luck		OMG	Oh, my goodness!
GMTA	Great minds think alike		QT	Cutie

SS	So sorry	^5	high five
TAL	Thanks a lot	<brrr>	That is sooo cold
TMA	Take my advice	<grrr>	I'm angry
TOOC	Totally out of control	@—)—(—	Rose (flower)
TOY	Thinking of you	:-#-	My lips are sealed
TTFN	Ta ta for now	>:-<	I am angrier than angry
VF	Very funny	(@@)	You're kidding
VVF	Very very funny	:-~(	I'm all choked up
WDYS	What did you say?	(: :)	Band-Aid
WML	Wish me luck	:-6	I'm sooo wiped out
YBS	You'll be sorry	0<| :-}}}	Santa Claus
YYSW	Yeah, yeah, sure, whatever	] - 8	Wearing sunglasses and
: -)	Happy		lip gloss
: -))	Very happy	-=#:-)/	Wizard and his wand
: -)))	Very, very happy	: - X	Sworn to secrecy
: - (	Sad	:-***	Smooches
=8-0	Shocked	<>)?	Huh?
{(i)}	Butterfly		
>^,,^<	Kitty cat		

Full disclosure: All of the above were used or invented in my From the Files of Madison Finn book series.

POINT & CLICK
REMEMBER THIS WHEN
YOU GO ONLINE

Y OU'VE PROBABLY HEARD SOME OF the bad stories about people who get tricked, lied to, or attacked online. Even when your computer has blocks on it to filter out material that is not suitable for you, the Internet can still be a very tricky and dangerous place. Though it is packed with vast amounts of facts, photos, and instant news . . . it is also a place that needs to be monitored.

A few very important DON'Ts:

DON'T ever agree to meet someone in person that you have met online. If someone asks you to do this, tell Mom, Dad, or an adult right away. Maybe it will be someone you can see—

under supervision—at a future date. But never agree to go somewhere alone. It's the equivalent of getting into a car with a total stranger.

DON'T ever give out your personal information. No exceptions. Although Web pages and blogs have become extremely popular, make sure you do not show your actual address or phone number. Don't e-mail it to strangers, either. And be careful of the photos you post.

DON'T ever spread bad rumors or bully someone. The increase in chat room environments has included an increase in bad behavior online. People make up things that are not true and then post it on message boards as if it's fact. Cyber bullies are even worse than bullies who get up in your face. Information that is spread virally (i.e. over the Internet) can reach thousands of people in a matter of moments. And the cyber bully can be a real coward, hiding behind his or her keyboard. Be aware. Take care.

NETIQUETTE

H AVE YOU EVER HEARD OF MISS Manners? She's newspaper columnist Judith Martin, who answers questions about how to be polite, have table manners, and all that important stuff that your grandmother always bugs you about. She's got a few things to say about cyber manners, too. "We have just as many ways, if not more, to be obnoxious in cyberspace," Martin says, "and fewer ways to regulate them."

Here are some things to think about before YOU communicate online:

• Never assume anything you write or do online is totally private. Once you've posted a message, you have no control over where it may go next. It could be forwarded to someone who shouldn't see it. OMG!

• Watch what you say. Although it's great to be able to send an instant note to someone, important details can get lost in translation. Like

tone of voice. Maybe you're making a joke, but without your winking, in-person facial expression to back it up, the written joke falls flat. Be sure that what you write cannot be misinterpreted. You don't want to leave someone hurt or confused by what you've written.

• DON'T USE ALL CAPS. When you do that, it's the equivalent of yelling. GOT IT!!??

• Check your grammar and spelling, but don't correct other people's text. If you're in a chat room, people type quickly, so mistakes are bound to be made. Other people in the forum may be rushing, or coming from a different country.

• Triple-check your e-mail before you hit SEND. Once that button is pressed, there is no turning back. Make sure the message you send contains all the information you need—and is not offensive in any way.

• If you're on a Web site and have a question, be sure to check the FAQs (Frequently Asked Questions) page before asking it. A lot of times, sites have already answered the question many times before. Use resources that already exist.

HOW TO

WRITE A LETTER TO THE FUTURE

AT THE END OF EVERY SUMMER, my mind would race about the upcoming school year. What would it be like? Would all my friends be the same? Who would I like? Who would I *like* like? What other surprises would be in store for me? I solved my curiosity by doing something deceptively simple: Writing myself a letter now—about the future. Of course, this kind of letter can be written anytime. It's a great way to record predictions and wishes for the new year.

1 Address your letter to yourself.

2 Write a quick status report: where you are writing, what you are wearing, how you feel, who you like, what you're doing for the weekend.

3 Ask a bunch of questions. What's bugging you? What do you wish for? What do you need? Make promises to yourself. Anything goes!

4 Look outside yourself. Make observations or predictions about life in the outside world, too. If you're feeling really inspired, tear out some headlines. The letter can be a mini-time capsule.

5 Write down the name of at least one person who you want to get to know better, one person you hope to meet, and one person you want to help.

6 Seal the letter in an envelope and decorate it.

7 Pick a date to read the letter. Put that date on the envelope: Open After _____. Then put the letter in a safe spot, like your jewelry box.

8 Sometime in the future, open it up and a) laugh, b) gloat, c) wax nostalgic, d) feel proud, or e) all of the above. Then do it again.

BODY LINGO

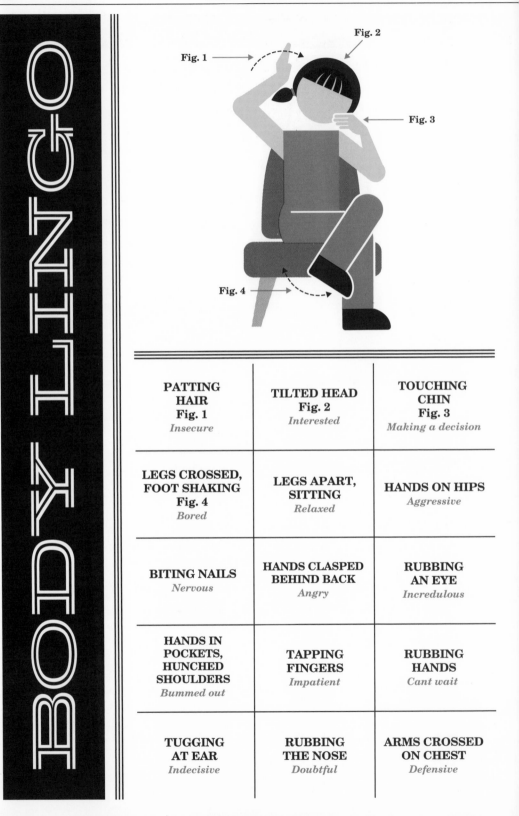

Fig. 1 · Fig. 2 · Fig. 3 · Fig. 4

PATTING HAIR **Fig. 1** *Insecure*	**TILTED HEAD** **Fig. 2** *Interested*	**TOUCHING CHIN** **Fig. 3** *Making a decision*
LEGS CROSSED, FOOT SHAKING **Fig. 4** *Bored*	**LEGS APART, SITTING** *Relaxed*	**HANDS ON HIPS** *Aggressive*
BITING NAILS *Nervous*	**HANDS CLASPED BEHIND BACK** *Angry*	**RUBBING AN EYE** *Incredulous*
HANDS IN POCKETS, HUNCHED SHOULDERS *Bummed out*	**TAPPING FINGERS** *Impatient*	**RUBBING HANDS** *Cant wait*
TUGGING AT EAR *Indecisive*	**RUBBING THE NOSE** *Doubtful*	**ARMS CROSSED ON CHEST** *Defensive*

COOL LETTERING

Coming up with new ways to write the alphabet seems like the best possible way to disguise your own handwriting and to give your cards, letters, and art a dash of personality.

DOUBLE   TRIPLE

DOTTY   FUZZY

HOT   COLD

WALKING   Loopy

SHADED   3-D

PUT A PATTERN INSIDE YOUR BLOCK LETTERS! LIKE THESE

PATTERNS

GRAPHOLOGY

Graphologists are experts who can identify forged (fake) documents. They can tell about someone's personality traits just from looking at handwriting. They look at different factors:

The pressure of letters. If you flip over a page that has writing on it, check for the impression left by the letters. Is it deep or dark? That means you have a lot of energy or confidence. Is the writing light? You may be shy or just feeling laid-back.

The size of letters. Small handwriting usually means you are research-oriented, methodical, and able to concentrate well. Large handwriting means you're outspoken and people-oriented.

Spacing of letters. Wide-open spaces between letters and words means you like your freedom. No space between letters and words means you put yourself under a lot of pressure.

Flourishes and embellishments. If you have a lot of loops and curls all over the place, you like to be the center of attention. See the list below for more specific explanations.

Slant of letters. If you write on an upward slant, you're feeling extra-happy. Slanted to the left? You are careful and cautious. Slanted to the right? Make way for success! If you don't slant but write straight up and down, you are very trustworthy.

A BRIEF HISTORY OF HANDWRITING ANALYSIS

There are references to handwriting analysis as far back as 4500 B.C.

Around 120 A.D., Roman historian Suetonius discussed Emperor Augustus's handwriting in his biography: "I have . . . observed this special peculiarity in his manner of writing: He does not divide words or carry superfluous letters from the end of one line to the beginning of the next, but writes them just below the rest of the word and draws a loop around them."

The first actual book devoted to handwriting analysis was published in 1622 in Italy by Camillo Baldi, a doctor of medicine and philosophy. It was called *How to Recognize from a Letter the Nature and Quality of a Writer.*

Modern graphology is now studied in university programs and used by jury selectors, forensic scientists, and others to determine an individual's state of mind. So the next time your teacher reminds you to cross your ts and dot your is, make sure you think about *how* you're doing it!

Ts crossed near the top Set for success.	**Many loop-de-loops and dips** Steadfast and determined.	**Squished letters and words** Afraid of social events.
t	*I'm very dedicated*	I'm kind of shy
Ts crossed with an enormous swoosh Excited. Totally.	**Big swoops on capital G and T** Overactive imagination.	**Teeny, tiny letters** Good concentration.
t	*G Y*	I'm focused
Ts crossed way down low Tired and blue.	**A little loop inside your O** Are you lying?	**Curly ends** So—emotional (sniff, sniff).
t	*O*	I'm a bit sensitive
Perfectly dotted Is Little Miss Perfection.	**Os open at the top** You're like Honest Abe.	**Letters looped over like an umbrella** Protective.
i	*O*	I'm watchful of my siblings
Is dotted with a dash instead of a dot Time to chill out.	**Space between all your words** Fearless.	**Wavy lines of text** Soulful and loving.
í	I'm not afraid!	Will you be my Valentine?

Graphology researcher Andrea McNichol states that nearly 99% of all people in the general population will line up their letters at the left margin of a page. But a higher percentage of criminals will *not*. She claims this is because criminals refuse to literally "toe the line" in society. What do you think?

PASSING NOTES...
OR NOT?

T HE DEBATE GOES ON: TO PASS A NOTE IN social studies class, or not to pass? Of course, your teachers would rather you paid attention and didn't pass anything around the room, but that might be a hard thing to do, especially when you are *just dying* to share a secret or ask a question of your pal in the third row, fifth seat over. My advice: Don't pass notes if you think it will seriously annoy your teacher. Be a good student above all other things. Don't mess with classroom karma.

BUT (oh, come on, there's always a *but*) . . . If the time is right and your friend is waiting for your note like a track star waiting for the relay baton, then here are some sneaky ideas:

- Fold a piece of paper into thirds so the top piece touches the bottom piece. Now, write a message on the edge between the two. When you open it up again, you'll only see half the word on either the upper or bottom portion. Your friend has to match it up to read your message.
- Make a decoy! Fold your note into a fan shape and pass it over to your friend. Upon opening the fan, she can read the message on the inside. Works best when the classroom is really hot. Does not work so well in January.
- Write your note on a tissue. Have your friend sneeze and pass the tissue to her. Just make sure you don't write on the tissue with permanent marker. It could get messy.
- Make a note "football." This is a variation on the paper airplane, but a little more reliable in terms of reaching its target. Don't forget to write the note inside *before* you fold.
- Stick the note in the side of your shoe. Kick the recipient's desk, and wait. That's your signal for your recipient to lean over and grab the note from your shoe (or sock). A-ha!
- Go for the tried and true: a paper airplane. But don't let your teacher catch the launch of this one. It'll be confiscated in a heartbeat.
- Write with invisible ink. See page 74 for more on this trick.

See page 74 for more on this trick.

HOW TO

MAKE A PAPER
FOOTBALL

1. Take an 8.5 x 11 sheet of paper and fold it vertically.

2. Fold it vertically again. You should have a long piece of folded paper.

3. Take the top-left corner and fold it diagonally.

4. Continue to fold the little triangle in the top downwards until there is a little rectangle in the bottom.

5. Fold the rectangle in to the little gap in the bottom to secure your paper football.

NOT-SO-PRACTICAL
NOTE-PASSING IDEAS

SLINGSHOT. A little obvious.

CARRIER PIGEON. A little messy.

FEDEX. A little over-the-top.

MORSE CODE. A little too secure? Not everyone speaks dash and dot.

REMEMBERING YOUR LOCKER COMBINATION

IF YOU'RE AFRAID OF FORGETTING your locker combination, try a memory trick to keep your brain abuzz. Write an encrypted number on the back of your lock with a permanent marker.

Encryption Option A: If your birthday is: 8 / 3 / 96 and your lock is 18 / 11 / 38, add the numbers together and write the total on the back: 26 / 14 / 134. When you forget your combo, subtract your birthday and—BINGO! You've got it.

Option B: Take your combination and add in a few 2s or 0s at the front, in the middle, and wherever else makes sense. How about adding 5 every second number? So if your combination is 18 / 11 / 38, your encrypted code would be 185115385.

Regardless of what combination you choose, pick something you can remember and use it consistently for *all* your locks.

OTHER TIPS:
Buy your lock a week before school, and practice at least five times per day.

Write down your combination twenty times in the AM. Do it again in the PM.

Make up a rhyme to memorize your combination. For example, if your combination is 3/12/28, say something like, "Three got me and twelve got thee, but twenty ate my honeybee." Sounds strange, but it works.

Write the combination in permanent marker on the inside of your backpack or somewhere else that's not so obvious where you can look at a moment's notice.

No matter what you do . . . do not tell anyone your combination, not even your best pals. Your locker should be your private, personal space at school.

Bonus! If all else fails! You can recover the combination online. Check out this very helpful site: *www.fusor.us/lockpick.html.*

OTHER WAYS TO IMPROVE YOUR MEMORY

WRITE THINGS DOWN: The act of writing something on a scrap of paper helps to cement the idea in your mind's eye (especially when you say out loud what you are writing). This way you are "seeing," "hearing," and "thinking" about the object or action. Most of your senses are engaged!
TEST YOURSELF: Test your short term memory for fun. Have Mom, Dad, or your little bro' put twenty random objects on a tray and cover it up (you can't peek yet!). They lift the cover (a scarf, a napkin) for exactly one minute. This gives you a chance to observe and hopefully memorize the objects there. Once it's covered up again, see how many you can recall. The more you practice this trick, the more you will recall.
USE AN ACRONYM: To remember a list of items, make up an acronym you will remember. An acronym is a word whose letters each represent the first letter of other words. One of the most popular memory acronyms I know is HOMES. This is an acronym used to recall all the names of the Great Lakes: Huron, Ontario, Michigan, Erie, and Superior.

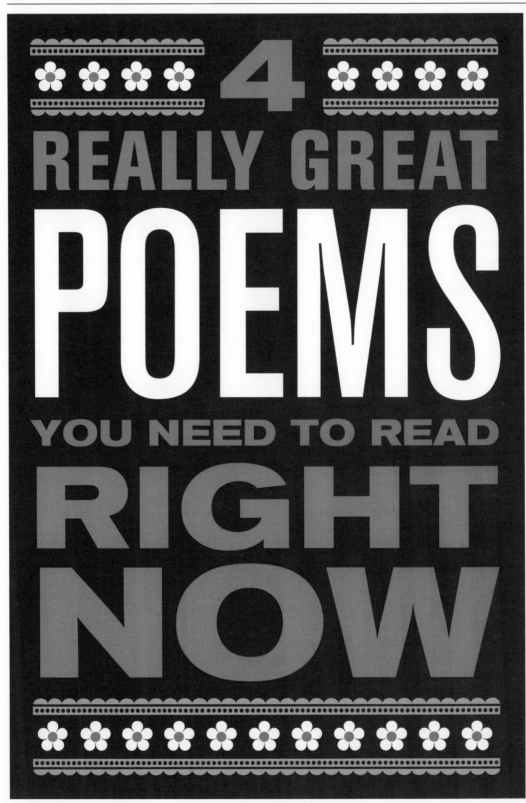

SOME PEOPLE SAY THEY DON'T "GET" POETRY. But here's the thing: What are you trying to get? Poems are way more about your *gut*. How does a poem make you feel? I think poems can be firecrackers, getting us to fire up and think differently. Poems can also be blenders, churning up emotions and telling us that we're not alone. Poems offer us language and music and humor and everything in between. Here are four short poems by women poets. Read them once. Then read them again.

ELIZABETH BISHOP
I Am in Need of Music

I am in need of music that would flow
Over my fretful, feeling fingertips,
Over my bitter-tainted, trembling lips,
With melody, deep, clear, and liquid-slow.
Oh, for the healing swaying, old and low,
Of some song sung to rest the tired dead,
A song to fall like water on my head,
And over quivering limbs, dream flushed
    to glow!

There is a magic made by melody:
A spell of rest, and quiet breath, and cool
Heart, that sinks through fading colors deep
To the subaqueous stillness of the sea,
And floats forever in a moon-green pool,
Held in the arms of rhythm and of sleep.

SARA TEASDALE
I Am Not Yours

I am not yours, not lost in you,
Not lost, although I long to be
Lost as a candle lit at noon,
Lost as a snowflake in the sea.

You love me, and I find you still
A spirit beautiful and bright,
Yet I am I, who long to be
Lost as a light is lost in light.

Oh plunge me deep in love — put out
My senses, leave me deaf and blind,
Swept by the tempest of your love,
A taper in a rushing wind.

ELIZABETH BARRETT BROWNING
The Best Thing in the World

What's the best thing in the world?
June-rose, by May-dew impearled;
Sweet south-wind, that means no rain;
Truth, not cruel to a friend;
Pleasure, not in haste to end;
Beauty, not self-decked and curled
Till its pride is over-plain;
Love, when, so, you're loved again.
Whats the best thing in the world?
—Something out of it, I think.

VALERIE WORTH
Stars

While we
Know they are
Enormous suns,
Gold lashing
Fire-oceans,
Seas of heavy silver flame,
They look as
Though they could
Be swept
Down, and heaped,
Cold crystal
Sparks, in one
Cupped palm.

WRITE YOUR

ARE YOU A POET AND YOU DON'T know it? Maybe you just got inspired by the page before this one and you want to take a stab at some poems of your own. Or, maybe you've got something important to say and a poem just seems like the very best way to do it.

Here are different (and relatively simple) poem-starting ideas.

#1: LIST POEM
The list poem can be a proper list, like a shopping list or a list of favorite places to go in the summer, with one or two-word lines. But not all list poems are that short. Some are longer, describing things. You can make a list poem of people you love or things in your closet or feelings you have when you get good news. You can make a list of just about anything.

What I Dreamed About Last Night
The wind against the window
Swimming in the ocean
A window to nowhere
The boy who sits next to me in English
Swimming in the sky
A rock

A duck
A frog who talks
A princess without a castle
A castle
And you, whispering, whispering

Check out Elizabeth Barrett Browning's short list poem on the preceding page. She names a few things she considers the best in the world. What would you put on your "Best Things in the World" list?

Other list poem ideas:

- Homework tasks
- Things that smell good
- Things that taste good
- Things you wear
- Achievements
- Your grandmother's kitchen
- Things that make you squirm
- Famous people you like
- Things that are noisy
- Things that are cold
- Things that are hot
- Funny objects
- Bedtime things

OWN POEM

(OR TWO)

- Embarrassing moments
- Lucky things
- Things to do when I'm alone
- Mistakes I've made
- Things I love about my pals

#2: POEM OF ADDRESS

This is the kind of poem you want to write *to* someone or something. It doesn't have to be something alive or even something concrete. You could write a poem to your best friend, the mail delivery person, the soap in the bathtub, your glass of chocolate milk, or a puffy cloud. You could write an ode to unhappiness or to your bicycle.

In Sara Teasdale's poem of address on the preceding page, she writes to a person she loves. Who or what would you write to?

- An empty box
- A bunch of bananas
- The fog
- Lipstick
- Your teacher
- Bumblebees
- Skyscrapers
- Shoes

- Your hometown
- Your grandfather
- The baseball game you just won
- An octopus
- The beach
- Halloween
- War
- Peace
- Love
- Getting older
- Cutting your hair
- Your pet
- Sandwiches

Whenever you write any poem, be specific. Use words that employ all your senses. Come up with powerful descriptions. Elizabeth Bishop's poem about music on the preceding page uses language that—when read aloud—sounds mellifluous (that means like honey). Valerie Worth's poem *Stars* uses only a few words to describe stars, but each word has been carefully chosen. If you remember anything about poem-writing, remember this: less is usually more. Say a lot by choosing just the right words.

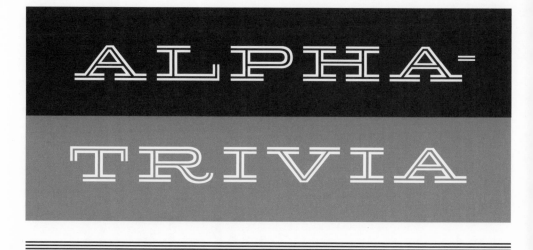

- In the English language, the single longest word that is spelled by displaying all of its letters in alphabetical order is "almost."

- If you spell out the names of every number from one to 999, you will find every vowel except A.

- What seven-letter word lets you spell out seven complete words in the same order in which their letters appear in the original word? The answer is "therein," which can be broken down into there, the, he, her, here, rein, and in.

- Which English word begins and ends with the letters "und"? The words "underground" and "underfund."

- The highest-scoring word in Scrabble is "quartzy." This will score 164 points if played across a red triple-word square with the Z on a light blue double-letter square. It will score 162 points if played across two pink double-word squares with the Q and the Y on those squares.

- The English word with the most consonants in a row is "latchstring."

- The word "girl" appears only once in the Bible.

- "Rhythm" and "syzygy" are the longest English words without vowels.

- The longest word in the English language, according to the *Oxford English Dictionary*, is "pneumonoultramicroscopicsilicovol-canoconiosis," pronounced (noo-muh-noh / uhl-truh / my-kruh-skop-ik / sil-i-koh / vol-key-noh / koh-nee-oh-sis). It is a sickness caused by the inhalation of very fine silicate or quartz dust.

- The second-longest word in the *Oxford English Dictionary* is "floccinaucinihilipilifica-tion," pronounced (flok-suh-naw-suh / nahy-hil-uh / pil-uh-fi-kay-shun) which is the act of estimating as worthless.

- The third-longest word in the English language is "antidisestablishmentarianism," which means opposition to the withdrawal of support for an established church.

- One out of every eight letters used in written English is an E.

- The dot over the letter i is called a tittle.

- There are only three words in the English language with the letter combination "uu," muumuu, vacuum, and continuum.

100+

MOST COMMONLY ~~MISPELED~~ MISSPELLED WORDS

You might want to copy this list into your English notebook, just in case.

acceptable
accidentally
accommodate
acquire
acquit
a lot
amateur
apparent
argument
atheist
believe
calendar
category
cemetery
changeable
collectible
committed
conscience
conscientious
conscious
definite(ly)
disappear
discipline
drunkenness
embarrass

equipment
exhilarate
exceed
existence
experience
fiery
foreign
fourth
gauge
generally
grammar
grateful
guarantee
harass
height
hierarchy
ignorance
immediate
independent
indispensable
intelligence
its / it's
judgment
knowledge
leisure

library
lightning
maintenance
maneuver
memento
millennium
miniature
mischievous
noticeable
occasion
occasionally
occur / occurred
occurrence
official
parallel
parliament
pastime
pigeon
possession
preferable
principal / principle
privilege
questionnaire
receive
recommend

referred
reference
relevant
religious
restaurant
ridiculous
rhythm
sandal
schedule
scissors
sensible
separate
special
success
to / too / two
tomorrow
their / they're / there
twelfth
tyranny
until
vacuum
vicious
weather
weird
you're / your

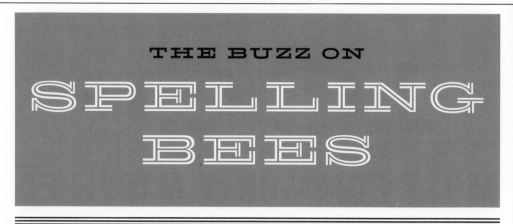

THE BUZZ ON

SPELLING

BEES

O F THE EIGHTY-THREE CHAMPIONS in the annual Scripps National Spelling Bee, girls have won the most—so far. As of 2006, forty-three champs have been girls and forty have been boys. And what were the winning words? You might want to pull out your dictionary while you look at this list. Use it to practice for your own school bee.

1925: gladiolus
1926: abrogate
1927: luxuriance
1928: albumen
1929: asceticism
1930: fracas
1931: foulard
1932: knack
1933: torsion
1934: deteriorating
1935: intelligible
1936: interning
1937: promiscuous
1938: sanitarium
1939: canonical
1940: therapy
1941: initials
1942: sacrilegious
1946*: semaphore
1947: chlorophyll
1948: psychiatry
1949: dulcimer

1950: meticulosity
1951: insouciant
1952: vignette
1953: soubrette
1954: transept
1955: crustaceology
1956: condominium
1957: schappe
1958: syllepsis
1959: catamaran
1960: eudaemonic
1961: smaragdine
1962: esquamulose
1963: equipage
1964: sycophant
1965: eczema
1966: ratoon
1967: chihuahua
1968: abalone
1969: interlocutory
1970: croissant
1971: shalloon

How do you know if you are a spelling bee wannabe? You couldn't look at this list without taking out your dictionary.

1972: macerate
1973: vouchsafe
1974: hydrophyte
1975: incisor
1976: narcolepsy
1977: cambist
1978: deification
1979: maculature
1980: elucubrate
1981: sarcophagus
1982: psoriasis
1983: Purim
1984: luge
1985: milieu
1986: odontalgia
1987: staphylococci
1988: elegiacal
1989: spoliator

1990: fibranne
1991: antipyretic
1992: lyceum
1993: kamikaze
1994: antediluvian
1995: xanthosis
1996: vivisepulture
1997: euonym
1998: chiaroscurist
1999: logorrhea
2000: demarche
2001: succedaneum
2002: prospicience
2003: pococurante
2004: autochthonous
2005: appoggiatura
2006: Ursprache
2007: serrefine

For more on spelling bees, check out the official study site: www.myspellit.com. You, too, can be a word champion, otherwise known as a beater, conqueror, master, subduer, trimmer, vanquisher, whipper, or winner. *Whew.*

*There were no spelling bees held during World War II in the years 1943, 1944, and 1945.   Source: Scripps National Spelling Bee

20 WAYS TO JAZZIFY* YOUR JOURNAL

A JOURNAL DOES NOT NEED TO BE all words, although words are a great place to start, of course. Journals can be so much more: things you find on the sidewalk, photographs, doodles, pie charts, and just about anything that expresses your feelings and thoughts in some way. Adding art to a journal adds a whole other dimension of color, texture, and emotion.

You don't need an expensive leather, fur-trimmed journal to say what's on your mind. Any old composition notebook will do. (Hint: If you put packing tape on the spine, it'll stay together better.) Sometimes you can turn an old book into a new book, too, to make your journal. How? Go to a used bookstore and find a sturdy edition of some old, illustrated book you can get for a buck. Tape or glue pieces of wrapping paper, newspapers, magazine photos, drawings, and anything else you like onto the cover and the pages inside. There is something magical about covering up some of the words on the page—and leaving others. Inspiration guaranteed.

And now, without further adieu, the short list of twenty more cool ideas.

Drum roll, please. . . .

*Okay, so *jazzify* won't be showing up at any spelling bees in the near future. It is not actually a real word. But that doesn't matter—this is your journal. You're allowed to make up stuff in here—including *words*. Invent your own language if you want. Your entries will certainly stay secret if no one else is able to read them!

1 Glue an envelope into your journal and fill it with interesting bits and scraps: stuff you tear out of a magazine, a note from a friend, a piece of junk mail, or whatever else strikes your fancy.

2 Find a photograph of someone you've never met (and don't know). Write about that person. And yes, you have to make stuff up. Journals don't have to be a line-by-line reporting of your day. They can be free-flowing stories, too, about people you never met.

3 If you had to write down ten cool rules that you follow (or break!) in your life, what would they be? Write them here.

4 Draw a diagram of your room, labeling all the important places and objects.

5 Eavesdrop on someone's conversation in the lunchroom. Write down everything they say.

6 Write a letter to someone you admire. P.S. If you want to send it, for real, then send the original and paste a copy here.

7 Write down 100 things you want to do in your lifetime.

8 Find a picture of yourself as a young child. Make a copy and paste that into the journal. Now draw on it, in the style of a young child.

9 Close your eyes and write a journal entry without looking. Or, if you're a righty, write with your left hand instead. Lefties, try writing with your right hand.

10 Make a graph that charts your moods throughout the day or the week.

11 Write up a list of instructions for how to get through the school day.

12 Write about one single, inanimate object for a half hour. Describe it in detail without actually naming it.

13 Your closet is being reviewed by the glam police. What does the review say?

14 Write an entire journal entry in pig Latin. Or maybe cipher code. You decide. (Check out how to make a cipher on the next page).

15 Write down at least five things you would pack in your desert island suitcase.

16 Write your own recipe for creativity stew, whatever that means to you.

17 Collect flat objects from nature (leaves and flowers can be pressed in a hard book for a day or so) and paste them into an all-natural journal collage.

18 Make a list of the places you have ever visited or lived. Draw a map to show them.

19 Write one journal entry in the smallest letters you can write. Then make an entry in the LARGEST letters possible. That should be good for a few pages.

20 Cut a bunch of scraps from a magazine. Now make them into an interesting "this is me" collage, filled in with words between the pictures.

SECRET JOURNAL HIDING PLACES

Worst Case Scenario #1: Your younger brother discovers your journal and rips all the pages out.

Worst Case Scenario #2: Your older brother discovers your journal and scans the pages onto his computer so he can blackmail you.

Worst Case Scenario #3: Your mom finds your journal and she wants to see you later to "talk about it."

Yeeps! No matter which scenario comes up, one thing is clear: The most important thing you need to do when keeping a journal is to find a safe place to stash it. Some potential hiding places:

Under the mattress	Pro: Easy access. Con: Too obvious a hiding spot.
Inside the freezer	Pro: No one will ever find it under the ice cubes. Con: The ice cubes. Brrrrrr!
Your underwear drawer	Pro: Absolutely off limits to *everyone*. Con: You might forget it's there, too.
In your school locker	Pro: It gets mixed in with your other notebooks. Con: Someone discovers it and reprints your secrets on the front page of the school paper.
Locked up in a safe	Pro: Only you have the key. Con: Only you have the key—and it's missing.

HOW TO

MAKE A CIPHER CODE

- Draw a circle. Draw another circle inside the first one.
- Draw "pizza" lines to split the circle into twenty-six "slices."
- In the outer circle, write the alphabet.
- In the inner circle, write the alphabet again, but start A next to the outer circle's letter K or another letter.
- Switch to code mode when you write by substituting one alphabet for another.

WRITE THE BEST
THANK-YOU NOTES

EVER SINCE YOU COULD WRITE, you've probably heard it after every birthday, holiday, and sometimes other days, too: "Did you write your aunt a thank-you note for that _____?" My usual response to this question was a groan followed by a muffled, "Um . . . no. Do I have to?" And the answer to that was always a resounding: "OF COURSE YOU DO!"

Writing thank-you notes does not have to be tough stuff. There's a formula to it. Here's how to whip out a personalized and heartfelt note in ten minutes flat.

1. IN THE CARDS

Keep a cool supply of pens and note cards on hand. Lack of supplies is the number one reason most thank-you notes never even get started. And keep those cards small. You don't need to be wordy, just grateful. Postcards are even easier—and cost less postage, too.

2. NO CHEATING

Writing a thank-you in the body of an e-mail message is a nice sentiment, but it just doesn't mean as much. You need to send a real card.

3. SAY THE RIGHT STUFF

Address your note. Dear _____ .

Open with "hello" or any nice, informal greeting. For example, if you're a cowgirl, "howdy do" will do.

Right after that say "thanks," and how much you like the gift. "I love my sweater," or "The books are great." Never say things like, "Thanks, but I already have one of those," or "I wish it were a different color, but I guess I'll live with it." (Helpful hint: If the gift was cash, don't mention money by name. Instead say, "Thank you for your generous gift.")

Add some detail about how you will use the gift—but make it genuine. Don't go overboard trying to convince the giver that you love it if you don't. Don't say, "Wow, I couldn't believe it when I opened up the package and saw that amazing electric blue sweater vest. I'll be the fashion queen at school." Say something true but noncommittal like, "Your gift arrives right in time for the cold weather. Thanks!"

End the thank-you note with a one-liner about getting back in touch. Maybe you can hint at a future conversation or meeting. For example, "I hope to see you soon," is pretty foolproof.

Sign off with one last thank you. You really can't say those two words enough. In a way, you could just create a card with a single message in huge type, all capital letters. It would be different—and get the job done.

Dear Cousin Jesse,

THANK YOU.

Love,

Me

One last note about your note: Try not to go off on any tangents. This is not the place to muse about what you're doing in school or at basketball practice or what you had for lunch. This is all about sending a proper thank you. Do it. Mail it. Done. And now Mom won't bug you.

YOURS TILL THE...

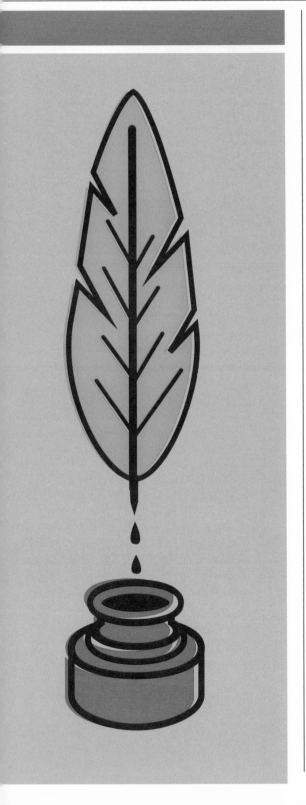

butter flies	friend ships
chocolate chips	candy canes
root beer floats	light bulbs
nail polishes	coffee cups
moon beams	season's greetings
ping pongs	wedding bells
candle sticks	Hershey's kisses
gum drops	heart aches
Web links	rain falls
ice skates	baby sits
home works	horse shoes
nose blows	trail mixes
peanut butters	pony expresses
scare crows	banana splits
pumpkin pies	ice creams
wind blows	carrot cakes
puppy loves	side walks
turkey gobbles	powder puffs
autumn leaves	Niagara Falls
potatoes mash	French fries
pumpkin pies	lemon drops
snow caps	sweater sets
mail boxes	Graham crackers
snow drifts	web sites
bees wax	dodge balls
duck quacks	door bells
pop stars	note books
life boats	orange ades
super stars	dew drops
spring rolls	shoe laces
flower pots	black berries
swimming pools	dust bunnies
road trips	smoke signals
globe trotters	ink wells
sun tans	soda pops
bubble gums	heart attacks
fire crackers	ice cubes
lip sticks	rain bows

CAR

THE GOOD, THE BAD, AND

You're hitting the road with your family for a looooong car trip. But the thing you really want to hit . . . is your brother! Fear not. There are many ways to pass your car time without having to resort to backseat violence. You can whip out the electronic game or your iPod, but face it, even that is going to get boring after a while. So (drumroll, please) here are a few clever games that should keep you and your sibs in the fun zone—and keep the grown-ups in the car *very* happy indeed.

 = BEWARE! MOM'S DRIVING!

SPOTTERS

Look out the window and notice what's zooming by. See all those other cars' license plates? There are games to be played *everywhere*! Have everyone in the car look for license plates with certain letter or number combinations. Who can spot a plate with the numbers of his or her birth date or initials? Who can spot a plate with a sequence of at least three numbers (like 234 or 567)?

Who sees a license plate from out of state? The spotter with the most states wins.

Can you turn a license plate's letters into words for a funny phrase? For example, if you see the letters BMD on a plate, you might say, "Beware! Mom's driving!" Use this game idea with signs along the road, too. Who can make up a sentence for the longest sign word you see? Spot away!

FLUBBER

(or any nickname will do)

Does one of your little brothers or sisters—or anyone traveling in your car—have a fun or unusual nickname? Did you say the nickname was Flubber? Great! Use it and have some fun. One player picks an item that he or she usually sees along the road more than once (like a truck, bicyclist, shrubs, fence, etc.). Every time the player sees that item he or she yells out, "Flubber!" or whatever funny nickname was selected. All the other players in the car need to guess what object the nickname stands for. The first person to guess correctly gets to pick the next "Flubber."

GAMES!

THE TOTALLY ANNOYING

CAR CHARADES

YOU'VE HEARD OF THE "regular" version of this game. It can be challenging enough when you stand up. What if you had to play while *sitting* in a car?

The object is to guess the famous person, movie, book, or song while seatbelted in the car. You can only use hand or foot gestures (no words and no mouthing words) and fantastic facial expressions to offer clues.

Gesture to show *what* category you'll be doing (like movie, song, etc.).

Show how many words are in the title by holding up that number of fingers.

Start to pantomime the title. If you're acting out the entire title with one action, make a wide sweeping motion with your hand (trying, of course, not to hit your sister in the head.) If you're doing one word at a time, hold up fingers to also show which word you're acting out.

If the word is very tough, you may want to break it into syllables. Use the gesture for syllables (fingers pressed on hand) to indicate a) how many syllables, and then b) which one you're acting out. Each time you offer a gesture, make sure the others guess correctly before moving on.

To have someone guess non-acted-out words like "a" or the" you should pinch together your fingers to indicate small word. Then everyone guesses small words to see if they get the right one. Remember that each correct guess gets a pointed finger at the guesser to say, "You got it!"

You can use a karate chop motion to show a word that is shorter than one that may have been guessed, or stretch out an imaginary cord to show that the word guessed needs to be longer.

The person to guess correctly wins. That person will choose the next title in the game.

Use the hand signals to encourage, make faces to show when someone's wrong—you can use all body motions available to you. Unfortunately jumping is not a possibility since you're car-bound. What will you do instead?

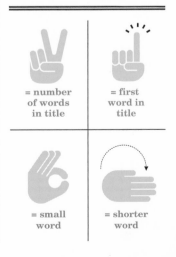

= number of words in title

= first word in title

= small word

= shorter word

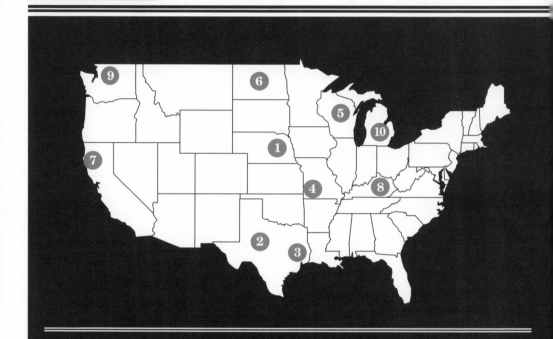

ALLIANCE, NEBRASKA
(Fig. 1)
Carhenge was created by farmer Jim Reinders, who wanted to build a memorial to his dad, he used thirty-eight cars rescued from farms and dumps. At first, the town wanted to rip it down, but they soon realized it was a regular tourist attraction.

KATY, TEXAS (Fig. 2)
A year-round exhibit built for an estimated $20 million by a former Hong Kong business-man, Forbidden Gardens includes a koi (fish) pond and 40,000 square feet of tiny model palaces and people, including a small-scale repro-duction of Emperor Qin's 6,000+ man terra-cotta army. Why in the middle of Texas? Houston, just twenty-five miles away, boasts the third highest Asian population in the U.S.

PARIS, TEXAS (Fig. 3)
Ooh! La! La! In the middle of Texas, a state of oil platforms, sits an enormous replica of France's Eiffel Tower. But this one's topped by a gen-uine, oversized cowboy hat.

SPRINGFIELD, MISSOURI (Fig. 4)
Home to the world's biggest fork! An advertising company left it there when its previous owner, a restaurant, went belly-up. It stands as tall as a three-story building. One catch: The spoon appears to be missing. Under suspicion: the dish.

LAKE NEBAGAMON, WISCONSIN (Fig. 5)
When he's not working at the town dump, James Kotera is working on his ball of twine—one of the biggest ever. He began his ball back in the late 1970s. At last count, the ball's weight was nearly 20,000 pounds.

NKNOWN, U.S.A. ★ ★

NEW SALEM, NORTH DAKOTA (Fig. 6)

Moo! Not only does this small town boast the largest cow anywhere in the world—named Salem Sue, the enormous cow measures thirty-eight feet high and fifty feet long and is made from six tons of fiberglass—New Salem also boasts a bevy of sports teams named . . . you guessed it . . . *the Holsteins.*

BAKER, CALIFORNIA (Fig. 7)

Somewhere in the high desert sits the world's largest thermometer. It's there to mark the place in the U.S. with the highest temperature ever recorded: In 1913 the mercury hit 134 degrees in Death Valley.

LOUISVILLE, KENTUCKY (Fig. 8)

Where can you find a 120-foot baseball bat? Just outside the Louisville Slugger Museum, of course. The gigantic bat was erected in 1995 and weighs thirty-four tons.

WINLOCK, WASHINGTON (Fig. 9)

If I were craving the biggest omelet ever, I would rush to Winlock, home of the world's largest egg.

ALLEN PARK, MICHIGAN (Fig. 10)

Roll with it! The world's largest tire sits near the Detroit Metro airport—all eighty feet and twelve tons of it. An urban legend says that once when it was moved, the tire broke loose and rolled across the highway.

NEXT STOP: MUCK

There are some pretty interesting names for some towns and cities around the world. How about a vacation in one of these hot spots?

- Anger, Ethiopia
- Antelope, Zimbabwe
- Asbestos, Canada
- Baa, Indonesia
- Bent, Iran
- Berry, France
- Black Tickle, Canada
- Blue Hole, Belize
- Boring, USA
- Cadillac, France
- Coffin Bay, Australia
- Deception Island, Antarctica
- Egg, Austria
- Energetik, Russia
- False Point, India
- Fish, Namibia
- Goodhouse, South Africa
- Heart's Content, Canada
- Hope, USA
- Horn, Iceland
- Karma, Niger
- Moodyville, Canada
- Mosquito Coast, Honduras
- Muck, United Kingdom
- Of, Turkey
- Ogre, Latvia
- Outlook, Canada
- Penny, Canada
- Pest, Hungary
- Polar Bear, Canada
- Pukë, Albania
- Putty, Australia
- Resplendor, Brazil
- Rich, Morocco
- Rum, Jordan
- Runaway Bay, Jamaica
- Salt, Spain
- Searchlight, USA
- Sauce, Argentina
- Show Low, USA
- Song, Thailand
- Speed, Australia
- Ten Degree Channel, India
- Thorn, Poland
- Turbo, Colombia
- Umbrella Mountains, New Zealand
- Wee Waa, Australia
- Wink, USA

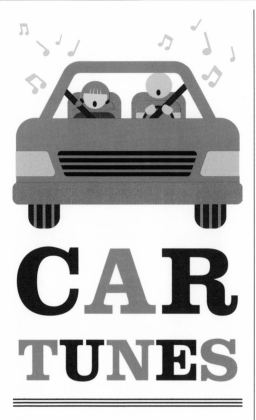

CAR TUNES

The car radio can also be the source of a lot of fun on long road trips. You can channel your inner Kelly Clarkson and do "car-a-oke" as you sing along with a top-40 song, or just lip-synch making funny facial expressions. You can also play "Name that Car Tune." Here's how:

1. Get a grown-up to help out. He or she must be sitting up front to change radio stations.

2. Tune into a random radio station. Listen to a few seconds of a song and then lower the volume to see who can guess the song.

3. Try a speed round flipping between stations: As soon as one person guesses the song, quickly speed to the next one.

4. If you run into stations that are all advertising stuff or too much talk radio, then guess what kind of song will come up next (rock, country, etc.).

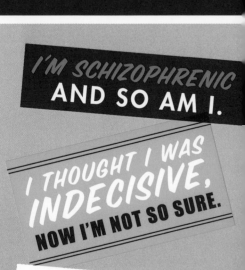

FUNNY

I'M SCHIZOPHRENIC AND SO AM I.

I THOUGHT I WAS INDECISIVE, NOW I'M NOT SO SURE.

WITHOUT GEOMETRY, life is pointless!

STABLE RELATIONSHIPS ARE FOR HORSES.

EVER STOP TO THINK, AND FORGET TO START AGAIN?

I'M DIAGONALLY PARKED IN A PARALLEL UNIVERSE

BUMPER STICKERS

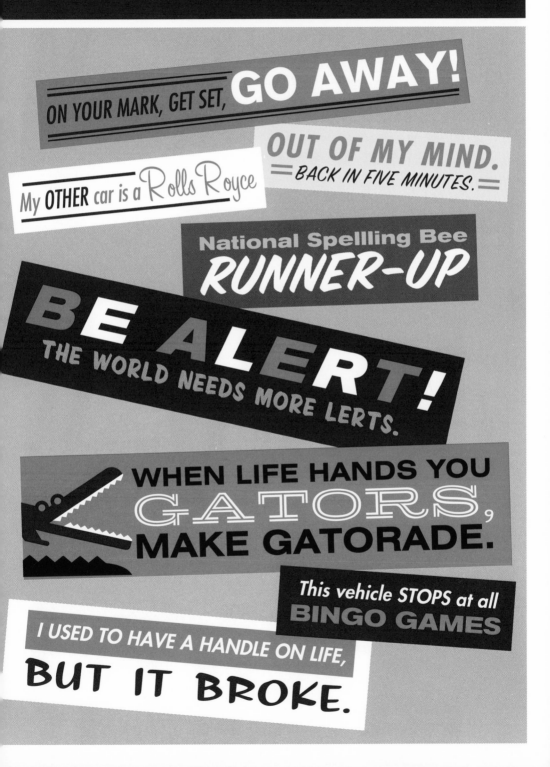

ON YOUR MARK, GET SET, **GO AWAY!**

OUT OF MY MIND.
BACK IN FIVE MINUTES.

My **OTHER** car is a *Rolls Royce*

National Spelling Bee
RUNNER-UP

BE ALERT!
THE WORLD NEEDS MORE LERTS.

WHEN LIFE HANDS YOU **GATORS,**
MAKE GATORADE.

This vehicle STOPS at all
BINGO GAMES

I USED TO HAVE A HANDLE ON LIFE,
BUT IT BROKE.

MAY I TAKE YOUR

Menu of the ~~World~~ Weird

Appetizers

BAALUT
(The Philippines)
Fertilized chicken egg that's been
buried in the ground for a few
weeks (also known as "the treat
with feet").

SEA SLUGS
(Korea)
Crunchy, served raw.

TAKOYAKI
(Japan)
Flour balls with octopus centers.

MONKEY TOES
(Indonesia)
Deep-fried toes eaten directly
from the bone.

ALLIGATOR ON A STICK
(Southern United States)
Chunks of gator tail rolled in
cornbread.

TURTLE EGGS
(Nicaragua)
Appearing like boiled ping pong
balls, these eggs are served with
hot sauce and a shot of rum.

Soups and Sides

BIRD'S NEST SOUP
(China)
Actual nest from the cave
swallow, which secretes a strange-
tasting liquid that holds the nest
together like glue.

FISH-EYE SOUP
(Southeast Asia)
Scoop out an eyeball,
suck out the juices, and spit out
the cornea. Repeat.

SCRAPPLE
(United States)
Take all the leftover parts of a pig
(lips, snout, organs), add a touch
of cornmeal, and cook in a block.
Served by the slice, fried.

GREEN ANTS
(Australia)
Munch on small green ants.
To eat: Pick up the bug, squash
the head, and take a bite.

HU HU GRUBS
(New Zealand)
Fat, white bugs that taste a
little like peanut butter.

ORDER, PLEASE?

Menu of the ~~World~~ Weird

Main Course

SURSTRÖMMING
(Sweden)
Herring that's been sitting for a year (or more) in a barrel. You gut the fish on your plate and eat over potatoes and thin, hard bread. But don't forget to pinch your nose. The smell will knock you out.

GEODUCK CLAMS
(Northwest United States)
Also called "Gooey Duck," these clams with the very long necks are a little odd-looking.

SQUIRREL BRAIN
(Southern United States)
The squirrel's head is baked with the other parts of the body. To eat, crack the skull and dig out the brain. Tastes a little like mushrooms.

HAGGIS
(Scotland)
Sheep's stomach stuffed with oatmeal and sheep's organs and steamed, usually served with chappit neeps (also known as turnips).

BOREWORS
(South Africa)
Sheep or cattle intestines stuffed with spices and grilled.

TACOS SESOS
(Mexico)
You've had tacos with hamburger meat; now try them with cow brains. Talk about smart food.

TARANTULA
(Cambodia)
These roasted furry eight-legged critters are a delicacy in many places all over the world.

Dessert

PIG BLOOD PUDDING
(Trinidad)
Add pig's blood to rice and bread crumbs and you've got something different for dessert.

UBE ICE CREAM
(The Philippines)
Purple ice cream made from purple yams.

MOVE OVER, BIG MAC

ONE MENU THAT'S ENJOYED WORLDWIDE is the one found under the golden arches: McDonald's. But McDonald's *isn't* the same everywhere. Its menu changes depending on the country. Who knew?

MAHARAJA MAC—a Big Mac made from lamb or chicken (because Hindus cannot eat beef) and the *McAloo Tikki*—a vegetarian burger.

McLAKS—a sandwich made from grilled salmon and dill sauce.

McPOLLO, JR.—a chicken sandwich served with mashed avocado.

GREEK MAC—a sandwich of two burgers served in a pita with yogurt sauce, tomato, and onions.

McKROKET—a deep-fried roll with beef ragout that's served on another bun.

McOZ—made from Australian beef and beetroot—with Vegemite (yeast spread) on the side.

McSCHWARMA—a kosher version of the Big Mac (because meat and dairy cannot be served together).

CROQUE McDO—a hot ham and cheese sandwich prepared like a traditional Croque Monsieur, a French grilled snack served in cafés.

KOROKE BURGER—made from mashed potato, cabbage, and katsu sauce, and the EBISU BURGER—made from fish and shrimp.

RICE BURGERS—a regular beef patty that's served bun-free, between two patties of rice instead of bread.

INDIA

NORWAY

CHILE

GREECE

THE NETHERLANDS

AUSTRALIA

ISRAEL

FRANCE

JAPAN

HONG KONG

THE REAL KINGS

King	Company	Year	Best in Show	True!
Dr. James Baker (U.S.)	Walter Baker Chocolate	1780	Semisweet baking chocolate	After the Boston Tea Party in 1773, patriots drank Baker's chocolate instead of tea.
Stephen Whitman (U.S.)	Whitman's Candies	1842	Whitman's Sampler (1915), assortment of chocolates which let people "sample" the chocolates they liked best	Introduced America to cellophane, which was used to wrap the candy boxes.
John Cadbury (England)	Cadbury Limited	1847	Cadbury Dairy Milk chocolate bar and the first Valentine's Day box of chocolates (1868)	In 1854, the company received orders to be the official manufacturers of cocoa and chocolate to Queen Victoria of England.
Domingo Ghirardelli (Italy)	Ghirardelli	1852	Signature Squares	In San Francisco, where the chocolate factory is located, there is a landmark named after the chocolate company: Ghirardelli Square.

OF CHOCOLATE

King	Company	Year	Best in Show	True!
Milton Hershey (U.S.)	Hershey's Chocolate Company	1871	Great American Chocolate Bar (1900); and Hershey's Kiss in its silver foil (1906)	Hershey's makes twenty to twenty-five million Hershey's kisses per day.
Heinrich Nestle (Germany) who changed his name to Henri Nestle (Switzerland)	Nestle	1875	Nestle Crunch, the first candy bar to combine taste, texture, and sound (1938) AND chocolate chips (1939)	Nestle was a trained pharmacist who created baby formula for mothers who were unable to breastfeed.
Rodolphe Lindt (Switzerland)	Lindt & Sprungli International	1879	Lindor Truffles	Invented the "conche," a vessel designed to melt and blend chocolates.
Joseph Draps (Belgium)	Godiva Chocolatier	1926	Shell-molded chocolates and gold foil packages	Named after Lady Godiva, whose cruel husband promised to lower taxes if she rode naked in the streets. She did! Her boldness inspired Draps to name his chocolates after her.

JUST THE
CHOCOLATE
FACTS, MA'AM

AS A GIRL, I CAN SAY WITH FULL CONFIDENCE that most of my girlfriends (ages tween and up) would do just about anything for a handful of M&M's, myself included. But what is it exactly about chocolate that has had us in its spell for centuries?

Cacao beans were like cash in ancient Mexico. The Maya, Aztec, and Toltec civilizations used them to pay for supplies and taxes.

In the seventeenth century the first recorded case of "Death by Chocolate" occurred in San Cristobal de las Casas, in Chiapas, Mexico. The Bishop of Chiapas was found dead. Poison had been secretly added to his daily cup of hot chocolate.

Chocolate was such a luxury that Louis XIV of France, also known as the "Sun King," established a job called Royal Chocolate Maker to the King in the seventeenth century.

By the eighteenth century, every European country from England to Austria made products from the cocoa tree, or (in Latin) the Theobroma Cacao. Translated literally, that means "food of the gods."

During World War II, the U.S. government asked Hershey's to make a chocolate bar especially for soldiers. During the Persian Gulf War, Hershey was asked to make another candy bar that could withstand very high desert temperatures.

As of 2006, American consumers spent more than $7 million annually on chocolate-related products. Apparently, we each consume twelve pounds of chocolate per year. Do you remember eating that many candy bars?

American chocolate manufacturers use about 1.5 billion pounds of milk annually. The only people who use more are cheese and ice cream makers.

A single chocolate chip provides sufficient food energy for an adult to walk 150 feet. It would take about thirty-five chocolate chips to go a mile, or 875,000 chips for an around-the-world stroll. Ready?

Contrary to very popular belief, chocolate does NOT cause zits. Overactive oil glands, heredity, dead skin cells that lodge in pores, hormonal changes, and even stress are what cause acne.

Ten Excuses for Eating Chocolate

1. I love it.
2. I love it.
3. I love it.
4. I love it.
5. I love it.
6. I love it.
7. I love it.
8. I love it.
9. I love it.
10. I *really* love it.

(But who needs an excuse? Pass the Snickers, pronto!)

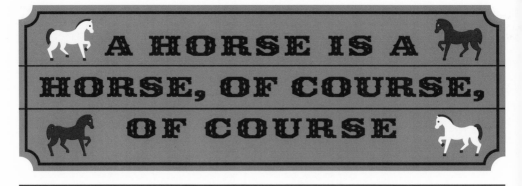

A HORSE IS A HORSE, OF COURSE, OF COURSE

ONCE UPON A TIME, HORSES FREELY roamed all over the continents, except for Antarctica. But the Ice Age changed all of that. Horses disappeared from North America. Around 3000 B.C. in Europe and Asia, people began to tame horses, to domesticate them, and to use them to carry things. Horses made a big difference in people's lives. They could be used in war as weapons and transportation. Around 1519, horses finally reappeared in North America, brought there by invading Spanish conquistadores (conquerors).

Over time, horses have become a girl's best friend due to their strength and elegance. Here is a list of some of the most popular breeds.

Do you *collect* horses? I mean, of course, the pretend kind, the ones that sit on your shelf, pose for pony photo ops, and roam the range that is your bedroom floor. These are the top five favorite collectible horses available now from Breyer, the collectible horse company:

1. Black Beauty
2. The Black Stallion
3. Misty of Chincoteague
4. Spirit: Stallion of the Cimarron and Rain
5. Cloud's Legacy

Breyer Animal Creations® was founded in 1950 and makes more than five million model horses and accessories each year for play and collecting. Visit them at www.BreyerHorses.com.

Rain®, Spirit: Stallion of the Cimarron™ © 2002 DreamWorks L.L.C.

- **American Saddle Horse:** The most beautiful show horse, which can learn to walk, trot, and canter for competition.
- **Appaloosa:** This spotted horse was used by American Indians to hunt buffalo.
- **Arabian:** Bred in the desert and swift, these were the horses that fought wars, carrying great leaders from history like Genghis Khan, Napoleon, Alexander the Great, and even George Washington.
- **Belgian:** Two Belgian horses could pull a massive load of 4,275 pounds, making them even stronger than a tractor.
- **Clydesdale:** This horse looks like it is wearing white fur boots; it's the national horse of Scotland.
- **The Morgan:** This fearless horse is often used by policemen.
- **Mustang:** As wild as a tornado, these horses live in the open range of the mountains and have jobs as bucking broncos for Wild West shows.
- **Palomino:** Queen Isabella is supposed to have sent five golden Palominos to New Spain (Mexico).
- **Percheron:** The horse you're most likely to see under the circus tent.
- **Quarter Horse:** Bred to race.
- **Thoroughbred:** A racer with a strong will, whose ancestry goes back to the three original sires: Byerly Turk, Darley Arabian, and Godolphin Arabian.
- **The Standardbred:** Horse you see at harness races.

EXTRAORDINARY HORSES

THERE ARE SO MANY REASONS TO love a horse. Their majestic beauty is inspiring. And you can gaze for hours into a horse's deep, brown eyes. Sigh. Some of the best horses from real life, books, and movies:

- **Black Beauty:** From the classic novel of the same name by Anna Sewell, about a Victorian horse sold to a series of owners (book; movie)
- **The Black Stallion:** "The Black" is a brave horse who rescues a boy from a sinking ship and then lives with him on a desert island (movie)
- **Seabiscuit:** A gifted, winning horse that beats the odds and captures the hearts of people during the Great Depression (real life; book; movie)
- **Kentucky Horse Park:** A Pilgrim horse is traumatized by an accident, but healed by "The Horse Whisperer" (book; movie)
- **Spirit, Stallion of the Cimarron®:** A free-roaming Mustang is caught by the U.S. Cavalry but learns to love again (movie)
- **Misty of Chincoteague:** Based on the ponies coming from Virginia's Assateague Island, a nature preserve; Misty was created by one of the best-loved authors of horse stories, Marguerite Henry (real life; book; movie)
- **Barbaro:** Winner of the 2006 Kentucky Derby who shattered his leg and later died, making his life and death one of the most heart-wrenching horse tales in years (real life)

WHAT A HORSE NEEDS TO BE HAPPY

A pasture to roam (without loose wire fences or rusty farm equipment).
Grass for grazing, and hay, too.
Unlimited supply of water.
Unlimited supply of minerals and salt. Horses need salt
    licks to keep their bodies working properly.
Shelter and shade.
A dry place to lie down.
Someone to watch for illness or injury.
Companionship with another horse or a sheep, dog, or goat.

HOW TO

GROOM YOUR PONY

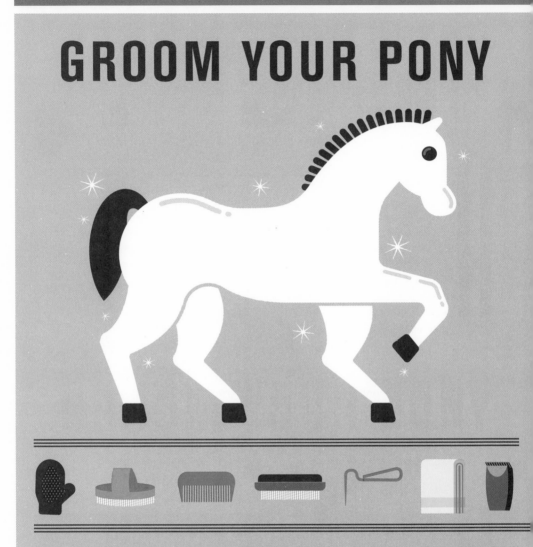

INSIDE YOUR GROOM-ING TOOL BUCKET

- A curry comb or grooming mitt
- A stiff-bristled body brush
- Mane and tail comb (plastic lasts longer)
- Soft bristle finishing brush
- Hoofpick
- Soft cloth or sponge
- Clippers

Step #1: Be sure to place your tool bucket in an area where the horse won't knock it over.

Step #2: Secure the horse with a safely tied release knot.

Step #3: Clean the horse's hooves. Slide your hand down the left foreleg and squeeze at the tendon, gently saying

"up," or whatever word will get the horse to respond. Hold the hoof carefully and use the pick to pry out dirt, manure, or anything else lodged in the areas of the foot. When done, place the hoof down gently. Repeat for all four hooves.

Step #4: Curry your horse. Start on the left side, using

#1 #4 #7

#2 #5 #8

#3 #6 #9

the comb or mitt to loosen dirt on the horse's coat. Use circular motions all over the body. But use a lighter touch in the bonier areas of the horse's body. Take note: If the horse lays back his ears or swishes his tail, he's communicating with you. Stop brushing too hard.

Step #5: Comb out tangles in the mane and tail.

Step #6: Whisk away any more of the loosened dirt. Use the body brush.

Step #7: Use your finishing brush across the entire coat.

Step #8: Use the soft cloth to very gently clean the ears, muzzle, and eyes.

Step #9: Finish up with grooming spray (if you have it) or whatever other soft touches you have to give. Don't forget the kiss on his head at the end.

BABY ANIMALS

ANIMAL	BABY	GROUP
Alligator	hatchling	congregation, pod
Bear	cub	sleuth, sloth
Bee	larva	hive, swarm (in flight), bike, drift, grist
Camel	calf	flock
Cat	kitten	clutter, clower
Cheetah	cub	coalition
Crow	chick	murder, muster
Dog	pup	litter, pack, kennel
Dolphin	pup, calf	herd, pod, school
Duck	duckling	badelynge, brace, bunch, flock
Elephant	calf	herd, parade
Ferret	kitten	business, fesynes
Fish	fry, fingerling	draft, run, school, shoal
Fox	kit, cub, pup	skulk, leash
Frog	tadpole, polliwog	army, knot
Goat	billy	herd, tribe, trip
Gorilla	infant	band
Hamster	pup	horde
Hedgehog	piglet	array
Horse	colt (M), filly (F)	stable, harras, herd
Hummingbird	chick	charm
Leopard	cub	leap, prowl
Lion	cub	pride
Llama	cria	herd
Otter	whelp, pup	family, raft, romp
Oyster	spat	bed
Penguin	chick	rookery
Pig	piglet, shoat, farrow	drove, herd, litter
Pigeon	squab, squeaker	flock, kit
Rhinoceros	calf	crash
Shark	pup	school, shiver
Sheep	lamb, lambkin, cosset	drift, drove, flock, herd, mob, trip
Tiger	cub, whelp	ambush, streak
Turkey	poult	rafter
Turtle	hatchling	bale

POPULAR vs. WACKY PETS

POPULAR PET	WACKY PET	WHY SWITCH?
Cat	Alpaca	Although the alpaca takes up a teeny bit more space than a cat, these are calm, curious animals that are very easy to watch. Trade in your feline purr for an alpaca hum.
Dog	Hedgehog	Although her back is covered with spiny stuff, the hedgehog's belly is as soft as your dog's.
Hamster	Degus	A lot like chinchillas, degus like to chew on everything and take daily dust baths. For dinner, serve degus pellets, hay, and certain fresh veggies.
Fish	Wild Scorpion	You can reuse the fish tank for the new pet—but be sure to have spots (rocks, branches) where the scorpions can hide. You must keep the tank super-hot, but that's easier than keeping a fish tank super-clean.
Guinea Pig	Pot-Bellied Pig	Pigs are smart, easily trained, affectionate, and odor-free—and they do *way* more than their guinea pig cousins. They are, however, on a constant quest for food and they like to root with their snouts (which can cause damage). So, get thee to a pig-trainer, pronto!
Parakeet	Tarantula	Tarantulas are easy to care for and they don't need a lot of handling. Think about that next time you clean the birdcage. And what sounds cooler: exotic spider or little birdie? Even your big brother will think you've gone cool.

Worth noting: Some exotic critters are illegal in areas. Check with local regulations before getting an alternative pet.

6 MORE PETS, VIRTUALLY

- **FURBY:** An electronic toy that speaks Furbish, until you teach it English.
- **NEOPETS:** Virtual pets cared for online. You buy them food, toys, and accessories with Neopoints.
- **TAMAGOTCHI:** A handheld pet housed in an egg-shaped case that needs you to a) feed it, b) clean up after it, and c) have playdates with it.
- **MY LITTLE PET SHOP:** The VIP versions of these mini animals can interact online with other cyber pets.
- **WEBKINZ:** Stuffed animals that come with a special code on their labels to get into "Webkinz World" where you can "adopt" a virtual version of the pet for virtual interaction.
- **ROBOT DOG:** A robot built like Goddard from the series *Jimmy Neutron*.

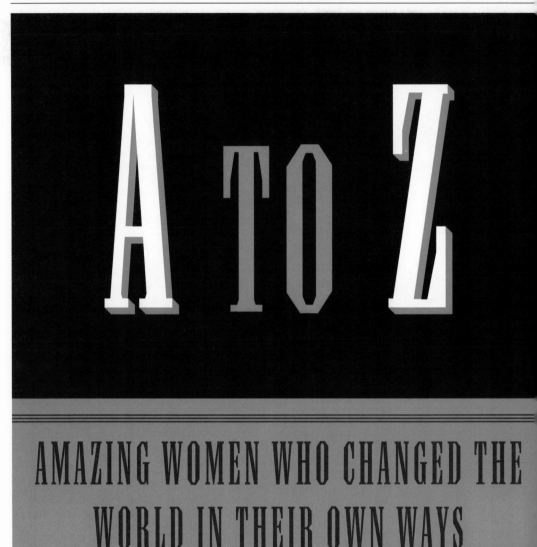

A TO Z

AMAZING WOMEN WHO CHANGED THE WORLD IN THEIR OWN WAYS

"Life shrinks or expands in proportion to one's courage."
—Anaïs Nin, author

WHEN YOU'RE LOOKING TO GET inspired, or seeking someone different to write about for that next school essay, or just trying to impress (and inspire) Mom at the dinner table, consider these fascinating—and truly courageous—women from history. Many appear in school history textbooks; many do not. But in her lifetime, each woman here went out of her way to make the most of her talent and ability, to do something extraordinary.

P.S. Someday your name will belong on this list, too. Believe it.

ELEANOR OF AQUITAINE

- **BORN 1122—DIED 1204**
- **POINT OF ORIGIN:** Medieval France
- **BEST IN SHOW:** Strong and single-minded for a woman of feudal Europe, she is reported to have dressed like an Amazon warrior and ridden her white horse into the Crusades battlefields to boost morale.
- **TRUE!** Sponsored "courts of love," where men having trouble in love came before a tribunal of ladies with their questions. Based on an idea from her forward-thinking daughter, Marie de France.

NELLIE BLY

- **BORN 1864—DIED 1922**
- **POINT OF ORIGIN:** Pennsylvania, U.S.
- **BEST IN SHOW:** Journalist who fearlessly traveled where no American woman had gone before: to Mexico as a foreign correspondent; inside Blackwell Island for its bad treatment of mentally ill patients; and around the world in seventy-two days.
- **TRUE!** Born Elizabeth Jane Cochran, she was nicknamed "Pink" for the clothes she always wore. In later life, she invented and patented a steel barrel and became one of the country's leading industrialists.

RACHEL CARSON

- **BORN 1907—DIED 1964**
- **POINT OF ORIGIN:** Pennsylvania, U.S.
- **BEST IN SHOW:** Writer, scientist, and ecologist whose prize-winning book, *The Sea Around Us*, brought public awareness of the natural world and our responsibility to it.
- **TRUE!** One of Carson's biggest triumphs: taking on the big chemical companies. She testified before Congress about the dangers of pesticides, especially DDT, which was killing birds and wildlife.

DOROTHEA DIX

- **BORN 1802—DIED 1887**
- **POINT OF ORIGIN:** Maine, U.S.
- **BEST IN SHOW:** Traveling across the country, she campaigned for the rights of the mentally ill. She fought to increase the role of government in social welfare.
- **TRUE!** In the Civil War, Dix was appointed Superintendent of the Army of Nurses. Even after she was relieved of duties, she was remembered as an example of kindness to Union and Confederate soldiers.

MARY BAKER EDDY

- **BORN 1821—DIED 1910**
- **POINT OF ORIGIN:** New Hampshire, U.S.
- **BEST IN SHOW:** Influential American author, teacher, and religious leader, noted for her groundbreaking ideas about spirituality and health, which she named Christian Science.
- **TRUE!** A healer named Phineas Quimby introduced her to alternative medicine. After a bad spinal injury, she read the Bible and recovered unexpectedly. Inspired, she became the first woman to start her own religion!

ANNE FRANK

- **BORN 1929—DIED 1945**
- **POINT OF ORIGIN:** Germany during World War II
- **BEST IN SHOW:** The diary of her family's two years in hiding during the German Nazi occupation of the Netherlands was discovered by her father, Otto, and published after the war. To date, it has been translated into more than fifty languages and is perhaps the best known diary of the Holocaust.
- **TRUE!** Anne wrote, "In spite of everything, I still believe that people are really good at heart." She died of typhus with her sister Margot in a concentration camp, weeks before it was liberated.

MARTHA GRAHAM

- **BORN 1893—DIED 1991**
- **POINT OF ORIGIN:** Pennsylvania, U.S.
- **BEST IN SHOW:** Influential American dance pioneer, teacher, choreographer and the mother of Modern Dance.
- **TRUE!** For more than fifty years she created dances, choreographing more than 180 works—and dancing in most of them!

QUEEN MAKARE HATSHEPSUT

- **DIED 1458 B.C.**
- **POINT OF ORIGIN:** Ancient Egypt
- **BEST IN SHOW:** One of the most successful female pharaohs, she reigned twenty-two years, longer than any other woman of an Egyptian dynasty. She was a great "builder-pharaoh," constructing hundreds of projects.
- **TRUE!** Hatshepsut's royal titles included: King of the North and South, Son of the Sun, the Heru of Gold, Bestower of Years, Goddess of Risings, Chief Spouse of Amen, and the Mighty One. There were so many statues made of her likeness, that most museums in the world have at least one. The Metropolitan Museum in New York City has an entire room dedicated to her.

QUEEN ISABELLA I

- **BORN 1451—DIED 1504**
- **POINT OF ORIGIN:** Medieval Spain
- **BEST IN SHOW:** In her quest to make Spain Catholic, Isabella unleashed the Roman Catholic Inquisition, which sought to convert—or else expel—scores of Spanish Muslims and Jews.
- **TRUE!** Her influence is far-reaching for this period in history: She had five children who would greatly impact sixteenth-century history and she's the one who paid Christopher Columbus to set sail when he "found" the so-called New World.

QUEEN JINGA (SOMETIMES GINGA OR NZINGHA)

- **BORN 1583—DIED 1663**
- **POINT OF ORIGIN:** Matamba, West Africa
- **BEST IN SHOW:** A member of the ethnic Jagas, a militant group that waged an inspiring, thirty-year war against the Portuguese slave-traders.
- **TRUE!** Using both the strength and will of male leaders, combined with the gentleness of women, she formed clever alliances with foreign powers, and pit them against one another to free Angola of European influence.

HELEN KELLER

- **BORN 1880—DIED 1968**
- **POINT OF ORIGIN:** Alabama, U.S.
- **BEST IN SHOW:** Blind and deaf author with incredible accomplishments in the face of physical handicaps: learning Braille and lip-reading; receiving a cum laude degree from Radcliffe College; writing best-selling books; and lecturing around the world. She is one of history's best advocates and inspirations for people with disabilities.
- **TRUE!** The story of Helen's life, *The Miracle Worker*, won the Pulitzer Prize and two Academy Awards. Her teacher, Anne Sullivan, lived with and assisted Helen for nearly fifty years.

QUEEN LYDIA LILIUOKALANI

- **BORN 1838—DIED 1917**
- **POINT OF ORIGIN:** Hawaii, U.S.
- **BEST IN SHOW:** The last reigning monarch of the Hawaiian islands, who wanted to preserve the islands for her people, but had to relinquish her throne when the U.S. annexed the islands for themselves.
- **TRUE!** In additional to her political fame, Liliuokalani is also known for composing many Hawaiian songs, including the popular "Aloha Oe," or "Farewell to Thee."

RIGOBERTA MENCHU

- **BORN 1959**
- **POINT OF ORIGIN:** Guatemala
- **BEST IN SHOW:** Self-educated activist and social reformer whose fight for the rights of her country's peasants earned her a Nobel Peace Prize in 1992. She was the youngest and the first indigenous person to receive the prize.
- **TRUE!** Her father founded the CUC (Committee of the Peasant Union), but Rigoberta celebrated its cause, educating the massive peasant population against the guerilla fighters who were taking over her country.

AMALIE "EMMY" NOETHER

- **BORN 1882—DIED 1935**
- **POINT OF ORIGIN:** Bavaria, Germany
- **BEST IN SHOW:** Although she showed no interest in math as a small child, Emmy went on to be an esteemed mathematician who worked with algebra theorems. Albert Einstein said that she was, "the most significant creative mathematical genius thus far produced since the higher education of women began."
- **TRUE!** Emmy's father, Max, was a mathematics professor at Erlangen University. Although women were not admitted to the school, Emmy was able to take classes and become a mathematics professor in her own right.

GRACE O'MALLEY

- **BORN 1530—DIED 1603**
- **POINT OF ORIGIN:** Ireland during the Tudor re-conquest of England
- **BEST IN SHOW:** The daughter of a wealthy, seafaring family whose "tough girl" exploits are the stuff of Irish legend, she once met face-to-face with Queen Elizabeth I to petition the release of her jailed sons and half-brother.
- **TRUE!** O'Malley earned the nicknames "The Sea Queen of Connaught" and "The Pirate Queen" because of her brave and brazen role in the Irish rebellions of the time, which attacked English ships and fortresses near Ireland and Scotland.

EMMELINE PANKHURST

- **BORN 1858—DIED 1928**
- **POINT OF ORIGIN:** Victorian England
- **BEST IN SHOW:** One of England's greatest activists, she and her three daughters founded the Women's Social and Political Union (WSPU), aggressively fighting for women's rights, including suffrage, or the right to vote.

(continued)

• **TRUE!** Whenever a suffragette was released from prison, the WSPU would be there with a flower-decked wagon and a parade! Pankhurst also brought attention to the cause with pageants, torchlight processions, and hunger strikes. Many American suffragettes considered her their role model.

HARRIET QUIMBY

• **BORN 1875—DIED 1912**
• **POINT OF ORIGIN:** Michigan, U.S.
• **BEST IN SHOW:** America's first licensed female pilot and the first woman to pilot her plane across the English Channel; she made aviation accessible to *all* women.
• **TRUE!** Quimby was a noted journalist and author of five screenplays directed by the legendary D.W. Griffith. She met an untimely death when, while performing at an air show, she was pitched out of her plane. Her likeness was put on a postage stamp in 1991.

ELEANOR ROOSEVELT

• **BORN 1884—DIED 1962**
• **POINT OF ORIGIN:** New York City, U.S.
• **BEST IN SHOW:** The original First Lady activist during her husband Franklin Delano Roosevelt's presidency (1933–1945), Roosevelt was later made a delegate to the United Nations.
• **TRUE!** Her roster of volunteer and humanitarian efforts is unparalleled. She supported women's suffrage; volunteered for the Red Cross; helped provide financial aid to students through the NYA (National Youth Administration); worked with the NAACP (National Association for the Advancement of Colored Peoples); and drafted the Universal Declaration of Human Rights for the United Nations.

MARGARET SANGER

• **BORN 1879—DIED 1966**
• **POINT OF ORIGIN:** New York, U.S.
• **BEST IN SHOW:** A controversial figure, she fought for the rights of all women to have access to birth control; opened up numerous family planning clinics; and founded the American Birth Control League.
• **TRUE!** An avid defender of free speech, Sanger was arrested at least eight times while speaking publicly. She toured and lectured to as many women as possible—from halls and churches to socialites—getting millions of letters from women who sought advice and information.

VALENTINA TERESHKOVA

- **BORN 1937**
- **POINT OF ORIGIN:** Maslenikov, Russia (USSR)
- **BEST IN SHOW:** A Soviet cosmonaut who was the first woman to ever travel into space, aboard the *Vostok 6*.
- **TRUE!** Even though she had no formal space or flight training, Valentina was an amateur parachutist and engineer who beat out more then 400 applicants for the historic ride into space.

WINIFRED (FREDA) UTLEY

- **BORN 1898—DIED 1978**
- **POINT OF ORIGIN:** London, England
- **BEST IN SHOW:** Author, scholar, and leader of the anti-Communist movement who sought to usher in a new era of human freedom through political activity.
- **TRUE!** Formerly a Communist, she became a leader in the anti-Communist movement when her husband was arrested and disappeared in Moscow. She wrote pioneering theories on international events in China, Japan, Germany, the USSR, and elsewhere in the world.

ELIZABETH VAN LEW

- **BORN 1818—DIED 1900**
- **POINT OF ORIGIN:** Richmond, Virginia, during the Civil War
- **BEST IN SHOW:** Also called "Crazy Bet," she is known as one of the greatest spies of all time, serving during the Civil War.
- **TRUE!** Although born in the South, Van Lew worked for the Union, helping prisoners to escape. She ran a twelve-person spy ring, including a contact inside the Confederate White House. She got the nickname "Crazy Bet" because she would sometimes pose as a crazy person with overgrown hair. She was inducted into the Military Intelligence Hall of Fame.

SARAH BREEDLOVE WALKER

- **BORN 1867—DIED 1919**
- **POINT OF ORIGIN:** Louisiana, U.S.
- **BEST IN SHOW:** Born to a slave in the cotton fields of the South, Madame C. J. Walker (as she was popularly known) transformed herself from uneducated laborer to entrepreneur. America's first self-made, millionaire businesswoman, she was an innovator in the field of African-American cosmetics and hair care; and pioneered corporate responsibility and charity.
(continued)

• **TRUE!** Walker created her own beauty products, including Madame Walker's Wonderful Hair Grower, a scalp conditioner and healing formula, when she began to lose her hair at a young age. Selling her product door to door, she eventually built her own factory, hair and manicure salon, and training school, settling outside New York City.

XENOBIA, QUEEN OF PALMYRA

• **DIED AROUND 274 A.D.**
• **POINT OF ORIGIN:** Syria
• **BEST IN SHOW:** Upon the death of her husband, she became ruler of the empire and conquered Egypt with her brains and beauty.
• **TRUE!** Well-educated, she knew Greek, Aramaic, Egyptian, and Latin; the works of Homer, Plato, and other writers from Greece; and enjoyed hunting animals and drinking. At the end of her life, Xenobia lived in luxury and became a prominent philosopher, socialite, and Roman matron. Many prominent Romans are counted as her descendants.

ROSALYN YALOW

• **BORN 1921**
• **POINT OF ORIGIN:** New York, U.S.
• **BEST IN SHOW:** Co-winner of the Nobel Prize in Physiology or Medicine in 1977, Yalow was one of the most valuable research scientists of the twentieth century.
• **TRUE!** Although her prize-winning procedure (called radioimmuneassay; used to detect levels in the bloodstream) had commercial potential, Yalow and her partner did not patent it. They wanted to develop it for the people, not for financial gain.

MARGARETHA ZELLE

• **BORN 1876—DIED 1917**
• **POINT OF ORIGIN:** Leeuwarden, Holland
• **BEST IN SHOW:** Born Margaretha Zelle, she was a free-spirited dancer recruited in World War I as a German spy and given the name Mata Hari.
• **TRUE!** Many believe that Mata Hari may have been a double-agent, spying for Germany and France. Her dead body was left unclaimed, so she was delivered to the Museum of Anatomy in Paris for medical studies.

SO YOU WANNA SAVE THE WORLD?

10 THINGS YOU CAN DO RIGHT NOW

1 Don't open and close the fridge too much. A refrigerator uses almost five times more electricity than a television. Every time you open the refrigerator door, up to 30% of cold air escapes.

2 Recycle your cans and bottles. Recycling just one aluminum can saves enough energy to keep the television on for three hours.

3 Turn off your computer monitor when not in use for more than twenty minutes, and your computer when not in use for more than two hours. Consider getting a laptop. A laptop uses half the energy of a desktop computer.

4 Don't throw away plastic bags into the regular garbage. Worldwide, an estimated four billion plastic bags end up as litter each year. Tied end to end, that's enough to circle Earth sixty-three times. When those bags get loose, they kill hundreds of thousands of sea turtles, whales, cows, goats, and other animals who accidentally ingest them.

5 Take off your shoes when you enter the house. Every chemical and pesticide from the street and lawn comes inside with you when you walk in!

6 Don't let the tap run while you brush your teeth. Did you know that more than 70% of Earth's surface is covered by water, but less than 1% of it is drinkable? Conserve!

7 Recycle at home. Organize plastics, paper, and metals separately. Have them ready on garbage day for the recycle truck to pick up. If no recycle truck comes to your part of town, check your city's Web site to see if your location can be added to the route. If not, look for a listing of local recycling drop-off spots in your city.

8 Drink tap water instead of bottled water. In addition to the energy cost of producing, bottling, packaging, storing, and shipping bottled water, there is a huge environmental cost as the millions of bottles are disposed-with nowhere to go.

9 Totally avoid Styrofoam. It does not break down in the environment. At all. Plus, it contains chemicals that can build up in the body and cause health issues over time and with continuous exposure (even in small amounts).

10 Take shorter showers or ask Mom or Dad to install a low-flow shower head, which will limit the hot water and conserve more energy.

Sources: Con Edison NY, Health.com, treehugger.com

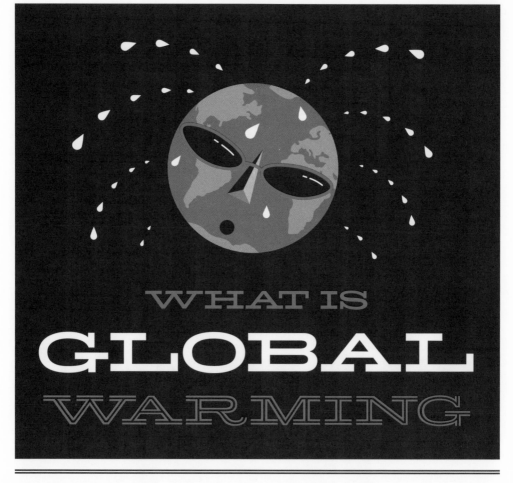

WHAT IS GLOBAL WARMING

IN THE PAST FIFTY years, humans have overloaded the atmosphere with heat-trapping gasses from cars and factories and power plants. More carbon dioxide is now in Earth's atmosphere than in the past 650,000 years. This carbon stays in the atmosphere, acts like a warm blanket, and holds in heat. That's why it's called "global warming." All this warming means that we're facing severe weather, extreme temperatures, and rising sea levels due to the melting of polar ice sheets. Ever wonder what it would be like if New York City was underwater? It's not impossible.

TAKE A GREEN SEAT

GROW A GRASS CHAIR IN YOUR BACKYARD. Take an old wooden chair and cover it with sod. Once it's grown, you won't be able to move it considering the more than 1,000 cups of soil it needs, but you'll be able to say that you're the proud owner of the greenest chair on the block. Of course, *mowing* the thing is another thing altogether, isn't it?

EVERYTHING
YOU WANT TO KNOW ABOUT
BARBIE

- *Who invented Barbie dolls?* Ruth Handler, co-founder of Mattel, in 1959.
- *What does Barbie stand for?* Barbara Millicent Roberts. The doll is named after Barbara, Ruth's daughter.
- *What does Ken stand for?* Ruth's son, Ken, inspired the Ken doll, which was produced in 1961.
- *Where are Barbie dolls supposed to live (besides your closet!)?* According to Mattel, Barbie attended Willows High School in Willows, Wisconsin.
- *Does Barbie have any sister dolls?* Five! Their names are Skipper, Tutti, Stacie, Kelly, and Krissy. She also has a best doll friend named Midge.
- *What was Barbie's first career?* Teenage fashion model. (She's had more than eighty doll careers altogether from rock star to presidential candidate.)
- *What special Barbie doll was introduced during the Gulf War in 1992?* Army Barbie.
- *Has there ever been a Barbie doll in a wheelchair?* Yes. In 1997, Mattel produced Share-a-Smile Becky, a fashion doll like Barbie who uses a wheelchair.
- *What's going on with Barbie dolls around the world?* Every second, two Barbies are sold somewhere on this planet. She's available in more than 150 nations. She has also been sold as forty-five different nationalities, including Quinceanera Teresa (Mexico), Spanish Barbie, and Freundshcafts, or Friendship Barbie (German).
- *How many outfits have been created for Barbie's closet?* Since her first appearance, close to one billion different fashion items have been created for Barbie and her whole doll family.
- *What unusual thing did Barbie dolls get for the first time in 2000?* Belly buttons!
- *What dolls have recently overtaken Barbie as the number one selling fashion doll?* Bratz dolls, with oversized heads, glam and rock looks, and flashy accessories.

SOLVE A MYSTERY LIKE NANCY DREW

WHEN I WAS NINE OR TEN, THE thing I loved most in life was getting a new Nancy Drew book. I ingested those suckers like candy. If I had to name anything I wanted to be when I grew up, it was a girl detective, just like Nancy. After all, how else would I be able to:

• Have the coolest friends ever who would drop everything and come sleuthing with me like George and Bess?

• Drive in a blue roadster at high speeds along gravel roads, in pursuit of the bad girl/guy/beast/ghost?

• Carry a flashlight everywhere just in case I need to shine a light on a sticky situation—or maybe throw some shadow figures on the wall?

• Trespass, break and enter, pick locks, and other sneaky stuff—without ever having to get in an ounce of trouble?

• Have an unlimited bank account so I can jet or ride all over the place collecting clues and getting a tan?

• Join my friends on wild adventures around River Heights, all while waiting for Ned Nickerson to notice that I *like* like him?

• Guess secret passwords in a snap, especially to places like Larkspur Lane, the Lilac Inn, Red Gate Farm, the 99 steps, and all those other quaint but oh-so-dangerous hot spots?

• Know everything there is to know about old clocks, ciphers, mysterious letters, tapping heels, crumbling walls, whistling bagpipes, moss-covered mansions, and everything else mysterious?

You just can't be a girl detective until you read all of Nancy's books. Here is a handy dandy checklist for the first thirty books in the series:

- [x] 1. *The Secret of the Old Clock*
- [x] 2. *The Hidden Staircase*
- [x] 3. *The Bungalow Mysters*
- [x] 4. *The Mystery at Lilac Inn*
- [x] 5. *The Secret at Shadow Ranch*
- [x] 6. *The Secret of Red Gate Farm*
- [x] 7. *The Clue in the Diary*
- [x] 8. *Nancy's Mysterious Letter*
- [x] 9. *The Sign of the Twisted Candles*
- [x] 10. *The Password to Larspur Lane*
- [x] 11. *The Clue of the Broken Locket*
- [x] 12. *The Message in the Hollow Oak*
- [x] 13. *The Mystery of the Ivory Charm*
- [x] 14. *The Whispering Statue*
- [x] 15. *The Haunted Bridge*
- [x] 16. *The Clue of the Tapping Heels*
- [x] 17. *The Mystery of the Brass-bound Trunk*
- [x] 18. *The Mystery at the Moss-covered Mansion*
- [x] 19. *The Quest of the Missing Map*
- [x] 20. *The Clue in the Jewel Box*
- [x] 21. *The Secret in the Old Attic*
- [x] 22. *The Clue in the Crumbling Wall*
- [x] 23. *The Mystery of the Tolling Bell*
- [x] 24. *The Clue in the Old Album*
- [x] 25. *Ghost of Blackwood Hall*
- [x] 26. *The Clue of the Leaning Chimney*
- [x] 27. *The Secret of the Wooden Lady*
- [x] 28. *The Clue of the Black Keys*
- [x] 29. *The Mystery at the Ski Jump*
- [x] 30. *The Clue of the Velvet Mask*

If *you* dream of being a girl detective, there are a few unofficial tips for solving your mystery Nancy-style.

✦ *Make a list of clues!* Call it your sleuth "cheat sheet." It's like those guys on CSI when they crawl through a crime scene jotting notes onto a pad—even the smallest detail can mean something big. Nancy knows how to take notes.

✦ *Beware red herrings!* No, I'm not talking about a kind of fish. I'm talking about the big dupe, the wool pulled over our eyes, the one that got away: Clues that lead us the wrong direction. How to avoid a herring? Follow each clue as far as it will go before jumping to any conclusions. And if you reach a fork in the road, a good detective will find some way to follow both paths—just in case. That way, you'll never be misled.

✦ *Know your cast of characters!* This is true of any adventure or mystery. You need to know who you're talking about, who you're talking to, and what everyone needs to accomplish. Keep a running list of possible suspects for each mystery you pursue, taking notes about appearance, attitude, and more.

✦ *Learn how to spot a villain!* One dead giveaway will be the villain's name. Benny No Good should be pretty obvious, right? And then there's the villain's voice: deep and raspy like gravel.

✦ *Light the way!* Yeah, you might as well carry that flashlight after all (and a pair of backup batteries, too). Detective work in the dark is tough stuff. As a groovy girl detective, you need to be enlightened (ha, ha, get it?) at all times.

✦ *Look out!* Beware of danger ahead! Nancy and her crew were always coming up against trouble in some form. Sometimes it was a one-way ticket to peril, like the time she was hopelessly lost in the mountains outside Shadow Ranch; or the time she nearly toppled off a ladder; or the hundred or so times she was pelted by rocks, attacked by someone's pet, or nearly hit by a car. What if that were you? Then what would you do?

✦ *Make up a clever alias!* Don't use a name too close to your own, though, just in case someone recognizes you. Combine the new name with a new look, too: Add a wig, makeup, and whatever props disguise you while you're on the case.

6 INSPIRING WOME

THERE ARE WAYS OF seeing the world, and then there are ways of seeing the world: painting, sculpting, sketching, shaping, and living through art. However, the history of women in art is sketchy at best before the eighteenth century. There are many reasons why this is true.

For one, women's primary artworks—weaving, embroidery, lace-making, and manuscript illumination—were unsigned, so we have few records of women's achievements in that area. Not to mention the problem with names! When women married, which they usually did at a very young age, they took their husband's names, creating a discontinuity of identity for these artists. Sometimes, too, paintings by women have been attributed improperly or women worked in art workshops where their identities remained unofficial while the name of the master artist (usually male) appeared on the canvas.

Despite all of this, there are many great women artists (and patrons of art) who we do know and admire.

These women put themselves out there bravely to paint, draw, take photos, and support the arts, even when it wasn't the popular choice.

MARIE TUSSAUD
• **Lived:** 1761–1850
• **Home:** Strasbourg, France
• **Her Story:** Her mother worked for a doctor skilled in wax modeling and he taught Marie how to model, too. During the French Revolution, she was arrested and her head shaved for execution by guillotine, but she was saved from death at the last minute. The condition? She was forced to make wax death masks of leaders like Robespierre, Marie Antoinette, and Marat, before they were killed.
• **Style:** Sculpture
• **Medium:** Wax
• **Famous Work(s):** During her lifetime, she personally sculpted many famous people in wax, including Voltaire and Benjamin Franklin. Madame Tussaud's Wax Museums remain popular tourist attractions all over the world today.

JULIA MARGARET CAMERON
• **Lived:** 1815–1879

• **Home:** Born in Calcutta, India, but lived in London, England
• **Her Story:** Cameron did not take a single photograph until she was forty-eight years old, when her daughter gave her a camera as a gift. Even more amazing, within just one year, she was a member of the photographic societies of London and Scotland, getting acclaim for her work. She smartly kept records of every photograph she took, which is why so much of her work remains intact today.
• **Style:** Closely framed portraits and allegorical photos based on religious works
• **Medium:** Photography
• **Famous Work(s):** Portraits of her family and friends, including Julia Jackson (her niece and the mother of author Virginia Woolf); Victorian society including Alfred Tennyson, Charles Darwin, Lewis Carroll, and Edward Lear.

MARY CASSATT
• **Lived:** 1844–1926
• **Home:** Born in Allegheny City, Pennsylvania, but later moved to Paris, France
• **Her Story:** The only American invited to exhibit with a

N WHO LOVED ART

group of independent artists later known as the Impressionists, she painted average women like herself out and about in Paris, or at home, taking tea, reading, sewing, writing letters, and engaging in common activities. In 1880, she began to paint mothers with children, which became her signature theme.
• **Style:** Impressionism
• **Medium:** Oils, pastels, printmaking, Japanese woodcuts
• **Famous Work(s):** *Mother and Child (Baby Getting up from His Nap)*, c. 1899

KÄTHE KOLLWITZ
• **Lived:** 1867–1945
• **Home:** Born in the Province of Prussia, now known as Kaliningrad, Russia
• **Her Story:** Strongly influenced by her grandfather's fierce religious beliefs and her young brother's death, Kollwitz suffered from anxiety. Her parents' solution to that problem? Art! Her father saw her talent and enrolled her in art school. During World War II, despite being harassed by Nazis, she remained in Berlin to continue her life's work.
• **Style:** Naturalism and expressionism
• **Medium:** Drawing, etching, lithography, woodcut
• **Famous Work(s):** She embraced all people affected (and afflicted) with poverty, hunger, and war, and her art shows the human condition (and inhuman conditions) in Germany during the first half of the twentieth century.

GEORGIA O'KEEFFE
• **Lived:** 1887–1986
• **Home:** Born in Sun Prairie, Wisconsin, but later settled in Santa Fe, New Mexico
• **Her Story:** She studied art from an early age, but soon realized she did not want her art to be traditional. After a friend sent a series of O'Keeffe's abstract charcoal drawings to photographer Alfred Stieglitz, O'Keeffe arrived on the New York art scene, exhibiting her work. She later fell in love with Stieglitz and began creating some of her most famous images of large-scale flowers. Her stark art was in great contrast to the chaotic art of the time. Later, when she moved to New Mexico, she painted images of the Southwest.
• **Style:** Abstract, bold colors, landscapes
• **Medium:** Oils, charcoal, pencil, watercolor, clay
• **Famous Work(s):** *Black Iris* (1926), *Poppies* (1927)

FRIDA KAHLO
• **Lived:** 1907–1954
• **Home:** Coyoacán, Mexico (near Mexico City)
• **Her Story:** Born Magdalena Carmen Frida Kahlo y Calderón, she contracted polio at age six and was in a bus accident at age eighteen that left her with numerous painful injuries. After the accident, Frida turned to painting full-time. Her works are often stark expressions of the pain she endured. As a young artist she met and married famous painter Diego Rivera. Kahlo painted with themes almost exclusively about women: women's bodies, birth, death, and survival. She herself was the subject of at least one-third of her paintings.
• **Style:** Surrealism
• **Medium:** Oils on canvas
• **Famous Work(s):** *The Two Fridas (1939)*

50 GIRLS
YOU NEED TO HEAR

LISTEN UP! YOU NEED to turn on the CD player and turn up the radio. There are some groovy girl bands, rockers, and divas out there just waiting to be heard.

- Mahalia Jackson
- Marian Anderson
- Billie Holiday
- Nina Simone
- Janis Joplin
- Tina Turner
- Celia Cruz
- Madonna
- Ani DiFranco
- Stevie Nicks
- Donna Summer
- Mariah Carey
- Celine Dion
- Patti Smith
- Joan Baez
- Aretha Franklin
- Laura Nyro
- Shania Twain
- Whitney Houston
- Agnetha Faltskog
- Alicia Keys
- Sarah Brightman

- Dusty Springfield
- Ella Fitzgerald
- Sarah Vaughn
- Björk
- Patsy Cline
- Kate Bush
- CeCe Winans
- Feist

- Edith Piaf
- Judy Garland
- Uum Kulthum
- Minnie Riperton
- Tori Amos
- Christina Aguilera
- Annie Lennox
- PJ Harvey
- Debbie Harry
- Dolly Parton
- Joan Jett
- Gwen Stefani
- Mary Wells
- Bette Midler
- Renée Fleming
- Pat Benatar
- Amy Winehouse
- Queen Latifah
- Ethel Merman
- Anita O'Day

5 CAN'T-MISS, ALL-GIRL BANDS

- The Go-Gos
- The Bangles
- Indigo Girls
- The Dixie Chicks
- Diana Ross and the Supremes

20 ROCKING GRRRL TUNES

- *Angelina* - Louis Prima
- *Barbara Ann* - The Beach Boys
- *Billie Jean* - Michael Jackson
- *Sweet Caroline* - Neil Diamond
- *Planet Claire* - The B-52s
- *Jack and Diane* - John Cougar Mellencamp
- *Donna* - Richie Valens
- *Come On, Eileen* - Dexy's Midnight Runners
- *Georgia* - Ray Charles
- *Gloria* - U2
- *Iris* - The Goo Goo Dolls
- *Jenny from the Block* - Jennifer Lopez
- *Proud Mary* - Ike & Tina Turner
- *Michelle* - The Beatles
- *Nikita* - Elton John
- *Rosalita* - Bruce Springsteen
- *Roxanne* - Police
- *Veronica* - Elvis Costello
- *Meet Virginia* - Train

THE PERFECT POP STAR NAME

Using the letters in your real name, discover what your new stage name could be. Take the first letter of your last name and find its corresponding star name in LIST A. Then take the letter of your first name and find its star name in LIST B.

LIST A		LIST B	
a.	Whitney	a.	Flowers
b.	Maggie	b.	Lee
c.	Delta	c.	London
d.	Chynna	d.	York
e.	Emerson	e.	Winter
f.	Lola	f.	Kite
g.	Brandy	g.	Fine
h.	Robyn	h.	Shay
i.	Shannon	i.	Bay
j.	Candy	j.	De Ray
k.	Lolita	k.	Best
l.	Tina	l.	Smile
m.	Tatum	m.	Stardust
n.	Fiona	n.	Dawn
o.	Cherry	o.	May
p.	Alyssa	p.	June
q.	Emma	q.	April
r.	Monique	r.	Tiger
s.	Krystal	s.	Fox
t.	Kiki	t.	March
u.	Raquelle	u.	Summers
v.	Joni	v.	Angel
w.	Summer	w.	St. James
x.	Cyndi	x.	La Donna
y.	Kara	y.	Roxy
z.	Bette	z.	Diamond

THINGS TO WRITE A SONG ABOUT

Your hometown, your best friend, the boy you like, the boy you don't like, rainbows, rain, religion, clouds, cliques, birds, a baseball game, loneliness, fear, the most embarrassing thing that ever happened to you, your Grampa, your dog, waterfalls, chocolate cake, outer space, movie stars, cowboys, pizza, a concert, and, of course, all of your deep feelings.

AMERICAN

FOR BE

HAVE YOU EVER WATCHED *American Idol* and thought one of the following things: a) I can do that, b) I wish I could do that, or c) That should be me? Have you ever stood in front of a mirror clutching a hairbrush and struck a pose like you were onstage at a live concert? Do you dream about applause and people holding signs that say VOTE FOR ALLYSON (or whatever your name is)?

Okay, take a deep breath. You have been diagnosed as having acute *American Idol*itis. It's not a big deal,

provided that you begin to take your interest in becoming a world-famous recording artist seriously. But you have to face some hard facts about breaking into the biz: It's a one-in-a-billion shot.

Are you a ready to face the music?

Ask yourself: Can I really sing? This question is not as easy as it sounds. You've seen the clips of people with the worst voices in the universe claiming they are actually superstars. Please. It's okay to love singing and have ter-

rible pitch. Just don't delude yourself into thinking you'll be the next Mariah Carey. Be content to sing because you love it.

Find out what you really love to sing. It's great to channel your inner Gwen Stefani. Just try other kinds of music, too. Find out what makes you grin or sigh with feeling. It could be a Broadway show tune or an operatic aria—or something else you don't expect.

Train your voice. Understand that you have muscles that

IDOL
GINNERS

BREAKING INTO THE BIZ

can be developed in the same way athletes train their muscles. Singing is fairly easy, with tiny muscles involved in coordinating the voice and subtle exercises required to develop their coordination. But like everything, it takes practice to get strong.

Increase your vocal range— and do your own thing. If you're really serious about making music (at least for now), then take voice lessons from a trained professional. Learn to sing in a higher register. Hold your notes for longer. Find something original to make the song "your own."

Always be prepared. Two of the key things you need to break into show business are determination and organization. Even if you're just practicing to audition for the school production, take your time to learn audition times, location, and requirements. When the details are handled, you can spend more time focused on . . . SINGING!

Find an agent. Chances are that you won't get any professional gigs unless a talent agent sends you out on auditions. How to get an agent? There are numerous books and Web sites that list agencies. Or just check the local Yellow Pages. Send a sampling of different agents your demo (a recording of your singing), along with a photo (a black-and-white headshot is the most professional), and a compelling letter to see if anyone is interested in representing you.

PLANN
ULTIMATE

Slumber-ific

[slum•ber•if•ik] adj.

Of, or pertaining, to the best slumber party ever.
Warm, fuzzy feeling you get while attending a slumber party with your best buds.
Alternative sleepover adjectives: awesome, major, cool, great, and FUN.

MY SLEEPOVER PARTY TO DO LIST

1 First things first: Pick a theme. Check out the ideas on the next page.

2 Make your invitation list. Try to keep your guest count low. No more than four or five of your closest pals.

3 Make and mail your invitations. Information you need to include:
* Theme of party
* Party location
* Date and time when party starts and ends (you need a pick-up time for the next morning)

4 Decide on a menu: dinner and breakfast.

5 Create or download a "soundtrack" for the party.

6 Purchase supplies.

7 Clean up your bedroom or basement-wherever the party will be held.

8 Make decorations or party favors.

9 Stock up on camera and film to capture the event.

10 Work out chaperone rules with Mom, Dad, or whomever is in charge.

11 Get a brand-new pair of PJs (of course).

12 Fluff up your sleeping bag and get set for FUN.

ING THE SLEEPOVER

Dream Theme:

STARLET

Invitation:
Make mini-movie clapboard with black construction paper and white pencil or chalk; or make a mini -replica of the Hollywood sign.

Main Activity:
Watching movies! Everyone dresses up in their most glamorous pajamas and settles onto the sofa and pillows for a three-flick fest.

Other Stuff to Do:
Make a red carpet catwalk, complete with fashion modeling (ask guests to come prepared with some glamorous things to wear). You could have everyone choose a movie star name out of a hat, too. Let everyone else at the party guess who's who.

Food:
Fifteen different flavors of popcorn: try butter, salt, parmesan cheese, or cinnamon sugar. Taste test and make your own combinations.

Decoration:
Silver and gold streamers.

Goody Bag:
Glam sunglasses for all guests for that Hollywood look.

Dream Theme:

CASTAWAY

Invitation:
Write your facts on a piece of plain, brown craft paper rolled up into a scroll and tied with a piece of twine-and don't forget to play off the idea of the TV show Survivor. Write at the top of the invite: Who will survive my party?

Main Activities:
Obstacle course, scavenger hunt, puzzles (with a timer to see who is the fastest), and other funny challenges like the ones you see on TV.

Other Stuff to Do:
Make a tiki totem pole or tie-dye T-shirts together.

Food:
Think about the challenges on TV shows like Survivor and Fear Factor. Plan your menu accordingly. Take ordinary foods and give them funny names like spaghetti that gets labeled as Worm Pie or something just as gross.

Decoration:
Think outdoors—big huts, tiki torches (fake ones, please), and other stuff you'd see on a desert island.

Goody Bag:
Rubber snakes aren't too girly, but a shell necklace is just perfect.

Dream Theme:

SPA-
TACULAR

Invitation:
Make the invite in the shape of a face or flower, something fresh.

Main Activity:
Spa central: Pedicures and manicures, washing each other's hair and then styling it silly, giving each other makeovers. Set up different "beauty stations" so everyone gets a chance to experience everything.

Other Stuff to Do:
Sample scavenger hunt-have everyone look for mini -samples throughout your house.

Food:
Fruit smoothies or homemade granola for breakfast!

Decoration:
Set the scene like a real spa: lemon water in pitchers, fresh towels, mellow music playing in the background.

Goody Bag:
Little soaps shaped like hearts, small-sized tube of body lotion, teeny tube of body glitter, hair clips, or even a jar of nail polish or nail art pens.

Dream Theme:

FEELING
SPORTY

Invitation:
Paper shaped like sports equipment looks cute and fun. Or try an invite based on a newspaper sports page, with a headline: PARTY TIME AT SHERRY'S HOUSE and sports lingo to describe all the activities.

Main Activity:
Playing soccer or swimming or doing anything athletic. You can plan an "Olympics" right in your living room with balloon volleyball, a long -jump, and a hoop shoot into a garbage can.

Food:
Since you're being sporty, try to eat healthy: Gatorade sports drink, orange segments, fruit salad, Power Bars, or bottles of water are good for starters. Then you need to have fresh vegetables and salad. If you want to serve pizza, make it fresh!

Decoration:
Netting, signs (like Football Crossing).

Goody Bag:
Cool laces for your sneakers, a terry-cloth headband, and maybe a fun plastic flying disc.

30 GREAT MOVIES TO WATCH WITH A GROUP OF GIRLS

1. The Breakfast Club
2. Bring It On
3. A Cinderella Story
4. Confessions of a Teenage Drama Queen
5. The Princess Diaries
6. The Princess Bride
7. Sixteen Candles
8. Mean Girls
9. Gone with the Wind
10. The Parent Trap
11. Freaky Friday
12. The Shop Around the Corner
13. Sense and Sensibility
14. Bend It Like Beckham
15. The Philadelphia Story
16. Little Women
17. The Secret Garden
18. Legally Blonde
19. Sabrina
20. Grease
21. Never Been Kissed
22. Splash
23. Clueless
24. Beaches
25. Say Anything
26. Ella Enchanted
27. Mermaids
28. Now and Then
29. Fried Green Tomatoes
30. Father of the Bride

HOW TO

GIVE SOMEONE A GROOVY

TIP BY TIP
WHAT YOU NEED TO KNOW

- Nail painting is an art and takes lots of practice. If you are willing, have your friends practice and experiment on your nails—and vice versa.
- Go super smooth for your base coat. It will be much easier to draw a design if the surface is smooth.
- If you're painting toes, you need to put dividers between each toe (a rolled up paper towel works well; weave it in and out between each toe). This will keep the toes from smudging as you paint.
- When you use the paint, dip the brush into the bottle, then wipe it against the inside of the bottle to get just the right amount of polish. Keep the coats thin!
- Apply your stroke of polish down the middle of the nail, starting at (but not on) the cuticle and brushing upwards. Then paint the sides with the remaining polish.
- Wait until the first layer has dried, then put on a second coat. But don't do more than two coats. It will get messy.
- If you make any smudges, dab them with nail polish remover on the edge of a cotton swab.
- Get yourself specially made nail rhinestones and stickers to add to your pedicure or manicure when you're done.
- Always paint nails in a well-ventilated room. You don't want to breathe in the polish fumes for very long.
- When using nail polish and removers, use alcohol-free whenever possible. Alcohol dries out your skin and nails.

What do you do if you spill nail polish on the carpet?

Don't panic. There are solutions to this problem besides moving a chair over the spot to hide it. You could use acetone nail polish remover, which works, BUT (and this is a big but) you may risk ruining the carpet. Acetone is strong stuff. Instead, try a *non-acetone* remover and a little elbow grease. And don't forget to neutralize whatever solution you use with a little water so it doesn't leave a stain. Your best idea of all? Don't do nails on carpet. Paint atop an old towel, newspaper, or on a tiled floor.

MANICURE (OR PEDICURE)

PAINT A GARDEN

ON YOUR FINGERS AND TOES

WHAT YOU NEED:
- Pale blue or pale peach/pink nail polish
- Assorted nail art pens (brown, yellow, orange, pink, green, purple, etc.)
- Clear topcoat
- Cotton swabs and polish remover (just in case!)

1. Paint the entire nail the background color you want. Let it dry completely before you add any colors.
2. Pick your favorite design and the nail. **Sunflower** (Fig. 1) Using your brown nail art pen, paint a half-circle shape over the corner of the tip of the nail. Color in. Let dry completely. Use your bright orange or yellow nail art pen to paint triangle shapes around the brown circle (the petals of your sunflower).
   Wildflower (Fig. 2) Using your pink pen, draw a circle on the nail and fill in the color. Then use the purple nail art pen to draw teardrop-shaped petals around the circle. When the center has dried, dot it with the yellow art pen and outline the petals in yellow. If you have space, draw a stem with the green nail art pen.
3. When the design has dried, apply one coat of clear topcoat to seal it.

Fig. 1   Fig. 2

OTHER DESIGN IDEAS

If a garden isn't your thing, try alternative art: a lightning bolt, skull & crossbones, kitty, fish, sunshine, moon and stars, rainbow, smiley face, rose, or a yin yang symbol. You can also stay super-simple with swirls and letters. If you're attempting a cool design, try it out on paper first and *then* apply to your nails. Paintbrush in a pinch: Unbend a bobby pin and use the rough end as a painting tool.

HOW TO

MAKE 3 AWESOME
FRIENDSHIP BRACELETS

Make a bracelet for yourself, an ankle wrap for your BFF, or a collar for your kitty! Each bracelet shown here should take between 10 and 30 minutes to make. Get your materials at any craft or sewing store: supply of many-colored embroidery floss, scissors, measuring tape or ruler, safety pin, masking tape, and beads (optional). You will also need a tape or a clipboard with a secure clip to hold the bracelet while you weave it.

KNOT! KNOT!

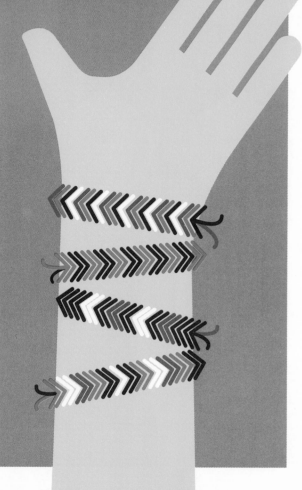

- Keep embroidery floss organized. Wrap it around flat pieces of cardboard to keep it from getting knotted and useless.
- For each bracelet, a measurement of each thread is indicated. This length of thread should be folded in two and knotted at the top. This "overhand" knot is where you pin/tape/hold the bracelet and where you tie the bracelet onto your wrist when it's done. Leave at least two inches to tie it off.
- The more strands of floss you use, the fatter the bracelet will be.
- As you weave, continue to push up the knots to keep the bracelet smooth and tight.
- Know your basic friendship knots.

BASIC FRIENDSHIP KNOT

Right Hand Knot	Left Hand Knot

Fig. 1   Fig. 2   Fig. 3   Fig. 4

DIAGONAL STRIPES

Use three colors of strings, three strings of each color, each about three feet long.

1. Start with the overhand knot. Arrange your strings in the order you would like to see your stripes. (Fig. 1)

2. For your first knot, use the first strand on the left and make a basic knot over its neighbor string, twice. (Fig. 2)

3. Take that same knotting string and continue making double basic knots over each of the other strands in the row. (Fig. 3)

4. Now you're ready for row two. Do the same as above using the new first string on the left as your knotting string. (Fig. 4) Continue this way until the end of your bracelet. Tie it off by joining the bottom to the top with another overhand knot. Trim the loose ends if you want.

Fig. 1   Fig. 2   Fig. 3

RAINBOW

Use four colors of string— two strands of each color, each about one yard in length.

1. Start by making the overhand knot and securing the strings, paired off by color, on your clipboard or table. (Fig. 1)

2. For this project, the two strings of the same color will be used together as if they're one string.

3. Start with the first two strings on the right and use them together to do the basic knot around all the other strings held together as a group. (Fig. 2) Pull the knot tight. Repeat these

knots until you have a single color slide about one inch long.

4. Then use the next pair of strings to knot around all the others for an inch length, also. (Fig. 3) Continue this way until your bracelet is as long as you wish. End your bracelet as usual with the overhand knot.

Fig. 1   Fig. 2   Fig. 3

Fig. 4   Fig. 5   Fig. 6

VERY Vs

You start this bracelet a little differently from the others. Use four different color strands, each at least six feet in length. Holding all four strands, fold them in half and make an overhand knot forming a loop in the middle. (Fig. 1) Slip this loop under the clipboard gripper or tape and you will have eight strings to work. Arrange the strings in a mirror image (see diagram). It's time to knot!

1. Start by doing the basic knot twice, knotting the first string on the left over its neighbor (Fig. 2) and then over the next string and the next until you reach the center (Fig. 3). Now do the same starting with the first string on the right.

2. When you reach the center (the two center strings should be the same color), make another double basic knot with the right hand string over the left (Fig. 4). Wow! Row one is complete. Time for row two.

3. Do row two exactly as you did the first row, and then row three, row four, etc. (Fig. 5) Do all the rows until you finish your bracelet. (Fig. 6) Tie it off, trim the ends, and wear proudly!

Bead Variation

This is the perfect bracelet to add beads. When you have finished the center joining knots, simply slip the strings through a bead and then knot again. Continue making V rows without joining the center knots until you've gotten to the bottom of the bead, then continue V rows, making the center joining knot just as you did above until you want to add another bead, then repeat.

THE INCREDIBLY UNSCIENTIFIC BUT SURPRISINGLY ACCURATE

FOR GIRLS ONLY

SUPERQUIZ

IS THERE A SCIENCE TO QUIZ-TAKING? Many experts think so. Myers-Briggs Type Indicator (MBTI) test has been used for many years to identify cool things about people's personalities. The famous test, created by researchers Katharine Cook Briggs and Isabel Briggs Myers, is based on the teachings of philosopher Carl Jung. Jung introduced important concepts to psychology. He coined the words "introverted" (shy or reserved) and "extroverted" (outgoing) to explain why people act the way that they do.

Meyers believed that although we are all born with the same basic personality traits, we prefer some qualities more than others. Think about it like this: although you have two hands, you probably prefer one hand over the other to write, eat, or bat a ball. (Unless of course you're ambidextrous, meaning that you use both hands!) Meyers decided there were four main areas of our personality. She decided that those four qualities could be combined in numerous ways; sixteen possible ways, in fact!

Now, you're probably wondering where you fit on this spectrum. Which crazy combination of letters (personality traits) represents you?

Unfortunately, the Myers-Briggs test isn't meant to be used by girls or boys under the ages of fourteen. (That's because up until that point your personality is still taking shape.) But, fear not! In the absence of the actual test, I've developed this uniquely unscientific For Girls Only (FGO) quiz.

It's a teeny bit like the MBTI. There are four parts. Answer all of the questions in each part, tally your answers, and total your points on a separate piece of paper. After getting your number totals, you will then get four different letters; one for each part. It is the combination of these letters that reveals your personality profile.

Whew. Sound complicated? It really isn't. Think of it as Meyers-Briggs Lite. Although it's not the real deal, I hope you will be pleasantly surprised by the quiz results. Follow the directions (in order) and most importantly... have FUN.

PART ONE:
FASHION AND STYLE

Below are 40 questions about your clothes and personality (as you see it). Answer each one based on the following scale:

c Totally (1 point) c Sort Of (2 points) c No Way (3 points)

1. My dream job is to be a fashion designer.
2. I usually follow trends.
3. I always stop to look when I pass a mirror.
4. I change clothes more than once a day.
5. My wardrobe is bigger than Barbie's.
6. Frizzy is not cool.
7. I wish designer labels filled my closet.
8. Thrift shops are off limits.
9. If I look good; I feel good.
10. My outfits always match.
11. If I were a shoe, I'd be the cutest pair of flats ever.
12. My screen name is FASHIONGRL (or something like that)
13. If I had a credit card, I could shop all day long.
14. On my dresser: jewelry box with twirling ballerina inside.
15. In my jewelry box: charm bracelets and rings.
16. I would never get a tattoo.
17. My friends and I dress a lot alike.
18. I always compliment my BFF on her outfits.
19. I love it when someone compliments me.
20. I cannot live without my lip gloss.
21. Sneakers are for gym class.
22. I get invited to every party.
23. I could host the show *What Not to Wear*.
24. I believe in bling.
25. Sometimes I wear makeup.
26. Sometimes I dream about being a model.
27. Favorite four-letter word? SALE.
28. I carry scented lotion in my backpack.
29. Happiness is a great haircut.
30. My parents sometimes call me Princess.
31. I like to decorate my locker or bedroom.
32. I paint my nails.
33. I borrow things from my mom.
34. I tear pictures of models out of magazines for ideas.
35. Everyone wishes they had my sense of style.
36. When in doubt, dress up.
37. I wish I could walk the red carpet.
38. On my birthday wish list: perfume.
39. I get a new wardrobe every season.
40. Being "Best Dressed" in the yearbook is my goal.

Your Total _____
If your total is less than 40, you are C for Casual
If your total is more than 41, you are F for Fashionista
If your total is 125+ or above, you are Fashionista Plus Plus, which means that you'd spend all day looking in a mirror and dressing up in diamonds if you could. Helpful hint: maybe it's time to drag out the sweatpants and just kick back? Your call.
Your letter _____

PART TWO:
ATTITUDE

What's your self-esteem like these days? Take a close look at the following 10 questions and choose your answers.

1. **You just found out that there will be a pop quiz—and you haven't studied or done the reading assignment. How do you feel?**

   a) My palms are sweaty; I'm a mess!

   b) Huh? What? My mind has gone blank!

   c) I quickly try to review the assignment and prepare as best as I can.

2. **When my crush says hello in the hallway, I feel:**

   a) Happy and excited, in a heart-beating-faster way.

   b) OMG. I could just scream!

   c) Relaxed and serene. Just call me yoga girl.

3. **If someone is rude to me or cuts me in the lunch line, this is I what I say:**

   a) Nothing. I avoid conflict wherever possible.

   b) "Hey, what do you think you're doing?!"

   c) "Way to be friendly."

4. **If a teacher asks me to "come and talk" after class, I immediately think:**

   a) Ack! I'm in deep trouble!

   b) Yay! I'm a superstar!

   c) Gee, I wonder what's up?

5. **While waiting on a long line, what do I do?**

   a) I haven't got time to wait. I'll come back later.

   b) Stare at everyone. Talk to someone.

   c) Just wait.

6. **Whenever someone compliments me, I feel:**

   a) Like a ~~million~~ trillion bucks!

   b) Totally embarrassed.

   c) Sort of good; sort of uncomfortable.

7. **When I write my name down on a piece of paper, the letters look:**

   a) Pretty, open, and round cursive. In other words, *perfect*.

   b) Scribbly, and unreadable.

   c) Like I wrote it in 2nd grade.

8. **If I had to describe the way I think people see me as a critter, here's what I'd be:**

   a) A Bengal tiger.

   b) A butterfly.

   c) A Labrador retriever.

9. **If someone says something that upsets me, I reach for:**

   a) An ice cream sundae.

   b) A box of tissues.

   c) A telephone.

10. When my friends start talking about someone else (in not a nice way), I immediately think:

   a) They're entitled to their opinions, even if they are wrong.

   b) I wish I could think of something mean to say about them, too. Revenge can be sweet.

   c) That is so not cool. But I'll just let it go. Sigh.

1.	a=1	b=2	c=3
2.	a=3	b=1	c=2
3.	a=1	b=3	c=2
4.	a=1	b=3	c=2
5.	a=3	b=2	c=1
6.	a=3	b=1	c=2
7.	a=2	b=1	c=3
8.	a=1	b=3	c=2
9.	a=2	b=3	c=1
10.	a=1	b=2	c=3

Your Total _____

If your total is less than 16, you are
   R for Reserved

If your total is more than 17, you are
   O for Outgoing

Your letter _____

OUTGOING

16

RESERVED

PART THREE:
FEARS AND EMBARRASSMENT

There's nothing worse than being afraid or being embarrassed. Unless, of course, you get afraid or embarrassed at the same time! Below are 30 statements. Answer Y (for yes, if it's true) or N (for no, if it doesn't apply to you).

1. I am afraid of snakes or anything that slithers.
2. If my hair looks messy, I freak out.
3. I remain calm during tests.
4. I have burped in public and survived to tell the tale.
5. Someday I could climb Mount Everest.
6. My worst nightmare is failure.
7. I dream about winning an Academy Award.
8. Whenever I eat, food gets on my shirt.
9. I usually ride the rollercoaster more than once.
10. I would love to be photographed by the paparazzi.
11. There is nothing worse than parents telling "when she was a baby" stories.
12. Ghosts are real.
13. I snort when I laugh.
14. I have had toilet paper stuck to my shoe.
15. I am super-ticklish.
16. I feel better being part of a clique.
17. I've shown up to a school dance in the same outfit as a classmate.
18. I was hit in the face with volleyball during gym class (or something like that).
19. When I fall, I usually pretend to be fine, even if I'm not.
20. I have worn shirts inside out by mistake.
21. I heard a rumor about myself once.
22. I've waved to someone—only to discover he or she doesn't know me.
23. When I see a spider, I usually scream.
24. I've gotten cafeteria applause for tripping with a tray of food—splat!
25. I lost my bikini top in the pool/ocean/water.
26. I have trouble speaking in public.
27. I would totally run for class president.
28. I have no trouble talking to boys in social situations.
29. I don't mind shopping for a bra with my mom.
30. When I get embarrassed, my cheeks turn scarlet.

1. Y= 1 N=2	11. Y= 1 N=2	21. Y= 1 N=2
2. Y= 1 N=2	12. Y= 2 N=1	22. Y= 1 N=2
3. Y= 2 N=1	13. Y= 1 N=2	23. Y= 1 N=2
4. Y= 2 N=1	14. Y= 1 N=2	24. Y= 1 N=2
5. Y= 2 N=1	15. Y= 2 N=1	25. Y= 1 N=2
6. Y= 1 N=2	16. Y= 1 N=2	26. Y= 1 N=2
7. Y= 2 N=1	17. Y= 1 N=2	27. Y= 2 N=1
8. Y= 1 N=2	18. Y= 1 N=2	28. Y= 2 N=1
9. Y= 2 N=1	19. Y= 2 N=1	29. Y= 2 N=1
10. Y= 2 N=1	20. Y= 1 N=2	30. Y= 1 N=2

Your Total _____
If your total is less than 31, you are E for Easily Embarrassed
If your total is more than 32, you are D for Daring
Your letter _____

PART FOUR:
FRIENDSHIP

You can tell a lot about your own personality from the friends you hang with—and the things you do with them. What qualities do you look for in a friend? What's the nicest thing you ever did for someone—or that someone did for you? Select the multiple choice option that suits you best and add up your points.

1. **A day late, you realize that you missed your friend's birthday. What now?**

   a) You get an enormous bunch of Mylar balloons, a stuffed Teddy Bear, a homemade cake with the words BEST FRIEND IN THE UNIVERSE on top and surprise her a day late.

   b) You find out what everyone else got her and vow to do the same.

   c) You text message her: "Sry I missed ur bday. It's not a big dl, is it?"

2. **If your friendship was a movie, what would it be called?**

   a) *Just Like Sisters*

   b) *Let's Hang Out*

   c) *See You Next Year*

3. **Your friend had a huge fight with her mother. She calls you up for advice and wants you to tell her what to do. Now what?**

   a) Although you want to help her to feel better, explain that you can't tell her what to say or do. But you are here to be a great listener.

   b) Change the subject. There's no use in getting her more upset.

   c) Ignore her.

4. **What qualities are most important to you in your friendship?**

   a) Honesty, trust, and compassion.

   b) Common interests and sense of humor.

   c) Someone who lets me borrow all of her cool clothes.

5. **You catch your friend cheating on a science test. When your friend begs you not to tell, what do you do?**

   a) Convince her to turn herself into the teacher before it becomes a huge deal, blown out of proportion.

   b) Tell her you're sorry, but you can't keep a promise like that.

   c) Avoid your friend for a while. You can't be associated with a cheater.

6. **Your friend just told you a huge secret. What do you do with the information?**

   a) Lock it up and throw away the key.

   b) Write it in my journal and then tell one or two people.

   c) Talk about it a lot so eventually, you've blabbed the secret to almost everyone you know.

7. **It's the holiday party at school. Your friend shows up in the ugliest dress you've ever seen. Do you tell her?**

   a) No way. You don't want her to feel self-conscious!

   b) You make a little joke about the reindeer pattern on the dress fabric, but that's it. Otherwise, you let her wear it with no trouble.

c) Absolutely! Friendship = honesty. You want her to know what people really think, even if feelings get hurt.

8. **You suspect that your friend has been talking about you behind your back. How do you deal with the situation?**

   a) Tell her what you've heard—and how much it hurt. See how she reacts when she sees how clearly she has hurt your feelings.

   b) Catch her red-handed in the act of talking again. Then lay on the guilt trip.

   c) Tell her you no longer want to be friends.

9. **A classmate has a big birthday party. Everyone has received an invitation—except your friend. What do you do?**

   a) Boycott the party. If your friend can't go—you won't go.

   b) Ask the person having the party why your friend didn't receive an invite. It might just be an oversight.

   c) Tell your friend that she can come anyway. Who cares?

10. **During art class, you develop a crush on a cute guy—and then your friend says she likes him, too. What do you tell your friend?**

    a) Tell her you agree that the guy's cute and maybe you can both like him. After all, it's not like anyone's going on a date.

    b) Even though you feel competitive, you don't say anything. Better for her to think she's the only one who likes the guy.

    c) "He's mine. Back off."

11. **How good a listener are you?**

    a) You make time out of each day to ask your friend how she's doing—and actually listen when she tells you.

    b) If your friend calls you, you talk for a little while.

    c) You'd rather just send an IM or e-mail later.

12. **You borrowed one of your friend's favorite shirts—and spilled a diet soda down the front of it. Now what?**

    a) You confess to the spill right away—and promise to get her a new shirt.

    b) You don't mention it when you return the shirt. If there's a problem; she'll tell you.

    c) Act like the spot was there before you wore the shirt.

13. **Someone in line for the cafeteria cracks a mean joke about your friend. She isn't there to defend herself. What do you say?**

    a) You loudly say, "Stop talking about _____." Plain and simple. A good friend like you is a good defense.

    b) You tell the person to stop, but you say it quietly, so you're not one hundred percent sure if the kid even hears you.

    c) You don't say anything. Better not to get involved.

14. **If you are sick in bed with a cold, your friend will usually do what?**

    a) Get your homework and bring it over to your house right away. She does everything she can to make you feel better!

    b) Make some joke about bringing

over a container of chicken soup; and check in on you by phone later that day.

c) Stay far, far away. She doesn't want to get sick, too.

15. **You both decide to hang out one Saturday, but you want to stay at home and study for a test while your friend wants to go to the movies. How do you resolve this conflict?**

a) You figure out a way to do both. Study for an hour and then head to the movie.

b) Go to the movie and then come back to study.

c) You don't resolve it. You do neither. She wants to have her way.

16. **Your friend decides to sit at a different table during lunch. How do you feel?**

a) Not worried. She's allowed to have other friends. You'll see her later.

b) A little jilted. She is your best pal, after all. What's she up to?

c) Angry. How dare she leave you at the other lunch table by yourself?

17. **You've been away all summer long. When you get home, your friend is giving you the cold shoulder. What do you say?**

a) Tell her you missed her and ask to spend some fun time together before school starts. You can find out what's bugging her then.

b) Get mad and call her up. Demand to know what happened.

c) Blow her off. Two can play this game.

18. **You're in a school play together. On stage, your friend forgets an important line. Everyone is waiting. You**

know the line. What do you do?

a) You whisper the line, hoping that she'll pick up the cue.

b) You stand still and try to send her psychic signals. She'll remember the line eventually, won't she?

c) You crack up.

19. **The ultimate day with your best friend would be:**

a) Anything. Just being together is the best part.

b) Doing as many activities as possible with other friends, too.

c) The "ultimate" day is just me, myself, and I.

20. **You've had tickets to go see a play and now the day is finally here! As you are getting ready to leave, the phone rings. Your friend is in tears. What do you do?**

a) Lend her support but tell her that you can only talk to her about what's happened after the play.

b) Tell her to deal with it. Things happen.

c) Shout, "I can't talk now. Sorry!" into the receiver and then hang up. Whatever it is can wait.

Mostly As—give yourself 3 points
Mostly Bs—give yourself 2 points
Mostly Cs—give yourself 1 point

Your Total _____
If your total is less than 40 you are L for Laid Back
If your total is more than 41, you are T for True Blue
Your letter _____

EVERYTHING GREAT
ABOUT TAKING A

FOR GIRLS ONLY

QUIZ

1. You can share this quiz with friends and laugh when the answers are right on the mark—or off base. Because that's what friends do best: cry, laugh and *understand* each other when no one else can.

2. No quiz is a crystal ball. It only records a few bits and pieces of you (ie. not the *whole* you). It only tells you how you're acting or feeling or existing *this* week. Results change from day to day. You have a lifetime of experiences— and quizzes—ahead of you. So don't give this one too much weight.

3. Any quiz responses are valid. All the letter types that define you after taking this quiz are good. Whoever you are on the spectrum is just fine. There's no judgment or criticism here. There is no "right" score.

4. Despite the fact that it isn't a perfect explanation of your future, a quiz like this *can* be a big help, even if it's just to cheer you up. And remember: you have the power to change any quiz result you may not like. Don't forget that. Re-take it, I say! That's why they invented erasers.

5. Quizzes are like potato chips. We can say they don't matter (and they really don't), but they still reel us in with their salty, wonderful, crunchy, and delicious answers. Hmmm. Is anyone else hungry?

Enough stalling! Turn the page and find out your personality type!!!!
Sorry. I meant to say, "Please turn the page? Thank you."*

*Never forget your manners, girls.

Still curious about the real MBTI? Look for more information online at www.myersbriggs.org.

YOUR FOR GIRLS ONLY PERSONALITY TYPE:

CASUAL	**EASILY EMBARRASSED**
FASHIONISTA	**DARING**
RESERVED	**LAID BACK**
OUTGOING	**TRUE BLUE**

CREL
You're a combination of Casual/Reserved/Embarrassed/Laid Back.
You shrink away from stressful situations and can hardly get through the day without one embarrassing moment, which is made triply hard by the fact that you don't have a lot of close friends to give you some recovery time. You're could use some big change—to fix your fashion problems, to help you to speak up, and give you more incentive to fight for the friends you do have. Don't let things pass you by!

CRET
You're a combination of Casual/Reserved/Embarrassed/True Blue.
Although you tend to be a little shy and even quiet, you are a steadfast friend. You get embarrassed easily, but that's okay because you surround yourself with good friends to help you feel better about what's going on. Let them help you to stand up and speak out. Don't be afraid to say what you feel or think. Friendship is the key!

CRDL
You're a combination of Casual/Reserved/Daring/Laid Back.
You're a study in contrasts. You like to wear low-key clothing, but your personality can be a little wild. You have to be careful not to step on anyone's toes because your daring nature can sometimes get in the way. You sometimes put your friends second, when they should be first. Try mixing it up a little bit more. Next time you step out...find someone to share the experience. Rock on!

CRDT
You're a combination of Casual/Reserved/Daring/True Blue.
Everyone likes your style: a combination of easygoing and daring that keeps friends interested in you. You have an appreciation for the quiet and loud things that make friendship work. Even more importantly, your sense of loyalty is sky high. You want to make a difference, but you don't need to hog the spotlight. You're happy to share it! Way to go!

COEL
You're a combination of Casual/Outgoing/Embarrassed/Laid Back.
Although you're no fashion plate, you try to assert yourself in all sorts of other, simpler ways. Sometimes this means that you take small risks that don't always pay off. Don't worry, though. You don't get too hung up on the details. It's the big picture that counts—and you're setting a course for success.

COET
You're a combination of Casual/Outgoing/Embarrassed/True Blue.
It's hard to keep your friendships on track because sometimes you want so much to do everything the right way—that you get too intense. But there's no denying: your sensitivity makes you a great listener—and, as a result, a special friend. Pay attention to those gut feelings. They are great guideposts for you!

CODL
You're a combination of Casual/Outgoing/Daring/Laid Back.
You like to stay comfortable; never formal, even though you love a party. You're not

touchy-feely, though, so friends probably don't come to you with their deepest secrets or strongest feelings. It depends. Mostly, you're here for a fun time. Enjoy the ride.

CODT
You're a combination of Casual/ Outgoing/Daring/True Blue.
Although you'd rather hang out in sweatpants than a dress, you are a girl's best friend: always plotting some fun activity, rarely letting things get you down or embarrass you, and sticking by your friends through thick and thin. Someone like you who marches to her own drummer always finds a profound path in life, too. Chances are you'll be the one to discover a cure for cancer or write a Pulitzer Prize-winning novel. You're the quiet trailblazer. Kudos!

FREL
You're a combination of Fashionista/Reserved/Embarrassed/ Laid Back.
You make a huge fashion statement when you walk into a room—but it's your clothes and style doing all the talking for you. When it comes to baring souls, you're a little tight-lipped. You'd rather stay calm and quiet. In some ways, even mushy feelings embarrass you. But your dramatic exterior and reserved attitude sometimes don't mix, but you keep things interesting. You could give lessons on being—and staying—cool.

FRET
You're a combination of Fashionista/Reserved/Embarrassed/ True Blue.
You love to dress up, although you don't have any attitude about it. You're the first one to jump in when there's trouble. And although you may get embarrassed easily yourself, you're quick to rescue a friend if she gets embarrassed, too. You put the "true" in true blue. Everyone could use a friend like you!

FRDL
You're a combination of Fashionista/Reserved/Daring/ Laid Back.
Bold colors. Cool accessories. You've got the sense of humor to go along with all the bold

statements you make. Everyone wants to be around you, too, but you tend to lay lower than the rest. You're more reserved than outgoing, after all. Your daring side combined with your tendency to be low-key about your friend's needs, may make you seem insensitive at times. But you're in it for the long haul. Friends forever!

FRDT
You're a combination of Fashionista/Reserved/Daring/ True Blue.
Although you know how to work a great outfit or hairdo, and although you like to take risks, you have a reserved side to you, too. It's this side that keeps you in check—and makes you more thoughtful. It's this part of your personality, too, combined with the "true blue" part, that makes you a fantastic listener. You're an ideal combination of girly-girl and tough—the kind of friend you can count on for almost anything. How did you get to be so great?

FOEL
You're a combination of Fashionista/Outgoing/Embarrassed/ Laid Back.
Sometimes friends might think you're in it all for show. You like the hot new outfits and feel a need to be noticed. In fact, you need attention so much that you'd even take a negative experience just to get noticed! You'll turn a nothing moment into a dramatic scene or make comments that might not be as kind to your friend as they should be. Remember to show people all the sides of you—out and in. It's not just about your shoes. It's about your heart—and yours is HUGE.

FOET
You're a combination of Fashionista/Outgoing/Embarrassed/ True Blue.
You're like the girl all dressed up to go to the party: you have the right dress, the right attitude, and you love your friends. But then, at the party, some of your insecurities show through a little. You need to trust all of the other qualities—and believe in yourself enough to toss those fears and embarrassments into the trash. You have so much to offer!

FODL

You're a combination of Fashionista/Outgoing/Daring/ Laid Back.

You've got the sparkle. You've got the quick wit. You're not even afraid of spiders! But here's the thing: sometimes you let all the stuff outside of you push down the feelings inside of you. You have so much to offer a great friendship. Make sure you're practicing your listening skills and taking seriously this great friend who needs you. Fly your banner high and be the leader everyone knows you can be.

FODT

You're a combination of Fashionista/Outgoing/Daring/ True Blue.

Nobody's perfect, although you are certainly trying very hard to be that way. Relax! You're usually stylin' and you're always up for adventure. You're not afraid to take risks and you're the best friend a girl could hope to have. Just make sure there's room—and time—for you. Keep a journal. Don't be afraid to be introspective once in a while.

EVERYTHING GREAT ABOUT TAKING A GIRL QUIZ

1. You can share it with friends and laugh when the answers are right on the mark—or off base. Because that's what friends do best: cry, laugh and *understand* each other when no one else can.

2. You know it's not a crystal ball. Not only does a quiz record just a few bits and pieces of you (ie. not the *whole* you), but a quiz like this only tells you how you're acting/feeling/existing *this week*. Results could change from day to day. And you have a lifetime of experiences—and quizzes—ahead of you. So don't give it too much weight.

3. All the quiz responses are valid. All the letter types are right. Whoever you are on the spectrum is just fine. There's no judgment or criticism here. There is no "right" score.

4. A quiz like this can be a big help. Sometimes we don't realize we're doing something annoying or goofy until we answer a few questions, tally our scores and see our result. But you have the power to change any result you don't like. Don't forget that. You have the power to believe in you. Use it.

Still curious about the real MBTI? Look for more information online at www.myersbriggs.org.

BIBLIOGRAPHY

Steven Caney's Kids' America © 1978 by Steven Caney. Workman Publishing. New York, NY.

Anna Banana: 101 Jump Rope Rhymes © 1989 by Joanna Cole, Ill. By Alan Tiegreen William Morrow & Co, Inc. New York, NY.

Album of Horses by Marguerite Henry, Ill. By Wesley Dennis. © 1951 by Rand McNally & Company, © 1993 Aladdin Paperbacks Edition.

The Curious Kids' Activity Book Boredom Busters © 1997 by Avery Hart and Paul Mantell. Williamson Publishing Company, Charlotte, VT.

Women Invent! © 1997 by Susan Casey. Chicago Review Press. Chicago, IL.

Scholastic Guides: How to Write Poetry ©1999 by Paul B. Janeczko. Scholastic Inc., New York, NY.

The Kids Guide to Fortune Telling © 1998 by Louise Dickson, Ill. By Pat Cupples. Kids Can Press, Ltd. Buffalo, NY.

Hopscotch, Hangman, Hot Potato & Ha Ha Ha: A Rulebook of Children's Games by Jack Maguire © 1990 by the Philip Lief Group. Simon & Schuster, New York, NY.

Folklore on the American Land © 1972 by Duncan Emmerich. Little Brown & Co. New York, NY.

Oxford Atlas of the World 12th Edition.

The Love magic book © 2003 by Gillian Kemp. Little Brown & Co. New York, NY.

Nike is a Goddess: The History of Women in Sports, © 1999 by Lucy Danziger.

The Book of Lists for Kids by Sandra and Harry Choron, © 1995 by Sandra Choron, Houghton Mifflin Co. Boston, MA.

Clever Letters: Fun Ways to Wiggle Your Words by Laura Allen © 1997 by Pleasant Company, Pleasant Company Publications, Middleton, Wisconsin.

The Encyclopedia of Dreams: Symbols and Interpretations by Rosemary Ellen Guiley © 1993 by Rosemary Ellen Guiley, Berkley Books, New York, NY.

"I Am In Need of Music" by Elizabeth Bishop from *The Complete Poems: 1927-1979,* and *"Stars"* by Valerie Worth from *All the Small Poems and Fourteen More,* reproduced with permission from Farrar, Straus, & Giroux.

ASSORTED WEB SITES:
www.Popculturemadness.com
www.Roadsideamerica.com
www.Snopes.com
www.Worldcocoafoundation.org
www.Costumegallery.com
www.About.com
www.Womeninworldhistory.org
www.Greatwomen.org
www.Rd.com (Reader's Digest)
www.spaceplace.nasa.gov
www.womenssportsfoundation.org
www.northnet.org/stlawrenceaau w/timeline.htm
www.poemhunter.com/org
www.discoverychannel.com/uk
www.mcdonalds.com
www.weird-food.com
www.womeninworldhistory.com
www.globalfundforwomen.org/cms
www.fashion-era.com
www.school.discoveryeducation.com
www.amic.com
www.girlscouts.org
www.gettech.org
www.engineergirl.org
www.mathpower.com
www.whitehouse.gov
www.usolympicteam.com
www.dictionary.com
www.sleepfoundation.org
www.britannica.com

Thank you for reading this FEIWEL AND FRIENDS book.

A special thanks to HEADCASE DESIGN for making this

G✿R✿E✿A✿T

BOOK

The Friends who made *For Girls Only* possible are:

Jean Feiwel
PUBLISHER

Liz Szabla
EDITOR-IN-CHIEF

Rich Deas
CREATIVE DIRECTOR

Elizabeth Fithian
MARKETING DIRECTOR

Elizabeth Noland
PUBLICIST

Holly West
ASSISTANT TO THE PUBLISHER

Dave Barrett
MANAGING EDITOR

Nicole Liebowitz Moulaison
PRODUCTION MANAGER

Jessica Tedder
ASSOCIATE EDITOR

Allison Remcheck
EDITORIAL ASSISTANT

Ksenia Winnicki
MARKETING ASSISTANT

Find out more about our authors and artists and
our future publishing at www.feiwelandfriends.com.

OUR BOOKS ARE FRIENDS FOR LIFE